When did things change? Lucy asked herself. *When did I start falling in love?*

The words may have been said silently, but to her, it sounded as if they'd bounced off the kitchen walls straight at Logan. The idea was frightening. She'd told herself that this was an affair, nothing permanent, and that she didn't want to remarry. This time more than her heart was in danger— so was her son's.

All that didn't stop her from looking at Logan as if he was the best thing in her life. He leaned against the counter, his hair as rumpled as his clothing due to a late-night emergency. He'd always been handsome, but when had he become downright irresistible? He fidgeted with a fortune- cookie wrapper.

Lucy covered the distance between them and took the cookie from him. "You don't need this to tell your fortune. I can tell you." Through a wicked smile she whispered in his ear, and instantly Logan swept her up in his arms.

For once in her life, Lucy wanted to take what she could get. Enjoy the moment and not worry about what might happen tomorrow.

If Scarlett O'Hara could do it, so could she.

Dear Reader,

When the Walker siblings first appeared in *My Little One*, I had no idea they would be featured in three more books. I've had a lot of fun creating the right soul mate for each sibling, but as you know, I didn't make it easy for them.

Lucy Donner was introduced in *Two Little Secrets* when she secretly set up her hairdresser, Ginna Walker, with her brother, Zach Stone. It seemed only fair that someone do the same for the single mother. I always knew it would be too predictable for Ginna to be the one finding Mr. Right for Lucy. Not when Lucy's son, Nick, now a teenager, could come up with a devious plan that involves local veterinarian Logan Kincaid. Before Lucy knows it, she has a terrier puppy and is working at Logan's animal clinic. And along the way, she falls in love with Logan.

As with the previous books, the rest of the Walker family are present to add to the mix.

I hope you've enjoyed reading about the Walkers as much as I've enjoyed writing about them.

Linda Randall Wisdom

SINGLE KID SEEKS DAD
Linda Randall Wisdom

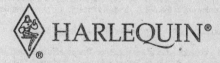

HARLEQUIN®

TORONTO • NEW YORK • LONDON
AMSTERDAM • PARIS • SYDNEY • HAMBURG
STOCKHOLM • ATHENS • TOKYO • MILAN • MADRID
PRAGUE • WARSAW • BUDAPEST • AUCKLAND

ISBN 0-373-75063-3

SINGLE KID SEEKS DAD

www.eHarlequin.com

Printed in U.S.A.

ABOUT THE AUTHOR

Linda Randall Wisdom is a California author who loves movies, books and animals of all kinds. She also has a great sense of humor, which is reflected in her books.

Books by Linda Randall Wisdom

HARLEQUIN AMERICAN ROMANCE

Prologue

The small, dimly lit room was a contrast to the bright lights and merriment in the nearby reception hall. It was the perfect meeting place for the two conspirators who faced each other.

"I have to say, young man, that your note was intriguing. Are you now going to reveal why we have to have this meeting in private?" The deep voice rumbled as the man settled back in a chair. He eyed the boy facing him. He was impressed that even under his stern gaze, the boy didn't waver as he spoke.

"It's very simple." The boy kept his voice low. "I have a single mom. You have a single son. We both want to see them married off. There's no reason why we can't work together to accomplish our objectives."

The man chuckled. "I suppose you have a plan."

"Yes, I do. We're already ahead because your son is hot for my mom."

The older man shook his head. "I've heard that she has told him she isn't interested."

The boy shrugged off his statement. "Yeah, but that can change. I did some research on your son and what I've learned about him tells me he's perfect for my mom. All she needs is some time to really get to know him."

"How do you expect to bring them together?"

Nick Donner smiled. "I've worked up what I feel is a fool-proof plan." He then proceeded to outline his idea.

The older man's skepticism soon turned to interest as he listened to Nick. "I admit that I'm impressed. Do you honestly think something that wild could work?"

"There is absolutely no reason why it won't as long as you're willing to do your part," Nick said with unshakable confidence.

An hour later, their plan was mutually approved with a handshake. Separately, the two participants slipped out of the room and returned to the reception hall just in time to watch Nora Summers Walker and her new husband, Mark Walker, cut the wedding cake.

For the balance of the evening, the young man and his older partner didn't do anything to betray their plan that, if successful, would bring them together for another wedding real soon.

Chapter One

The sun shouldn't be shining today. It should be cold and dark and dreary. Or raining. Rain would work.

With a sense of foreboding, Lucy Donner looked up at the modern-styled concrete-block building. She imagined the stairs leading to the front doors were actually steps leading to the gallows. The line of people patiently waiting to go through the security checkpoints in the courthouse lobby were the condemned waiting their turns.

She really needed to stop watching late-night movies where everyone ended up murdered.

She didn't want to walk up those steps even though she knew her son's fate hung in the balance up there.

"There you are, dear." Lou and Cathy Walker came up to her. Cathy immediately pulled her into a hug then cupped her hands around Lucy's cheeks. The older woman looked concerned as she studied Lucy's face. "How are you doing?" Cathy asked, clearly not missing the worry shadowing Lucy's eyes.

"I've gone through four bottles of antacids in the past two days," she whispered, gripping Cathy's arms as if she needed a lifeline. "What does that tell you? It's wonderful that you're here, but as I told you last night, you didn't have to come. I have an idea it's not going to be pleasant."

"Of course, we would come. You're family," Lou told her.

The relationship was only that Lucy's brother was married to their daughter, but Lou continued, "We Walkers stick together." He curved his arm around Nick's shoulders and tugged him against his side.

Lucy blinked rapidly. The threat of tears quickly dried up when she looked at her son. This was her darling baby boy. The light of her life. The reason they were spending their morning in court.

Once this was over she was grounding him until he was fifty.

And here she'd thought things would change for the better after they moved.

Lucy had seen it as a sign when she'd found a house not far from the Walker homestead in Sunset Canyon, California. She was even happier to find a school that believed in challenging its gifted students without giving them any special treatment just because their IQs happened to be higher than those of most of the rest of the human population. She was even relieved that puberty seemed to settle down Nick's mischievous nature now that he'd turned thirteen. He spent many of his free hours with Lou Walker during which he learned what went into renovating an antique automobile. Lucy had decorated their new house and made it into a home for herself and her son.

Life was great.

Until it took a crazy U-turn. Lucy received a call from the school's dean telling her that not only had Nick hacked into the school's computer, but that he'd deleted all student and personnel files and replaced them with new ones that bore no resemblance to what had been there. The dean explained that Nick's actions were considered a crime, which was why they would spend this morning at the courthouse.

Lucy was grateful Cathy and Lou had come to lend her moral support. Since the day the dean had called her, she'd alternated between fury at her son for what he'd done and fear he'd be sent to a juvenile facility that would make those late-night bad-boy movies look like a fairy tale.

Now they were in court to learn Nick's fate. Determined to look the part of the most responsible mother in the world, she'd chosen a black skirt and a cream blouse. She mentally cursed the black high heels that were killing her feet. She'd chosen the extra three inches for courage. Judging by the condition of her stomach, it hadn't worked very well. For once, she hadn't had to resort to threats to get Nick into a dress shirt and tie. Even his usually unruly sandy-brown hair was brushed into submission.

"What judge did you draw?" Lou asked.

Lucy had to think for a moment. "Judge Kincaid."

The man's face darkened.

"What?" Lucy felt her fears return. "How bad is he?"

"It's nothing like that, dear," Cathy soothed as she shot her husband a warning look. "Everything will be fine."

"The man should have retired years ago," Lou muttered.

"He's the same age as you are," Cathy reminded him.

"He has no heart."

The bantering was halted by the arrival of Lucy's brother, Zach, and his wife. They hurried toward her and Zach wrapped his arms around her for a warm embrace then hugged Nick.

"Everything will be fine," her sister-in-law, Ginna whispered.

Lucy wasn't as confident, but now was the time to find out. Together, they all walked up the steps and went through the security checkpoint, then they looked for the courtroom in which Nick's case would be heard.

Lucy was relieved to see Nick's attorney already there. She only wished he didn't look like Opie from *The Andy Griffith Show*. It didn't help that at their first meeting he had told her to call him Ritchey. All that did was bump him up to the teenager from *Happy Days*.

Oh my God, she wailed to herself, *I'd forgotten that my son's lawyer looks twelve years old!* She dredged up a faint sickly resemblance of a smile.

"Hey, Mrs. Donner." Ritchey grinned as he offered his hand. He nodded at Nick. "Are you ready, Nick?"

"Sure," the boy said, sounding almost adult.

"Maybe he is, but I'm not. But I guess that won't matter, will it?" She touched her stomach, which sent out burning signals again. "You don't think—" She found herself afraid even to say the words. "He won't be—" She stopped because she just plain couldn't go on and voice what had been giving her nightmares since this had all begun.

"I wouldn't worry, Mrs. Donner. I'm sure Nick will be put on probation and assigned to community service," he assured her. "We'll be in and out of here in no time."

Lucy breathed her first sigh of relief in days.

"I'm sorry, Mom," Nick said quietly as he touched her shoulder.

She didn't hug him, because she knew a display of affection would only embarrass him.

"No matter what the judge does to you, you are still grounded until you're a hundred and five," she told him as they went inside.

"You told me I was grounded until I was fifty," he reminded her.

"I changed my mind."

Lucy's sense that things would turn out all right disappeared the moment the judge entered the courtroom and settled into a high-backed black leather chair. Her blood turned to ice as she saw the man's stern expression.

We have Opie for an attorney and Boris Karloff for a judge. My son is going to Devil's Island!

The five adults sat in the front row with Lucy in the middle.

The judge leveled a piercing gaze at Nick.

"Come up here, young man, and let's talk," he ordered in a rumbling deep voice that rivaled Orson Welles's.

Lucy again silently vowed to stop watching late-night television. Her imagination was running away with her. She could see her baby being led off in chains to a dark and dank hole where he would spend the remainder of his life unless he managed to escape by digging through dirt and stone with a small spoon.

She was vaguely aware of Cathy taking her hand between her two.

"Frank's a fair man," Cathy whispered.

Lou refuted her assessment. "He's an idiot."

The judge's head snapped up and he scowled in their direction.

"If people can't respect the court and be quiet, they'll be thrown out," he threatened.

Lucy heard a small sound of distress travel up her throat. The last thing she needed was anyone putting Judge Kincaid in a bad mood.

As the judge questioned Nick, she vaguely heard his attorney interject a few times, but each time the judge ignored him.

Again he addressed Nick. "Young man, what you did was more than malicious mischief. You knowingly destroyed Fairfield Academy's computer files."

Lucy felt her heart sink down to her toes. This was it. Her baby was going to prison for the rest of his life. She was so lost in her misery she barely heard the judge's pronouncement.

"The dean and I had a long talk about this, young man," the judge said sternly. "Expulsion would be too good for you, namely because I don't believe that expulsion from school is a punishment. I'd rather see that student punished *in* school, loaded down with extra work. And that is what you will be doing for the rest of the school year. Be prepared to write a lot of book reports, young man."

Lucy's spirits started to rise. Lots of homework for Nick? Not a bad thing, in her eyes. She'd never believed in expelling students either. But she realized the judge wasn't finished.

"Along with your extra school work, you will have six months community service to be spent working at the Valley Animal Clinic and Shelter," the judge ordered.

"What?" She felt her neck crack as she whipped her head from side to side to look at Cathy and Ginna.

Lou shot to his feet. "Your Honor, may I speak?"

The judge scowled. "Why?"

"Young Nicholas has been working at my garage for the past four months. Is there any reason why he can't serve his time there?"

"There is an excellent reason why he cannot. I didn't order him to work there," Judge Kincaid snapped. "From what I can see, it didn't do him any good to work under your supervision if he felt he needed to find an outlet by committing this act. I can assure you he will be working very hard at the shelter, and he won't have the time or energy to think up ways to create mischief."

"An animal clinic? He refuses to clean the cat's litter box!" Lucy blurted out without thinking. "I'm sorry, Your Honor," she whispered, wilting under his condemning glower.

The judge focused on her. "Madam, it seems your son needs more supervision than you can give him. If he knows what's good for him, he will use this time to reconsider his actions. He will also tender a letter of apology to the Dean of Students at Fairfield Academy and will not be participating in any computer labs for the next semester." He turned back to Nick who looked about as solemn as Lucy had ever seen him. "Report to Dr. Kincaid at three-thirty tomorrow afternoon, young man. If you know what's good for you, you won't end up in my courtroom again. I can assure you the next time I won't be so lenient."

Nick didn't flinch under the older man's harsh regard. "I understand, sir."

After tendering his judgment, the judge dismissed the court.

Lucy was smart enough to keep her mouth closed. At the moment, she wouldn't have put it past the judge to sentence her to hard labor.

"There was no reason why he couldn't work under my supervision," Lou grumbled, as they filed out of the courtroom. "The old bastard just didn't want to appear human."

"Please, don't make him angry," Lucy pleaded.

"Don't worry, dear, they're two old fools who have been carrying on an old feud much too long," Cathy reassured her. "Come, let's stop somewhere for lunch. You need something more substantial in your stomach than antacids."

"She's right, Mom," Nick chimed in.

Lucy looked up at her son and saw his concern for her. Now that he'd passed his thirteenth birthday and sprouted several inches almost overnight, she had to look up at him. She must look bad if he was that worried.

Lou took charge. "Nick, you ride with me and Cathy will ride with your mother. We'll meet you at Stewie's." He called over his shoulder, "Ginna, Zach, are you going to join us?"

"We'll follow you over," Ginna said.

"Eating at Stewie's means he won't be watching his cholesterol." Cathy heaved a sigh. "I wouldn't worry about Nick, Lucy. Logan Kincaid's not the grump his father is. I'm sure you've met him at some of our parties."

"Logan's a sweetheart," Ginna added. "He went to school with my brother Brian."

"Logan Kincaid?" Lucy flashed back to the various Walker parties where she'd met the family veterinarian. He'd let it be known he was interested in her. In turn, she'd let him know she wasn't interested in him. "He's who Nick will be working for?" She closed her eyes. "I think I need more antacids."

"Is THERE A REASON I have to get all of your hard cases?"

Judge Frank Kincaid calmly ignored his son's outburst.

He dipped a tortilla chip in the spicy salsa and brought it to his lips.

"The best reason there is. You need additional help at the shelter. I provided you with a living body. Now you don't have to worry about finding someone." He perused the menu. "My stomach won't like anything I order, but I'm still ordering the shredded-beef enchiladas." He looked up at the waitress, gave his order and waited as his son gave his.

Logan picked up his beer and sipped the cold brew.

"The last person I need caring for my animals is some juvenile delinquent you've foisted on me."

"Chad Matthews worked out nicely."

"No, Chad Matthews broke into my drug cabinet and relieved me of all my Ketamine." The animal tranquilizer had apparently turned into a popular drug of choice. "Kristi and Jeremy worked out, but that's because they both love animals."

"There you have it!" Frank beamed. "I wouldn't worry about Nick Donner. He appears to be a good kid. He just needs some direction. That's the problem with single mothers of sons nowadays. They don't give their boys the firm structure they need."

"Donner?" Logan frowned in thought. "Is his mother named Lucy?"

Frank tipped his head back and momentarily closed his eyes in thought. "I believe that's her name. Why, do you know her?"

"Not exactly." He recalled sun-streaked light-brown hair and flashing green eyes along with a pair of kissable lips that had firmly told him she didn't require, nor desire, his attention. He quickly masked his thoughts. His dad had been trying to get him married off since his divorce had been finalized five years ago. The older man didn't seem to understand that while Logan didn't mind having a woman in his life, he wasn't looking for anything permanent. He preferred keeping the opposite sex tucked in a nice tidy compartment that wasn't long-term.

"The boy isn't your run-of-the-mill troublemaker," Frank Kincaid explained. "Psychologists would say he's one of those child geniuses who needs constant stimulus. I say forget the psychobabble. He just needs to put in some hard labor."

"Aha!" Logan held up his glass. "If you had your way you'd have everyone doing hard labor."

Frank recognized his son's sarcasm and blithely ignored it. "It didn't hurt you any."

Logan didn't bother saying any more. After all these years of verbal sparring with his father he knew he'd only lose. Instead, he settled on looking at the positive part of this deal. He'd have a chance of seeing Lucy Donner again.

"YOU KNOW, Mom, pretty soon you won't have to worry about picking me up from school," Nick said as he settled in the passenger seat of Lucy's pewter-gray Murano. He looked out and waved at a classmate. "Pretty soon I'll be able to apply for my learner's permit."

"Not in this lifetime, bud. Being grounded for the next forty years means no driving ever. I don't care if I have to drive you to your college graduation." She checked her side-view mirror and moved away from the curb. "There's a pair of old jeans and a T-shirt in the back seat." Her knuckles turned white as she tightened her grip on the steering wheel. "I should have sold you to the gypsies when I had a chance."

He grinned. "That threat hasn't worked since I was five."

"That's no threat. You have to work at that shelter for six months," Lucy muttered. "I guess it could be worse. Some hackers aren't allowed to use a computer for years."

His upbeat nature dimmed. "I can't use the computer lab at school. I have to go to study hall instead."

"Just be grateful the school didn't expel you." She mentally calculated the easiest way to drop Nick off at the shelter and make a getaway without having to deal with Logan Kincaid. She knew a conscientious mother would go inside and insist on seeing just where her son would be working. And she was a conscientious mother. But she was also a woman who found Logan Kincaid a little too attractive for her peace of mind.

Instead of running from him, she should be making herself available. The man had asked her out on a date, after all, and she'd turned him down without a good reason. Unless you counted deciding she couldn't handle anything resembling a love life right now. After what had happened with Nick, she knew she'd made the right decision. If she couldn't control her son, what made her think she could control her own life?

Lucy looked at the ranch-style building bordered by grass and colorful flowers. Farther back she could see a small house with what looked like a waist-high wooden fence around it. Off to one side was a wire-fenced-in area. She would have thought this was a lovely residence if it weren't for the sign out front declaring the premises to be the Valley Animal Clinic and Shelter—that and the cacophony of barking coming from the rear of the building.

"Maybe I should have taken you to the doctor first. For all we know you might require shots to work here," she mused aloud. "Was there anything in the court order about shots?"

"It's more like the animals need shots," Nick pointed out, as he opened the door. He glanced over his shoulder. "Aren't you coming in?"

For a second she saw the little boy she'd walked every day to the Sunny Day Preschool around the corner from their house.

"I guess I should." She climbed out and walked around the front of the vehicle.

They stepped inside a waiting area that was divided down the middle of the large room by a waist-high wall. Lucy noticed one side appeared decorated for the feline patients while the other side was indicated for dogs. She almost yelped when she saw a teenage boy seated on a bench with a python wrapped around his shoulders. She hoped the expression on the snake's face didn't have anything to do with hunger.

"Can I help you?" asked a young woman behind the counter. Light-blue medical scrubs decorated with tiny kittens wearing wings and halos covered a large pregnant belly. She smiled at the two of them.

"I'm Nick Donner. I'm supposed to be working here."

She nodded and pressed down on a button on the phone console. "Gwen, the kid is here." She looked at him. "The vet tech will be out here in a second."

"I'm Lucy, his mother," Lucy said, keeping as much distance from the snake as she possibly could. She transferred her attention to a silvery gray dog that looked like a husky that sat near the woman. What appeared to be a cell phone was lodged firmly between his jaws. She hoped the dog had been fed lately because he looked awfully hungry. Between the python and the dog, she felt like an afternoon snack.

"Nick Donner?" A spritely blonde walked out from the rear. She greeted him with a broad smile. "Hi, I'm Gwen." She introduced herself to Lucy and then explained, "Don't worry, Mrs. Donner, he won't be around anything dangerous. "He'll be under the supervision of our shelter staff along with Dr. Kincaid and myself."

Lucy was reassured by the young woman's matter-of-fact manner. "I'll be back at six, then. Nice meeting you." As she made her way out, she determinedly kept her eyes down instead of looking around for Logan Kincaid. With Nick working here for the next six months, she knew she'd be dealing with the veterinarian sooner or later.

She was hoping for later.

NICK FOLLOWED Gwen to the back. She walked swiftly while talking over her shoulder. "The shelter has two regular employees who work a rotating schedule. Kristi is working today. She'll show you the ropes. I'm sure Logan will come back to see you when he finishes with his patient."

"Okay." Nick looked at the framed color sketches of dogs, cats and exotic animals that lined the hallway walls.

"You're our youngest worker," Gwen told him as she pushed open the rear door. Barking and feline yowls greeted them as they stepped into the large room. "Just don't let Kristi scare you off."

Nick gulped as he entered the shelter. For a brief moment, he wondered if he should have found another way to accomplish his goal. It had seemed so easy when he'd mapped it out to the judge.

"Kristi, this is Nick Donner. We've got him for the next six months," Gwen announced.

Nick stared at the young woman dressed in a midriff-baring black tank top and camouflage pants tucked into Doc Martens. Light danced off the tiny gold ring hooked to one nostril and another bisecting an eyebrow, while a red stone sparkled from her navel. A barbed-wire tattoo circled one slender upper arm. Her short spiky hair was as black as her top. Dark-brown eyes surveyed him with clinical interest.

"You don't look like the typical juvie Judge Kincaid sends here," she drawled. "What'd you do?"

"I hacked into my school's computer system and gave them a whole new set of records."

She looked impressed. She gestured for him to follow her to the back of the large building. "Cool. Okay, here's how it goes. You do the dirty work. I supervise. Gwen or the doc handles any medications that need to be administered. Jeremy or I handle the records. That means you keep your paws out of the medication cabinet in case it's unlocked, which is pretty much never. What you'll be doing is hosing down and cleaning the kennels. You'll also exercise the bigger dogs, which means you take them out to the fenced-in dog park the doc set up out back. They can run free out there, but you still have to stay in there with them. Most of them enjoy chasing a ball or chasing you. You have a dog, right?"

"No, we have a cat. Luther." He eyed one rambunctious German shepherd with a trace of unease. "He's real old and cranky."

She shrugged. "You're a kid. You can handle a dog."

"Nick Donner?"

Nick turned around to see a tall man with dark blond hair coming toward him. Sunglasses hung from his T-shirt neck-line.

"Logan Kincaid." He held out his hand. "You're Lou Walker's grandson, right?"

"I guess you'd call me more a nephew or something by marriage. My uncle is married to Lou's daughter," Nick explained, taking his hand.

"And you reworked the school's computer records which now has you slaving away here." He shook his head. "You're going to regret it real fast. Work around here is pretty dirty."

"Don't scare him off," Kristi warned her boss.

"I don't have to. That's your job." Logan looked her over. "New tattoo?"

She glanced down at her arm. "It was time. You can't see my other one unless I'm wearing a bikini." She turned to Nick. "Don't even try to imagine where it is," she warned him.

"I know it's hard to believe, but Kristi's bark is worse than her bite," Logan told Nick.

"Yeah. Uh, yes, sir."

"Just call me Logan. We're pretty informal around here. Do you understand what we do here?"

"You're a veterinary clinic. You treat sick dogs and cats."

"That along with treating pretty much any other critter that shows up. We're also an animal shelter. The county shelter is usually overloaded. This area was growing enough that we needed a more local place for dogs and cats dumped on the back roads or given up by owners. We have a successful adoption program."

Nick must have looked uneasy, because the doctor gave him an assessing look and said, "Look, if you have a problem with this, I'll talk to the judge about putting you somewhere else. Just because you're ordered here doesn't mean it's written in stone, no matter what he says."

"That's not it. I'm not used to being around dogs except at the Walkers's and Jasmine's real low key." He mentioned Cathy and Lou's German shepherd. "We only have a cat."

"Then I suggest you make friends with the dogs first. Don't worry about them. They're all friendly and love the attention. Just make sure to read the tag on each door and always greet them by name. Also, if the tag has a warning about biting, don't do anything with them. Let Kristi or Jeremy handle those animals."

"Uh, boss." Kristi held up a broom. "The kid's got work to do."

Logan laughed. "Okay, he's all yours, Kris." He walked to the front of the clinic.

"Come on, it's time to earn your keep." Kristi chuckled. "So to speak."

She showed Nick how to clean out the first dog run then handed the cleaning tools over to him.

In record time Nick was wielding the hose, a heavy bristled broom and a bucket.

Kristi stood back and observed him at work.

Nick figured he was doing all right since she hadn't offered any criticism.

"Once the kennels are clean, take the dogs outside to the fenced area. They all play together pretty well, but we only take two or three out at a time. It's easier to keep them under control that way. We try to give them at least a half hour out there. When they're all exercised, clean up the area. Right now, we don't have any puppies and only a few cats. The cats are in what we call the cat palace. You'll find two litter boxes in there that have to be cleaned."

Nick nodded. "Okay. I'll get it all done."

Kristi studied him. "What are you? Thirteen, fourteen?"

"Thirteen and a half," he replied. "Have you been working here long?"

"About three years. Old Judge Hard Ass gave me the choice of working here or going to a youth facility. Trust me, juvie would have been easier." She started measuring dog kibble into metal bowls. "Logan worked my butt off."

"So you're under a court order, too?" Nick asked. He hated to think what she had done if she was still working here.

"Nah, I finished up a couple years ago. Logan gave me a real job here. It helps pay my college expenses."

"Gwen said someone else works here, too," Nick said.

"That's Jeremy. We work a rotating schedule. You'll meet him tomorrow."

Nick stared warily at a black-and-tan rottweiler sitting docilely by the gate. "Is he friendly?"

"That's Ginger and she's a sweetheart, aren't you, baby?" Kristi cooed to the dog as she opened the run. The dog stood up and greeted her with a slobbering kiss.

LOGAN REMAINED out of sight for a few minutes to see how the two got along. He'd had problems in the past when either Kristi didn't like her new helper or the helper wasn't too sure he or she could get along with a young woman who looked as if she just stepped out of a Goth club. Despite her tough exterior, Logan knew that Kristi had a true heart of gold.

He heard Nick speaking to the dogs in a low voice that didn't show any of the trepidation he'd first shown. He gave the kid credit for not flinching at the prospect of dirty work. He knew Kristi would find a way to make the tasks dirtier than usual. She claimed they might as well find out right off the bat that it wasn't easy. Seeing that the two were getting along fine, Logan went up front and stopped by the desk.

"Brenda, do me a favor. Would you let me know when Nick's mother shows up?"

The receptionist nodded.

Logan might not feel he needed another helper, but he might as well take advantage of the situation to see Lucy again.

LUCY PULLED INTO the clinic parking lot promptly at six. She noted a large sage-green SUV parked along the side of the building with a small compact car and a motorcycle parked next to it. When she stepped inside the building, the receptionist was on the phone. She waved her in.

"Go on back," she mouthed.

Lucy hesitated.

The receptionist covered the mouthpiece with her hand.

"It's okay. Just go all the way down the hallway to the end door. That leads to the kennels." She returned to her phone call.

Lucy kept an eye out for Logan as she made her way down the hallway to the rear door. The first thing she heard when she entered the shelter area was her son's laughter accompanied by a low, rumbling male voice that sent a shiver along her spine. She remembered that voice only too well. The last time she'd heard it had been at a barbecue at the Walker house. Not that she had a problem with the voice. Low-pitched with a slight rumble to it, it was the kind of voice that seduced a woman into feeling safe and cared for, two things Lucy didn't believe most men could accomplish. No, it wasn't the voice she was worried about. It was the owner of the voice that prompted her to keep her guard up.

She started to back out through the door, but the two noticed her before she could make her escape.

"Hey, Mom!" Nick called out.

Lucy stared at the dirt-covered lump that had called her Mom. He looked as if he'd rolled in the dirt. She doubted she'd find one inch on him that wasn't filthy.

"What on earth did you do?" She didn't think there was enough soap in the world to get him clean again. "Or should I say how much earth did you get on you?"

"Hello, Lucy," Logan said, looking cleaner than Nick but not by much.

She ignored the tingle starting in the pit of her stomach at the sight of his welcoming grin and brown eyes dusted with gold. "Hello, Logan. I hope Nick did an acceptable job today."

He looked more amused than put off by her formal tone. "He did fine. For a kid not used to dogs, he handled the pack without any problems."

"Pack?"

He gestured to the kennels. "I guess you could call these guys my pack."

Just then a young woman came out back. She stuck out her hand and said, "The kid did great. Hi, I'm Kristi."

"Kristi's in charge back here," Logan explained. "She and Jeremy keep things humming."

Lucy silently prayed that Nick wouldn't get the idea that a tattoo or body piercing was a good idea. It had taken a couple months for his self-drawn tattoo, courtesy of a semi-permanent ink marker, to wear off. She'd made him wear long-sleeved shirts any time he had to leave the house.

Her gaze skipped from one kennel to another. It seemed they were all filled with large dogs. Didn't anyone have a Chihuahua out here in Southern California's Riverside County?

"I cleaned all the dog runs then took the dogs out to this fenced area in the back where I can run with them," Nick explained with enthusiasm. "It's really cool!"

"And did you also roll in the dirt with them?" She indicated his dirty clothing.

He looked down. "I guess this is why you had me wear old clothes, huh?"

Lucy turned to Logan. "He's safe being alone with these animals?"

"No one's been bitten yet. And I guess Nick's had his shots so the animals are protected." He blew out a low breath. "It's a joke, Lucy."

"Yes, I gathered that." She mentally hated herself for acting so stiff but couldn't seem to stop herself.

"I have to clean up first," Nick told her.

"Use the antiseptic soap," Kristi reminded him.

Nick nodded as he loped off.

"He's not a typical juvenile delinquent," Lucy stated almost defiantly.

"I never thought he was," Logan replied mildly. "I read the judge's report, Lucy. It sounds like Nick has a knack with computers that will give Bill Gates a run for his money in a few years. I think the judge wants Nick to see a different side of life so he uses his skills only for good and not evil. Another joke."

"I know that! He's on the basketball team at school." Now she sounded defensive. "And he's worked on cars with Lou Walker since we moved here. He just has too much imagination and sometimes does something before thinking of what his actions might cause."

"And what have you done since you moved here?"

"I've taken kind of a sabbatical from my travel agent job in order to get my house in order. It's not an easy task," she replied.

"That's right, your other house was crashed into or something."

"The engine landed ahead of the jet," she said dryly. "Unfortunately, it landed inside my house. Luckily, the jet didn't."

"Since you've been so busy you probably haven't seen too much of the area," Logan surmised. "Perhaps one weekend you'd like to go for a tour."

"Right now you're in charge of my son's community service. I think that's enough interaction." She raised her voice. "Nick, I'll be in the car." The smile she directed at Logan was patently insincere. It turned more genuine as she looked at the young woman. "It was nice meeting you, Kristi. Dr. Kincaid." She made her escape.

"It's Logan," he called after her departing figure.

Before he could say anything further, Nick emerged, wiping his wet hands on his jeans.

"My mom's not usually this cranky," he explained quickly. "I think it's because I got in trouble. I'd promised I wouldn't get in any more trouble and then this happened. I think she was afraid I'd end up in jail." He leaned over to confide, "She kept saying my lawyer looked like Opie, whatever that means."

Logan chuckled. "I know who you're talking about. Ritchey Owens does look pretty young to practice law, but he's good. Besides, the judge doesn't like to send boys to jail. He believes in a strict work ethic."

"He just likes you getting free labor," Kristi teased her boss.

"The judge is your dad, isn't he?" Nick asked Logan.

"Guilty."

"You must take after your mom, then." He shot the vet a grin. "Good night, Logan. 'Night Kristi. See ya tomorrow."

"Good night, Nick." Logan turned to Kristi and cocked a questioning eyebrow.

"He did good," she told him. "He took orders without any arguments. He actually listened to everything I said. Of course, he hasn't given the dogs their baths yet." She grinned.

"The ultimate test." He looked around. "It all looks great. Go ahead and take off."

She sketched a salute. "See ya on Thursday." She snatched up a backpack and headed out the rear door. A few moments later the roar of a motorcycle could be heard.

When Logan walked into the reception area, Brenda was shutting down the computer and locking drawers. He looked at her big belly and winced. The fear she might go into labor during working hours had haunted him for the past month.

"I'm out of here," Brenda announced before breezing out the door.

"Good night," he called after her.

"Have you seen Beau?" Gwen asked, coming into the room.

He shook his head. "You know how he is when we're closing up."

"Come on, you little monster! Show yourself!" Gwen called out.

Beau, a bright red macaw with turquoise and green wings, waddled down the hallway. A flap of his wings bore him up to the counter. He cocked his head to one side.

"Tigger is in his bed, Beau." Logan held out his arm and the macaw hopped onto it, content that the cat he somehow believed to be his pet was down for the night.

"Magnum," Beau uttered in his raspy voice.

Magnum was Logan's Malamute.

"He's on guard."

"Like anyone would dare break in here," Gwen muttered. She eyed her boss. "So that's Lucy Donner."

"Nick's mother, yes."

"I heard she's one of the few women to turn you down." Gwen grinned broadly. "She shot you down again tonight, didn't she?"

"I didn't give her any reason to shoot me down," he defended himself.

"I really like her."

Logan huffed the exasperated sigh men expel when women think they have the best of them.

"Shouldn't you be nicer to the boss when you're due for a raise?" he asked as he set the macaw in a large black wrought-iron cage and secured the door with a lock; the macaw had a habit of escaping.

"I already gave myself a nice one last month. 'Night, boss." She waved her hand over her shoulder as she headed out the door.

"'Night, boss," Beau echoed.

"Right, like I'm in charge," Logan muttered.

Before locking up, he took one last tour of the clinic to make sure all was in order. He was impressed to find the bucket Nick had used rinsed out and hung on its hook on the wall, the broom set back in place and the hose neatly coiled in a corner by the faucet. No trash was left out and covers on trash cans were secured. He didn't think this was a boy behaving himself because it was his first day working here. He was positive Nick had acted like himself that day.

"I wonder if Dad would consider giving him to me for an additional six months. Magnum, guard!" he ordered the Malamute who lay on a dog bed in one corner. As always, the slightly chewed cell phone lay within reach.

For once, Logan left the clinic not thinking about work. Lucy Donner dominated his thoughts as he walked outside to the small house he used as his living quarters. He chuckled as an idea came to mind.

"Too bad Dad can't order her into community service."

Chapter Two

"How is Nick doing with his community service?" Ginna Stone asked when she met Lucy for lunch a week later.

Ginna had called her that morning and suggested that since she had the day off from the hair salon they get together for lunch. Lucy was always glad to see her best friend and new sister-in-law. Lucy had always thought Ginna would be a perfect match for her brother, Zach. She proved it when she'd secretly paired the two for an island getaway. Now they'd been married for months, and Lucy had never seen them happier. Ginna joked that she was going to return the favor by fixing Lucy up with Mr. Right, but so far her matchmaking efforts had failed.

"He's doing very well. He goes over to that clinic and cleans up after animals and cats and exercises the dogs, but he still won't go near Luther's litter box," Lucy told her. "His excuse is that he's so tired from his work at the clinic he only has enough energy left to do his homework."

Ginna chuckled. "But he finally acknowledges Luther has a litter box. I remember when he pretended it didn't exist. Isn't that a step in the right direction?"

"I guess so. I still don't understand why Nick did this. He's always had an inventive mind, but he'd outgrown that mischievous streak of his. He was really behaving himself. Until now."

"Zach once told me about some of Nick's more colorful antics." Ginna sipped her iced tea. "And to think you let Nick live," she teased.

"There were times when I wondered which one of us would survive his childhood," Lucy admitted. "When Nick was eight, the school psychologist told me that Nick was acting out because he didn't have a father figure. Zach had gone to the appointment with me and told the man that Nick had *him* as a male figure in his life. He felt the school needed to do its part by offering Nick and kids like him more challenges. That's why I was so happy when we moved out here and I found Fairfield. They offer just the right programs for a boy with his smarts. Until this happened. Now I'm just grateful they didn't expel him." She sighed.

"Look at it this way. Nick had a lapse of good judgment. He's becoming a teenager, Luce. Collectively, my brothers don't have intelligence anywhere close to Nick's. Trust me, they pulled some pretty wild stunts in their day. Mom claimed it's because of them that she had to start coloring her hair so young."

"No wonder I have highlights done so often." Lucy laughed. "How are Emma and Trey doing?" She mentioned her niece and nephew, Ginna's stepchildren.

"They both love second grade. The principal talked to us about putting them in different classes. They prefer splitting up twins unless the parents object. It gives the kids a chance to be more individual. Zach and I thought it was a good idea since Trey seems to follow in Emma's shadow too much. Now that he's in a different class he's had a chance to come into his own more. He stands up to her in ways he wouldn't have dreamed of before, and last weekend he even pulled a practical joke on her. It's great to see him turn into his very own little individual."

"For someone who didn't want kids, you've sure turned into Super Mom," Lucy teased. "And to think you were so mad at me for setting you up with Zach on your trip."

"Which you will never let me forget," Ginna verbally tossed back, but she looked very happy as she uttered the words.

Lucy grinned back. "You've loved every minute of it."

"Yes, I have. In fact—" she leaned forward "—it's nothing definite yet, but Zach and I are looking at property out this way." She held up her hand. "We haven't said anything to my parents yet. For Zach, writing his magazine column and now his books means he can work anywhere, and while I enjoy working for CeCe at the Steppin' Out Salon, the idea of having my own salon has been calling me for the past year or so. If it works out, Nora and I would look for local space. She and Mark are looking around here, too."

"Abby said she and Jeff found a house in the area. They don't want to say anything to Cathy and Lou until the escrow closes," Lucy said, mentioning Ginna's oldest brother and sister-in-law. "She said there's another fire station opening and Jeff has already put in for a position there. Lou said if the rest of the Walker sons would return to Riverside County he could have his very own fire-fighting department and paramedics." She grinned.

"They'll love having everyone around them. Dad used to joke about his Walker Dynasty," Ginna said. "Which, whether you like it or not, you are a part of."

"I learned that the day of Nick's hearing. I was very grateful for everyone's support," she confessed.

"That's the way they are. Dad always hoped that at least one of the boys would go into the auto renovation business with him, but he should have known better; Jeff wanted to be a fireman since the day he accidentally set the garage on fire, and Brian and Mark are naturals as paramedics. Now Dad hopes one of the grandkids has grease in his or her veins." She chuckled. "Don't you find it odd that Nick is working for the man you've avoided all these months?"

"Not the way my life is going."

"I thought for sure Logan was going to be successful at Grandpa's birthday party."

Lucy shook her head. "Luckily, Mark's proposal to Nora took the spotlight off us." She remembered that evening very well. It seemed every time she turned around Logan was there. While she was attracted to the blond, good-looking veterinarian, she was also wary. She had an idea the man knew just how cute he was and capitalized on it. Since Lucy's ex-husband had been blond and good-looking, she tended to stay away from the type.

Ginna peered at her closely. "Lucy. You're not—" She suddenly burst out laughing, "You are! You're blushing. Lucy, you're blushing!"

Lucy resisted the urge to feel her cheeks to see if they felt as warm to the touch as she sensed. "I am not."

"Yes, you are!" Ginna was delighted with her friend's loss of composure. "Logan is very good-looking."

"If you like the aging-surfer look."

"Blond hair and a tan don't automatically make you a surfer. Besides, I understand he gave that up after he graduated from veterinary school."

"That type plays the field as if they're still in high school," Lucy pointed out. "Besides, I don't need a man in my life."

"Yeah, right." Ginna held up her left hand with its sparkling diamond wedding band and engagement ring displayed on the third finger. "That's what I said and look what happened."

LUCY MENTALLY CURSED Ginna for planting ideas in her head. She even felt a little nervous when she arrived at the clinic to pick up Nick. She never suffered from paranoia until all her friends wanted to do some matchmaking for her.

As she walked into the clinic she steeled herself to come face to face with Logan. She hadn't seen him the past few days, but she didn't expect her luck to continue to hold.

"Mom, I need to come in real early tomorrow," Nick greeted his mother.

She wrinkled her nose at the smelly young man standing in front of her. "And you have to do this because…?"

"It's Adoption Day. The dogs have to be bathed and brushed and the cats have to get cleaned up," he explained. "Jeremy can't come in early because he's got an exam. I thought maybe you'd come in with me and help. You will help us, won't you?"

"Nick said you wouldn't mind helping us out, Mrs. Donner," Kristi spoke up.

Lucy wondered if the young woman owned anything other than black crop tops and camouflage pants. Each time she'd seen Kristi the wardrobe had been the same. Still, she doubted the young woman had trouble deciding what to wear when she got up in the morning.

Nick beseeched her. "Please, Mom?"

She could never turn him down when he used the magic word. "Just don't make a habit of this."

"We'd appreciate it, Mrs. Donner," Kristi said.

"Logan, Mom said she'll help us tomorrow," Nick called out.

When Logan walked into the kennel area a large macaw with green and turquoise feathers was perched on his shoulder. Lucy noticed that the hungry-looking Malamute trotted along beside him. He still had a cell phone in his mouth. The dog, that is.

"Maybe this is a silly question, but is there a reason why that dog has a phone in his mouth?" she asked, gesturing to the husky who watched her with an unblinking silvery-blue gaze.

"He's hoping to hear from a cute little collie who was in here a few months ago," Logan said glibly.

"He's better off without her. I heard collies can be fickle," she said. "Also high-maintenance with all that fur. So what's his real story?"

He looked down and grimaced. "I found Magnum on a side road about eight months ago," he replied. "Poor guy had been hit by a car and wasn't in good shape. When I was checking him over, I set my cell phone down on the ground. It started ringing and I guess Magnum didn't like the sound. He picked it up and growled every time I tried to get it back from him. To this day, I'm not sure if he's waiting for a call or still figuring out how to make one. Since he nominated himself as the clinic's guard dog, I decided he wants to keep it on hand in case he has to call nine-one-one."

"You mean you just let him keep your cell phone?"

"See that jaw? Those teeth? Trust me, you'd let him keep it, too."

Lucy studied the black-and-silvery-gray Malamute, a hundred pounds-plus of pure muscle. "I see your point."

"Here kitty, kitty, kitty," the macaw cooed. A faint meow sounded before a ginger-colored cat trotted up to Logan. The cat sat back on his haunches and raised a paw, batting at the air.

"That's Tigger, Beau's cat," Nick explained, stooping to stroke the cat, who immediately purred and arched under his touch. "He's really sweet."

"If only you paid that much attention to your own cat," Lucy pointed out.

"Luther's a hundred years old and hates me."

"Luther is fifteen years old and merely cranky," she said.

"Every boy should have a dog," Logan said.

"Not when I'd be the one who'd be cleaning up the backyard." Lucy looked at the kennels. She decided the dogs had grown even larger since the last time she'd seen some of them. "Are your Adoption Days successful?"

"Pretty much." Logan transferred Beau to a series of thick manzanita branches set up as a macaw playpen in one corner of the large room. "We have it all set up outside. We have volunteers to help out with the animals and assist people in filling out the adoption paperwork, but we can always use more live bodies to help out." He looked hopeful.

Lucy swore Logan's expression when he turned her way echoed Nick's. She feared he could prove as difficult to resist as her son was.

"I already said I'd come in and help wash the dogs when doing all this is actually his job and not mine," she said.

"I'd call it mother/son bonding."

"We already do plenty of bonding." She tried to keep her eyes off a world-class male butt as Logan turned around when Gwen called out his name. She felt a blush burn her cheeks when she noticed Kristi's attention was centered on her. The younger woman flashed her a cheeky grin. She held up her thumb and forefinger circled in a sign of approval.

Lucy was relieved when she and Nick were finally leaving the clinic.

"See you in the morning," Logan called after her.

"Yes." Why did she feel his words sounded more like a threat than a polite good-bye?

As they climbed into the Murano, Lucy looked at her son.

"The last thing most boys your age want is to spend more time with their mothers," she said. "Especially if they're working with a young woman like Kristi." *Please, do not have a crush on her!* she silently begged.

"Kristi is really cool," he said enthusiastically. "She's been working hard to get her grades up because she wants to be a vet. I've been helping her with her chemistry. She kinda sucks at that."

"Chemistry, terrific," she muttered, switching on the engine.

Lucy decided it was a good idea she was helping out at the shelter tomorrow where she could see just how her son and one of his bosses interacted.

"Oh yeah, we need to be there about five-thirty," Nick told her.

She almost slammed on the brakes. "In the morning?"

He patted her shoulder. "Don't worry, Mom. I have faith in you."

"Sweetheart, there are many things your mom can do. Being civil in the morning is not one of them."

She silently vowed she wasn't doing this because Logan had asked.

The first time Lucy had met Logan Kincaid she'd thought he was a good-looking man. He was the kind of male specimen who had her hormones sitting up and taking notice. Besides the blond hair, there wasn't a physical resemblance to her ex-husband, but he had the same charm Ross had always exhibited. She decided Logan was one of those love-'em-and-leave-'em types. It was too easy to imagine him as a man who was convinced all he had to do was flash his pearly whites and the woman would instantly swoon in his arms. Luckily, she wasn't the swooning type. Nor was she looking for a permanent man in her life. In fact, she wasn't looking for anyone short-term either. Since her divorce she'd closely guarded her heart.

Her ex-husband had left her long ago after finding out she was pregnant. He'd told her he wasn't father material and had no desire to learn how to be one. Her brother, Zach, and his first wife, Kathy, were there to help her get through her pregnancy and her new single state. Lucy did the same for Zach when his wife died in childbirth, leaving him with twins.

Lucy always regretted Nick not having a brother or sister. She thought her son might not have given in to his mischievous tendencies if he'd had a sibling. Then again, she rationalized, he also could have ended up with another partner in crime.

"MOM."

"Umph."

"Mom." A hand touched her shoulder and gently shook it.

"Go 'way," she mumbled, pulling her covers over her head to block out any hint of light.

"Mom, you have to get up."

"Mom doesn't exist."

A corner of her blanket was pulled back and something warm and aromatic was practically shoved under her nose.

Lucy opened one eye to see if the aroma was real or a dream. Nick held out her largest mug filled with coffee. Light streamed in from the hallway. At least he'd been smart enough not to turn on the light in her bedroom.

She kept her eyes slitted. "What time is it?"

"Four-thirty."

She groaned loudly as she pulled the covers back over her head. "I changed my mind. In fact, drive yourself to the shelter. I'm sure you can whip yourself up a fake driver's license in no time. I promise not to tell."

"Mom, you said you'd help us," he reminded her. "You always said we have to honor our promises."

Lucy bit back a curse. There was nothing worse than a son spouting back what a parent had taught him. She reached out and took the coffee mug from him. She sighed happily as she sipped the strong brew.

"I even turned the shower on for you, so by now it's a nice warm temperature," Nick said in a coaxing tone. "And I'm making waffles."

Lucy perked up a little. "Waffles?"

"And bacon and eggs scrambled just the way you like them."

She was starting to give in. "You hate getting up early just as much as I do."

"I need to help get the dogs ready for Adoption Day."

"And if you're not there, who knows what that cranky old judge would do to you." She pushed the covers back more. That was when she noticed that Nick was already dressed in a pair of ragged denim shorts and a faded T-shirt that she thought she'd thrown away a week ago. Considering what he'd be doing that morning, it was probably just as well he wasn't better dressed. She slurped more coffee and held the mug out. "Please refill this for me while I shower."

Nick took off. The refilled mug was returned before she finished crawling out of bed.

Lucy realized how important this day was to Nick when he cleaned up the kitchen after breakfast and she found Luther's litter box filled with fresh litter. The stormy gray cat peered at her through golden eyes filled with feline suspicion before he stalked off to his favorite corner in the family room where he always took his morning snooze.

Her only problem was what to wear. She knew she should wear something she wouldn't care about if it ended up ruined, but the feminine part of her didn't want to look like a hag in front of Logan. Just because she was leery of dating him didn't mean she didn't want to look her best.

She dug through her drawers until she reminded herself that she was over thirty and wasn't looking for the perfect outfit to wear to school, so she could impress the captain of the football team.

She also reminded herself that she wasn't interested in Logan. She had a full life and didn't need a man in it. A couple of times she'd considered getting back into the dating game, but it only took a few dates for her to realize dating wasn't anything like she remembered. She wasn't sure if she was dating the wrong men or she was the wrong woman for them. Either way, she'd come to the conclusion she was better off going solo.

"Just pick something." She finally closed her eyes and pulled out a pair of old cotton shorts and an oversize T-shirt that she knotted at her waist. "Nick, please pour the rest of the coffee in a travel mug for me!" she called out. "The really big mug."

"Already done. Like I'd let you leave the house without

enough caffeine to send you rocketing into another galaxy," he hollered back as he headed for the garage. "Come on, Mom! We're gonna be late."

Lucy started to leave her bedroom then paused and ran back to the bathroom to apply a hint of blush and lipgloss.

"Don't want to scare the dogs," she muttered to herself.

LOGAN HAD just checked on his patients who had remained in the clinic overnight when he heard shrieks and laughter coming from the kennel area.

"Bertie Beagle is starting to wake up," Gwen announced, looking into the closet-sized room that doubled as Logan's office. "He looks good, so does the pug. However, you look like hell. What time did you get to bed last night?"

He stretched his arms over his head. "Who says I got to bed? The Sullivans called about 2:00 a.m. and brought in their iguana. Sigfried wasn't doing well."

Gwen shook her head. "I guess you need this more than I do." She set a coffee shop to-go cup on his desk.

"Is that one of those fancy drinks you like? The nonfat, no-foam, double-shot whatever?"

"Just be darned grateful I'm willing to share, Logan. Unless you want to wait while I make what you consider coffee."

"Because I'm a wonderful boss who wouldn't dream of depriving his favorite vet tech of her beloved coffee, I'll wait for the coffee." He smiled winningly. "What's going on outside to cause all the laughter? Kristi isn't known for having anything even close to a funny bone."

"Nick Donner has one and it seems his mother does, too." Gwen picked up the coffee carafe and carried it out to the sink. "The dogs are giving the crew a run for their money."

Logan uncoiled himself from his chair. "Maybe I should take a look out there."

She shot her boss a knowing look. "Right."

Logan ignored her parting shot and headed down the hall.

"When Nick was little he hated baths with a passion, but he was never as bad as these guys!" Lucy laughed and jumped back but not fast enough as a wet soapy tail slapped her in the face.

"Thanks, Mom, just what I want people to hear." Nick stood at another tub hosing down a Labrador mix that was happily enjoying his bath.

"Mothers love to embarrass their kids," Kristi told him. "You should hear some of the sh—uh—nonsense my mom dishes out." She caught the expression on Lucy's face and quickly amended her words. "My mom told me I'll do the same when I have kids."

Kristi grabbed a tighter hold on the Labrador's collar as he twisted around under the stream of water she directed at the dog. "Joey, you are a true water dog."

Lucy drizzled shampoo on her rottweiler's head and lathered it up with a steady stream of water.

"Why not wear a bikini?"

At the sound of Logan's voice Lucy spun around from the tub, forgetting she still held the hose in her hand. Even though the water wasn't turned on high, it was strong enough to hit him square in the face. She gasped in shock and quickly turned off the faucet.

"I am so sorry!" she apologized, handing him a towel until she realized it was too damp to do any good. Without saying a word, he took it from her and mopped his face.

"Wish I'd done that," Nick chortled.

"No, you do not!" Lucy glared at her son.

"More than once we've all thought of soaking the boss," Kristi said, "but he always stays inside all nice and dry while we're out here getting as wet as the dogs."

"But you enjoy it so much," Logan reminded them as he tossed the towel to one side. He paused to look at Lucy. He'd seen her dressed up at a couple of local parties and he'd seen her dressed casually when she dropped Nick off here. But he'd never seen her like this. Her faded navy T-shirt with Basketball Mom From Hell on it, and her equally faded navy shorts were more wet than dry. He'd learned the hard way about the rottweiler's love for water, so he wasn't surprised she looked like the proverbial wet rag. Even wet, with her perky ponytail and lack of makeup, Lucy still looked cute, although he doubted she would want to hear that description.

Logan recalled that it was Lucy's laughter that had first caught his attention. Full-bodied like a heady wine, rich like pure gold, the throaty sound traveled along his spine.

"And you hold your Adoption Day here?" Lucy asked, picking up a dry towel and drying off the large dog.

"We've got wire cages set up outside for the cats and dogs and a tent overhead," Logan explained, watching Lucy put the rottweiler in his kennel then choose a medium-size terrier mix to bathe next. She picked him up and placed him in the tub. "If you're up to hanging around for the day, we can always use the help."

"I don't know anything about dogs," she pointed out.

"You have a cat."

"Luther isn't a cat. He's a thug in a furry coat," she explained. "I think he was a hit man for the mob in another life."

"Logan doesn't let just anyone adopt an animal," Kristi said. "He wants to know they're going to a good home. Who knows, maybe you'll end up with one of the dogs." She wrestled a young black Labrador onto a table and began drying him with a hair dryer.

Nick looked expectantly at Lucy. "A dog would be good. Every boy should have one," he piously announced.

Lucy rolled her eyes. "I'm sure after working here for six months you'll have your fill of dogs."

"Didn't you have any pets when you were growing up?" Logan asked her.

She shook her head. "My dad claimed he was allergic to

goldfish. My mom told my brother and me that he was my pet and I was his. We agreed it just wasn't the same."

"At least you didn't have to worry about fleas." Logan walked over and draped a towel over the terrier before picking him up from the tub and carrying him over to a table for drying.

"Or getting him neutered," Lucy said, tongue-in-cheek.

"Uncle Zach neutered." Nick snickered.

"It's not a word we guys like to hear," Logan told him. He stepped back and watched Lucy towel-dry the terrier and mutter nonsense words to the dog. For a woman who claimed not to understand dogs, she was doing a good job of using the dryer, brush and comb on the dog and talking to him in the slightly high-pitched tone dogs enjoyed. She laughed when the dog jumped up on his hind legs and offered her a wet kiss.

"Who couldn't resist a charmer like you?" she cooed at the dog.

Abruptly, he called out to Kristi, "Get one of the Adoption Day T-shirts for Lucy, will you?" Then he made for the door leading to the clinic.

He felt a tightening within his body at the idea of Lucy giving him the kind of attention she gave the dog. He wouldn't mind a kiss on the nose. Or any other part of his body...

Lucy hadn't missed the vibes practically jumping off Logan. If she didn't know any better, she'd swear he had looked at her the way a big ol' tomcat looked at a fat mouse. Not that she'd call herself fat. The man was interested. And why wouldn't he act interested now? she asked herself. She'd been tracking him like a cat who hadn't been fed in days.

"Three hours here and I'm already thinking in animal metaphors," she murmured.

"Animal metaphors?" Kristi said, walking up with a bright red T-shirt in one hand. "This could be interesting." She held out the garment.

"Cute." Lucy looked at the black-lined heart centered on

the shirt with "Adopt With an Open Heart" written inside it. "But there's nothing on here to advertise the clinic." She wasn't surprised to see that Kristi's shirt was black with a red heart.

"Logan doesn't have these adoption days to promote the clinic. He does it to find homes for the animals." Kristi stroked the head of the terrier who leaned contentedly against her leg. "Which is why I have two cats and a turtle at home. Jeremy has two dogs and Gwen has three. Brenda says she refuses to give in to the animals. But how can you resist these faces?" She bent down, cupped the terrier's face in her hands and gave him a smooch. "Huh, Sweetie Pie?"

"Kristi named her that because she's so sweet," Nick explained, coming out from the rear of the kennels, now wearing an oversized red shirt himself.

Lucy felt as if she was seeing a new side to her son. He'd quickly become a part of this group. He might have been thirteen to Kristi's nineteen, but the young woman treated him as an equal. Lucy felt a sudden constriction in her chest.

My baby's growing up.

She suddenly turned away to hide the tears she could feel forming in her eyes.

"I'll be right back." Her voice sounded thick to her ears.

"Lucy, are you okay?" Kristi asked.

"I'm fine. Maybe I'm allergic to one of the dogs," she muttered as she grabbed her tote bag and made her escape to a nearby bathroom.

When she left the small room later, her eyes were mercifully dry and she wore the T-shirt over black shorts she'd brought with her. She was walking with her head down, so intent on not looking for Logan, that she didn't realize she was on a collision course until she literally walked into his chest.

"Oomph!" She reared back so quickly she would have fallen on her butt if Logan hadn't grabbed hold of her arms. "Sorry." She tried to step back but he still didn't release her.

"Are you okay?" he asked.

"You have a hard chest," she said, and then could have kicked herself when she saw the amused glint in his eyes. She noticed they were deep, brown and dusted with gold.

Cat eyes. She mentally gave herself a good shake. *Stop with the animal metaphors!*

"Lucy."

It wasn't until then she realized he must have said her name more than once.

"Sorry. I'm not used to being dragged out of bed at the crack of dawn."

He grinned. "Not a morning person, are you?"

"Not even close. It usually takes four or five cups of industrial-strength coffee to get me going."

Logan's smile was slow and way too dangerous for Lucy's peace of mind. "I'll keep that in mind."

He walked away before she could ask for clarification. She decided she was better off not knowing.

Chapter Three

Lucy was in the midst of a sight and sensory overload. All around her dogs barked and cats meowed. There were even two hamsters racing on squeaky exercise wheels.

"Is it always this crazy?" she asked Kristi, who'd just presented a happy family with the equally happy Joey.

Kristi reached down and hugged the dog. "You be good, sweetie," she whispered in the dog's ear. Her smile was wistful as she watched them walk away. The dog danced alongside the little boy who held on to the leash. "I'm always glad when they're adopted, but I also feel as if I'm losing them." She looked around. "As to your question, yes, it's always this crazy. Probably why Logan only has Adoption Day once a month unless we're overloaded with animals."

"Excuse me, you're one of the adoption people, right?" A woman holding a furry bundle stopped Lucy.

"Yes, I am, can I help you with something?"

"That's why I'm here. Adopt this one." The woman thrust the dog into Lucy's arms.

"I, uh—" Lucy looked down at the white and black spiky fur surrounding a tiny muzzle and black shoe-button eyes. Small pointed ears—one white, one black—perked up as the puppy returned her studying gaze. An odd-shaped black patch covered one eye while the rest of his face was white. He looked as if he'd been hurriedly stitched up. She mentally searched the dogs they had brought out that morning. She knew she would have remembered this little one. "I'm sorry, but I don't recall this one—"

"Oh no! I'm not adopting him. I'm giving him to you to adopt out or whatever you do," the woman said in a bright voice.

Lucy instantly felt out of her depth. She looked around, desperate for some assistance. She breathed a sigh of relief when Logan looked her way and started walking over. "I don't think—" She tightened her hold when the puppy wiggled in her arms.

"Hello, Mrs. Crenshaw, it's nice to see you," Logan said smoothly.

The woman turned to him. "Hello, Logan. As I explained to your helper, I want you to find a home for this dog."

"What's wrong with him?" Lucy asked, tightening her hold on the wiggling puppy.

The woman stared at her as if she'd lost her mind. "You can't see it? All you have to do is look at him. He looks like a patchwork quilt. My house is French provincial, not country or even modern."

Logan smiled as the puppy stretched out his head and licked his fingers. "He looks like a healthy terrier to me."

"Oh, he is. It's just that Harry got it wrong again. Just as he did with that poodle. And the shih tzu. And that horrid little Pekingese with the strange face. You can understand, can't you?" she appealed to Lucy. "My husband feels we need pets in the house. He thinks because we live in a rural area we should act more rural. I love animals, but he just doesn't understand that they have to be the right kind of animal. This one isn't it."

Lucy looked over the woman dressed in pale-blue capris, a blue-and-pink striped boat-neck knit shirt and matching blue leather high-heeled slides. The designer sunglasses were propped on a nose that Lucy was positive had known a cos-

metic surgeon's skill. As a former travel agent, she'd dealt
with enough women who had too much time on their hands
and too much money to spend that she could understand their
convoluted thought processes. She held the puppy protectively against her chest and felt the warmth of a slightly rough
tongue sweeping across her chin.

"Have you thought about setting up an aquarium?" she
asked.

The woman looked at her. "An aquarium?"

Lucy nodded. "You might consider setting up a salt-water
aquarium. I'm sure you've been to the Caribbean." The
woman nodded. "Did you do any snorkeling when you were
there?"

"Harry enjoyed swimming in the ocean. I never liked getting my hair wet."

Lucy wasn't surprised to hear that admission. "Then I'm
sure he told you about all the colorful fish he saw while snorkeling. I don't know how your house is set up, but I can imagine you have a large living room where you entertain a lot.
The kind of room in which something unique can really stand
out." She paused long enough for the woman to nod her head.
"That is the kind of room that is perfect for a large aquarium
filled with beautiful exotic fish. You'll find that the fish in a
salt-water aquarium are more brilliant in color."

"I see," the woman drawled, her interest aroused. "I can
imagine that some of them would be very rare." *Meaning expensive*, Lucy thought.

"I've seen some rare fish that are just beautiful. Since the
upkeep isn't easy, I understand it's best to have a professional
come in to handle the upkeep of the aquarium."

Mrs. Crenshaw considered Lucy's suggestion. "With an
aquarium I could choose a color scheme that would go with
the furniture much better than I could with a dog," she mused
aloud. "I've seen those specialty fish stores. Someone there
could assist us in setting up a salt-water aquarium."

"Definitely."

Mrs. Crenshaw smiled just enough to show she was pleased with the suggestion but not enough to cause lines. "What a wonderful idea. Thank you, dear. I'll look into that." She patted Lucy's arm that still cradled the wiggling puppy. She turned to Logan as she pulled an envelope out of her purse and handed it to him. "Thank you, Logan. I'm sure you can find the right home for the dog." She started to walk away.

"Wait! What's the puppy's name?" Lucy called after her.

The woman looked over her shoulder. "He doesn't have a name." She gave a little wave and hurried over to her Mercedes convertible.

Hugging the puppy against her chest and stroking his back the way she would comfort a baby, Lucy watched the woman drive off.

She looked at Logan. "She's done this before?"

He nodded. "The poodle didn't like her. The Pekingese had an ugly face. Then there was the Afghan that didn't match the furniture. She said she couldn't bear to return the dogs to the breeders, so she always brought them to me to adopt out. The problem is she has a husband who indulges her every whim." He shook his head in frustration. "How did you know she goes to the Caribbean?"

"It was pretty much an easy guess. In my former life as a travel agent, I met women like her. I'd also say she enjoys Vienna, Paris and Geneva for their shopping and costly facial treatments."

Logan absently stroked the puppy's head as he opened the envelope and pulled out a check. Lucy glanced over. Her eyes widened at the amount written in a graceful script.

"She not only leaves the dog but gives you money to boot?"

"I think it's guilt money on her part. Thanks to Mrs. Crenshaw's donations I've been able to add four more dog runs, set up the cat palace and give Kristi and Jeremy much-needed raises," he told her.

"But she basically abandons her dogs here." Lucy looked down at the puppy, now happily snoozing in her arms. She didn't want to put the dog down.

"Better she leaves them here than dumps them on the road." Logan started to reach for the puppy but Lucy danced out of his way.

"He's fine with me." She cupped her hand over the back of the puppy's head in a protective manner. "Besides, he's upset. He just lost the person he thought was his mother. He needs some TLC before you can even think of putting him in one of those cages."

"I have to check him out before I can put him up for adoption," he pointed out in a low voice. "Besides, those cages keep him safe."

"I want to adopt him." The words left her mouth before her brain engaged. She took a deep breath as she looked down at the puppy snuggling contentedly against her. Feeling she needed him to understand she was serious, she repeated the words. "I want to adopt him."

Logan was silent as he studied her. Lucy felt the rest of the world around them recede as she returned his gaze. Looking at the way his red Adoption Day T-shirt covered his chest, she was convinced that red was most definitely his color.

"That's a pretty quick decision considering you said you know nothing about dogs."

"He doesn't deserve to be just dumped here like…like…" She found herself at a loss for words. "It's as if that woman returned a dress that was the wrong color."

"True, Mrs. Crenshaw isn't the most thoughtful woman in the county, but she does have her good points. She knows I'll find the puppy an appropriate home," he explained. "I'm just hoping the next time around I won't end up with a tank full of fish."

The puppy sighed with contentment as Lucy lightly scratched between his ears. "I don't think you will. It sounds like she's happier when she's spending her husband's money. She'll spend a small fortune setting up a salt-water tank that her friends will ooh and aah over. That's all she wants. Having a dog didn't give her that kind of joy."

"She didn't have that joy with a cat either," he said. "The Persian had a habit of shedding fur on the furniture and she was positive the Siamese didn't like her. Luckily, she didn't try exotic birds."

Lucy winced. "Then we'll just hope that she loves fish."

"Or the clinic will end up with a fancy tank in the waiting area."

"Just don't put it on the cat side," she quipped. "Now, where do I sign the papers to make this baby boy mine?"

"I'll stop by Mrs. Crenshaw's house tomorrow to have her sign the dog over to you," he told her. "And I'll give you some puppy food to take home."

She nodded. "After here, we're going shopping at the pet store," she cooed to the puppy. She studied the rhinestone-studded baby-blue leather collar with its matching leash. "She didn't name you, but she gets you a fancy collar that doesn't go with your personality. Don't worry, I'll find you a collar that's more you and all sorts of toys for you to play with."

"I have to say, when you decide to get a dog you don't do it by half measures."

Before she could reply, Jeremy called Logan and walked quickly away.

Lucy looked down at the puppy as he opened one eye and stretched his mouth in a jaw-cracking yawn.

"I wonder what Luther will think of you," she murmured.

"Hey, Mom, cute dog." Nick walked up to her. He frowned as he studied the puppy. "Where'd he come from?"

"You always said we should have a dog." She stared into the face that stole her heart right away. "Meet Domino. He's going home with us." She laughed at the shock on his face. "Once we're finished here we'll have to do some shopping."

Nick shook his head as he walked away. "When I said we needed a dog I was thinking more like a lab or German shepherd."

By the end of the day, Lucy was exhausted. She could only sit on a folding chair and stare at the ground. Domino lay curled up in a tiny ball on her lap. Nick had collapsed on the grass beside her chair.

"No wonder you only do this once a month. It takes that long just to recover."

"A lot of dogs found good homes and so did most of the cats," Logan said. "I want to thank all of you for your help."

"Forget the thanks, when are you feeding us?" Jeremy demanded.

Nick opened one eye. "Food?"

"Logan always orders pizza at the end of the day," Kristi explained.

"No mushrooms," Nick said.

Lucy looked down at her son. "We really should go."

"Stay and eat with us," Logan invited. "You don't need to make any stops tonight. As I said earlier, I'll send some puppy kibble home with you."

"Yeah, Mom," Nick said. "Besides, it's part of my community service."

"Do you really think I'll believe that eating pizza is part of your work?"

"I'm a growing boy."

"Tell me something I don't know." Lucy turned to Logan. "He can eat his weight in pizza," she warned.

His grin did strange things to her insides. "So can I."

SATED FROM sausage pizza and cheese garlic bread, Lucy sat back in the chair and allowed herself to relax. The puppy snoozed by her feet.

"You know Luther's going to have a fit when he sees the puppy," Nick said as he flopped down on the grass.

"Luther has issues, but he'll get past them," she said.

"Yeah, he hates everyone." The boy leaned forward and picked up the puppy, setting him in his lap. The dog stood up on his hind legs and licked the boy's face. "Okay, fella, time to run and play." He stood up, taking Domino with him.

"A boy and his dog," Logan said, taking Nick's place by Lucy's chair. "I guess I should say *your* dog."

"It's a shame I can't get him to work this hard at home," she commented, watching her son herd the puppy into the enclosed area. The puppy took off running.

"I always worked better anywhere but home." Logan swiped a slice of pizza off Lucy's plate.

"Did you always want to be a veterinarian?"

"Since I was five and watched our cocker spaniel have puppies. She had some difficulty with the birth. I thought the vet was magic because he helped her. My dad always wanted me to be a lawyer then a judge like him. He never forgave me for not going into the law."

Lucy studied him through a narrowed gaze. "I have a pretty good imagination, but I can't see you in a three-piece suit delivering an impassioned summation to a jury."

"Neither could I." Logan half turned when a cold nose nudged his arm. Magnum sat on his haunches with his eyes fixed on the pizza in his hand. Logan heaved a sigh and held out the remainder of the slice. It disappeared in one bite.

"So he does put down the cell phone," Lucy commented, watching the dog carefully pick the phone up.

"Only when he eats."

"Have you ever been tempted to call it and see what happens?"

Logan grinned. "I did that once. The minute it rang, he looked at me with one of those 'you should know better' looks. All he ever allowed me to do was take the battery out of it. At least he doesn't chew on shoes or furniture. Besides, he's a good guard dog."

"He's a lucky dog." She looked over to where Kristi and Nick played with her puppy. Domino stayed at Nick's heels.

Logan studied Lucy's face highlighted by the fading afternoon light.

Today was the first time she'd seemed fully relaxed around him. He didn't know exactly what there was about her that called to him. When he'd first noticed her at Cathy and Lou's house he'd sensed an incredible energy about her. It was apparent that while technically she was an in-law, she was considered a full part of the Walker clan. He could tell that even if her brother wasn't married to Ginna, the Walkers would still have gathered her into their family fold. Logan had gone to school with Brian Walker and knew how readily the family adopted any friend of their children's.

Today he saw a softer side to Lucy. Even after their long day, a faint hint of perfume drifted toward him. What little makeup she'd worn was now gone, but he doubted she wore very much.

"I want to thank you for all your help today," he said. "We sort of threw you into it and you didn't run off screaming."

She looked amused. "You mean some people have?"

"A few. I always thought a T-shirt and pizza was a more-than-adequate bribe, but some people didn't see it that way."

"Maybe the T-shirt wasn't their color," she kindly pointed out.

"That must be it," he agreed. "I'd still like to offer you more. Maybe we could have dinner."

"We just did."

"Actually, I mean dinner not served on paper plates with dogs begging for their share. A place with some ambiance." He silently prided himself on his choice of words.

"Ambiance," Lucy repeated. "If I didn't know any better I'd swear you were asking for a date…again."

"I'm stubborn that way. Think you'll give me a break this time?"

"Trust me, Dr. Kincaid, women with teenage sons aren't good prospects for dating. We have to worry about our sons' social lives instead of our own."

"Nick doesn't seem all that interested in the opposite sex yet."

Lucy flashed him a who-are-you-kidding look. "You were once a teenage boy. Can you honestly tell me you weren't interested in girls when you were Nick's age?"

"I was too busy bumming rides to the beach. I planned to have an animal clinic across the street from the beach, so I could go surfing anytime I wanted."

Lucy had an image of all those Sixties' beach movies, but this time Logan was the star on a surfboard instead of Frankie Avalon romancing Annette Funicello or Moon Doggie enchanting Gidget. She imagined a younger Logan, with a tanned bare chest and a surfboard by his side. He must have been a chick magnet.

She shook herself back to the present. She looked from left to right in an exaggerated manner. "There's something missing. Namely, the ocean."

"I worked here summers when I attended veterinary school and came back to work full-time after I graduated. When Dr. Mercer retired, he offered me a good deal on the place. I decided I'd just drive to the beach on my days off."

"Was the shelter a part of the clinic then?"

He shook his head. "That happened about four years ago when I found a box of kittens sitting by the clinic's front door one night. I was able to find them all good homes. I guess the word got out because it wasn't long before more animals turned up."

"A man who helps children and animals. In some circles you'd be considered the perfect catch." She smiled. "I'd think women would be beating down your door. So why me?"

"Maybe I like a challenge." He edged his fingers toward Magnum's cell phone. The dog's low growl was more than enough warning. "See?"

Lucy shook her head. "Maybe I just don't like you," she countered, even though she knew that was far from the truth. Whether she liked it or not, Logan Kincaid was growing on her.

"Are you kidding? You just said I'm a prime catch." He held his arms out from his sides. "Upstanding member of the community, respected businessman, kind to children and animals. You couldn't do any better."

"The children come courtesy of the juvenile court system." She pointedly glanced toward the dog park.

"My dad was the one to come up with the idea of some of the kids working here. Luckily, it's turned out well." The feel of a paw on his arm distracted him. He turned his head and found Magnum staring at his plate, or rather, at the slice of pizza still sitting there. "I should have named you Mooch," he muttered, handing over his pizza. The huge dog stared at his now-empty plate, stood up and moved on to another source of food.

"He's very well trained. Was that your doing?" Lucy asked.

"That's all Magnum. I think it's more he trained me."

"It's amazing no one claimed him. He's a beautiful animal." She smiled as she watched the large Malamute pause by Nick's abandoned plate and soon have it licked clean.

"Some people prefer puppies. Once the dog grows up, they get rid of the adult dog and start fresh." Logan's voice hardened. "Or they end up as pawns in a divorce case. Sometimes the one getting the family pet isn't the one who really wanted him. It's not just the kids who can end up the losers."

"Luther didn't have that problem. I was the one who wanted him and I got him." Her airy voice didn't totally hide the old pain.

"And here I thought you were the loser in the battle for Luther the Wonder Cat."

Lucy chuckled. "Ross and Luther didn't get along at all and that was putting it mildly. Luther's idea of fun was shredding Ross's favorite ties."

"It sounds like you got the better deal."

"I did." Lucy pushed herself out of her chair. "I should go. Nick!"

Her son waved at her to indicate he heard. "I've got to put the dogs back first," he called back.

"Don't forget to get out a bag of puppy kibble," Logan told him.

"Thank you for the pizza," Lucy said. A smile curved her lips. "And the puppy."

"I don't think I had a choice where the puppy was concerned."

She crouched down as the puppy ran over to her. She picked him up and cradled him in her arms. "You're probably right."

It wasn't long before Nick returned from the shelter with a bag of kibble draped over one shoulder. Logan walked them to Lucy's car and watched them drive away.

"See you Monday, Logan," Kristi called out as she headed to her motorcycle with Jeremy following her.

In no time, Logan was alone. After he checked on Magnum in the clinic, he walked to his house, a short distance behind the clinic.

The small two-bedroom cottage suited his purposes for living quarters. He also liked the idea of living close to the clinic in case of emergency.

He hadn't expected Lucy to throw herself into helping out today. Nor had he expected her to go home with a puppy.

He pulled his clothing off and changed into cotton pajama pants and a T-shirt then padded barefoot into the kitchen to get something to drink.

He usually enjoyed these solitary hours. Tonight was different. Tonight he felt restless and in need of company. Not just any company either.

But the lady he wanted had a son and wouldn't be the kind of woman he'd invite back here for some his-and-her quality time.

Lucy Donner had him feeling conflicted. While he'd like to know her much better, he knew she was a dangerous proposition. Even if she stated she had no desire to date, she still spelled *commitment* with a capital *C*.

Chapter Four

"This isn't fair, Brenda! You cannot have the baby now. We're not prepared!" Logan shouted into the phone with panic coloring every word. He held on to the receiver with a death grip. "Besides, you said it's not due for another three weeks."

"You are not listening, Logan. I already had the baby," Brenda explained, using the long-suffering tone she tended to use with Logan. "I told you two months ago we needed to bring someone in so there would be plenty of time for me to train them."

"Okay, I'll call a temp agency and you'll be available to explain things to the temp, right? We'll do just fine."

"Listen to what I'm saying, Logan!" She laughed. "I just had an eight-pound-six-ounce baby girl. You should be grateful I even called you to tell you I wouldn't be in. I'll make it easy for you, Logan. The appointment book is easy to maintain and all the records are in order. If you can't get a temp in right away Gwen can help."

"You want Gwen to work the front? Are you nuts? You know very well she's no good with people."

She sighed. "Good-bye, Logan. I'm starting my maternity leave as of now. Call the temp agency!"

A dial tone hummed in his ear.

"She hung up!" He stared at the receiver with disbelief. "She hung up on me!"

"Brenda's allowed to be cranky. She told me she had to have an episiotomy." Gwen said as she breezed by. "Want me to explain what that is?"

"I'm a doctor. I know what it means," Logan muttered. He looked at her speculatively. "Gwen, Brenda said everything out there is all set up."

"Oh no, I'm not working the front desk." The tech opened a cabinet drawer and pulled out several tubes of medicated ointment. "When I took this job I told you I refuse to deal with Homo Sapiens."

He muttered a few choice words under his breath as he heard line one then line two start ringing.

"I'm not getting that," Gwen sang out.

Logan had a bad feeling the day was only going to get crazier.

"COME ON, Domino," Lucy coaxed the puppy out of the vehicle. "Don't worry, I'm not leaving you here," she assured him as she gently tugged on the leash.

She knew she could have waited until she dropped Nick off that afternoon, but she told herself they were in the area. Which was why she'd bundled the puppy into the SUV and driven to the clinic where she found a number of vehicles parked in front of the building.

"We'll just make an appointment for a checkup and your shots," she told the puppy as they stepped inside.

Lucy took one look and almost backed out of the room. She'd clearly stepped into what any sane person would call sheer chaos. Several people stood in front of the desk; others sat on the benches lining the walls. They all shared the impatient expression of someone who'd waited for some time. Ringing phones added to the confusion.

"Could someone, *anyone,* please answer the damn phone!" Logan's roar could be heard from the back.

Since no one jumped to his plea, Lucy took matters into

her own hands. She walked around the desk, grabbed the phone and punched a lit button.

"Valley Animal Clinic." She glanced at the appointment book as she listened to the voice on the other end. She made an appointment for the following day. She only had to look at the filled columns to see Logan didn't have any free time that day. After she hung up the phone, she looked out at the sea of faces—human, canine and feline, along with one reptile. A faint sound coming from behind alerted her to a new presence. She turned her head to see Magnum standing in the hallway opening.

"Tell you what, I'll answer these phones, so you only have to worry about yours. How's that?" she told the Malamute. The dog turned around and walked back down the hallway as if telling her the job was all hers.

Lucy turned back to the human and animal contingent.

"Let's see about doing this in an orderly fashion, shall we?" she announced, picking up a pen with one hand while looping the end of Domino's leash around the chair arm with the other.

"THANKS for your patience, Harvey," Logan told the owner of a basset hound named Ralph who'd come in for booster shots. "What with Brenda's baby coming early, we're a little crazy today."

"Things got sorted out," the elderly man told him. "Wasn't sure there for a while, though."

"Yeah, Gwen surprised even me."

"Gwen?" Harvey chuckled. "Everyone would have run for the hills if Gwen was out there. No, it was that pretty little gal with the black-and-white puppy who took charge out there. If I was you, I'd see about keeping her around. See ya, Doc."

Curious about Harvey's words, Logan walked out of the examination room. As he glanced at the examination room doors he noticed the formerly overflowing chart holders were now empty. If he hadn't emptied them and Gwen hadn't, then who had? That pretty little gal Harvey mentioned?

He stopped Gwen when she walked past. "Did you empty the chart holders?"

She stared at him as if he'd just lost his mind. Considering the way the morning had gone, it could easily have happened.

"Right, as if I've had time to take a breath. I thought you did it."

Logan slowly shook his head.

"Right about now I don't care if little gremlins stole in here and did it," she said.

"Harvey said a 'pretty little gal' was out front." Logan closed his eyes and prayed there was plenty of aspirin in his desk drawer. "What does the reception area look like?"

Gwen shot him one of her patented looks. "How would I know? I thought you were funneling them back here." She pulled a protein bar out of a drawer and tore open the wrapper.

They stared at each other for a few moments before it sunk in.

"Harvey's pretty little gal." Logan turned and almost ran for the front.

The last thing he expected to find at the counter out there was Lucy accepting a check from Harvey.

"Yeah, Doc, she got things in order out here in no time," the elderly man told Logan as he walked out. "She's a real keeper."

Logan looked around the now-empty reception area. "What happened?"

"You had a lot of cranky humans out here. I just went through the appointment book and sent them back in order. Your phone was ringing like crazy, too, so you can expect all week to be the same since I made a lot of appointments. People would think you're the only veterinarian in the county." She picked up Harvey's chart and set it to one side. "What happened to Brenda?"

"She had an eight-pound baby girl three weeks early," he replied.

Lucy clucked her tongue. "Been there, done that, loved the drugs. I'm surprised she didn't arrange for a replacement for while she's gone."

Logan shifted uneasily and looked off into space. "We talked about it."

"Meaning she told you someone needed to be brought in before she left on maternity leave and you kept putting it off," she guessed correctly.

He occupied himself with studying a chart. "I'd say that's pretty close to what happened."

Lucy shook her head. "No wonder she's looked so frazzled these past few weeks. You never did anything about it. What she should have done was go ahead and just bring someone in."

"I had a temp here this morning," Logan explained.

"Really?" Her voice sounded skeptical.

"She walked in, took one look around and announced she's allergic to cats and left."

Logan considered Lucy. "You did a great job and we appreciate it."

Lucy didn't need a college degree to see where this was going.

She asked, "First my son, now me? Even the judge wouldn't do this to me."

"Actually, he would if he could, but I'll go one better. I'll pay you." He named an hourly rate. "And free medical care for the puppy and your cat."

"That's why I came in, to make an appointment for a checkup for Domino. Luther hates vets with a passion. You only have to mention Luther Donner to any vet in Orange

County and they'll tell you he's the cat from hell. Some vets were known to drag out stakes, silver bullets and holy water before seeing him."

"Cats from hell are my specialty. At least stay this afternoon. I'll get a temp in for tomorrow."

Lucy thought of the excuses she could make: She had to wash her hair, she had an important appointment in another country. But she knew she couldn't make any of them sound convincing. Besides, lately she'd felt restless. She'd closed down her travel business when she and Nick moved out here because she'd felt the need to look for something new. So far, she hadn't decided what she wanted to do with herself other than getting the house and property together. She'd worked with a landscaper to get the front and back yards into shape. It took six months to get the property the way she wanted, but now she had areas meant for relaxing even if she hadn't spent as much time as she'd like there.

She had invested what was left of the money from the settlement from the airline along with the sale of her other house, so she didn't have to worry about getting a job in the next few days. But she wasn't used to being idle and with the house finished, she was finding she had too much time on her hands.

She hadn't planned on returning to her work as a travel agent. Maybe working here was what she needed just now.

"Domino is welcome to come in with you," Logan added.

"You're desperate, aren't you?" She couldn't resist torturing him a little.

He didn't lie to her. "Desperate is an understatement."

"How long is she staying out?"

"A few months."

Lucy nodded. "All right, I'll help out for a while, but I'll need to leave in the afternoons to pick Nick up from school."

"No problem. And we're closed from twelve to two. Voice mail will pick up the phone calls then. Gwen or I stay around in case there's an emergency, but you're free those two hours.

Kristi and Jeremy come in after their last class. Just let me know when you're leaving to pick up Nick." He unwound the leash from the chair and picked up the puppy. "How did he do?"

"Luther wasted no time letting him know who's boss. He didn't like sleeping in a box, so I let him sleep with me." Lucy smiled fondly at the puppy, who was happily chewing on Logan's fingers. "I know, I'm spoiling him already, but he's so cute and lovable."

"Lucky guy," he murmured. "So you named him Domino?"

"With the black and white, it seemed fitting. Naming him Patches sounded too predictable."

Logan studied the terrier. His stubby tail was white tipped with black. The puppy uttered a happy yip.

"I'll check him out, but knowing Mrs. Crenshaw, the pup is in perfect health," he said.

"She called a little while ago. She wanted you to know she's having someone come out to set up a salt-water aquarium. She just loves all the colors fish come in." Lucy's lips twitched. "I told her I took the puppy. She's going to drop off all his things this afternoon."

"Be prepared for pretty much everything including a complete wardrobe. Her husband buys all new accessories for each dog," Logan said, handing the puppy over to her. "Domino will be set for life."

Their fingers brushed as she accepted the dog. For a moment, Lucy felt the air inside her grow still. She reminded herself blond-haired men were dangerous. At least, they always had been for her.

She'd even told herself that Logan Kincaid was nothing more than a typical wolf on the make. She knew she was lying to herself.

It was said any man who loved children and animals couldn't be all bad. Even better, Logan treated Nick as a person, not a kid who didn't know anything. She'd already seen him around animals. He took his vocation seriously because he truly cared about the animals in his care.

She cradled Domino against her breasts. She felt the warm gentle rasp of his tongue on her chin.

"Within five minutes of meeting me, you hit on me. Why?" Her question was made in a hushed voice as if she was afraid of being overheard even though they could hear Gwen walking around in the back of the clinic.

"Why not? You're a lovely single woman."

Even though he'd said she was lovely, she felt disappointed by his answer. "A reflex action, then." She turned away and bent down to pick up her purse. "Okay, I'll be back a little before two."

Logan felt off balance. He wasn't sure what had just happened, and he felt the need to know. "So you'll take the job?"

She looped the strap over her shoulder and headed for the door. After three steps, she paused and turned around. "I don't have to wear scrubs with puppies and kittens on them, do I?"

He looked at her; she was dressed in a pair of slim-fitting jeans topped by a pink T-shirt. Just as she had on Saturday, she'd threaded her ponytail through the back of a denim baseball cap. She was more than lovely. She was beautiful. He grinned at her. "Only if you want to."

"Then I choose not to." She opened the door and stepped outside. A moment later, Logan heard an engine start up and Lucy's vehicle leave the parking lot.

"So she's staying?" Gwen asked as she entered the reception area.

Logan turned around. "Yep."

"Better than training a temp every five minutes."

"We wouldn't have to do all that training if you didn't scare them away. For someone claiming to be allergic to cats, that temp this morning wasn't even breathing hard," he pointed out. "It wasn't until she spoke to you that she practically ran out of here."

"I told you I'm no good with Homo Sapiens." She disappeared into the back rooms.

"No wonder you don't date," he muttered.

Gwen stuck her head in through the doorway. "Trust me, boss, I date a lot more than you do. There are a few Homo Sapiens I'm willing to deal with on a more personal level. For you, having Lucy Donner around here will be a good thing since it's obvious you have the hots for her."

"I do not have the hots for her!"

"Oh, come on, boss, wake up and smell the pheromones." Her laughter mocked him. "I've got a lunch date. See you later."

"Bring me back something, will you?"

When a low rumble sounded by his side, Logan looked down to see Magnum watching him with silvery-blue eyes.

"I don't see you having any lady friends," he grumbled to the dog. "Oh, that's right. I took that joy from you."

The big dog replied with a slight curl of the lip.

"Nothing worse than a dog with no sense of humor."

"YOU'RE WORKING at the clinic?" Nick stared at his mother as if he'd just heard the worst news in his life. "Mom, you don't need to check up on me like that. Logan told you I'm doing a good job. I'm not getting into any trouble at school. The dean even said he's proud of me for taking responsibility for my actions. Please, Mom, don't do this to me," he begged.

His mom took her eyes off the road for a second and looked at him patiently. "I explained it to you. Brenda had her baby early and they need someone organized to man the front desk. And who's more organized than your old mom?"

He slumped down in the seat, pouting like a five-year-old.

"It's only short-term," his mom said.

He stared out the window. "This sucks."

"I promise not to call you my very special baby boy in front of them."

Now he was downright horrified. "Mo-o-m!"

"You're still so easy to fool." She grinned as she pulled into a parking space alongside the clinic and she held up her right hand. "I vow not to call you my special pet names or tell any of those cute little stories that embarrass you. In fact, I won't even tell anyone you're my son."

"You made all those promises when I was in the second grade and you were Room Mother. Next thing I know you're acting like I'm Cute Kid on the Block," he said with remembered distaste.

She airily waved off his reminder. "I couldn't help it. It was Christmas and you looked so cute in your elf costume for the play."

Nick pushed open his door and slid out of his seat.

"This is not good," he muttered as he made his way around the building to enter through the rear door.

The moment Nick passed through the door his disgruntled expression was replaced with a satisfied grin. His plan had taken a good turn, one even he hadn't foreseen.

"Thank you, Brenda," he whispered, whistling as he walked over to the dog runs. "Hey, guys! Who's ready for a clean kennel and some playtime?"

LUCY WAS GRATEFUL the afternoon was a little quieter so she could familiarize herself with the clinic's computer programs and records.

"Thank you so much," Gwen whispered, coming up to give Lucy a one-armed hug. "If you hadn't stayed, he would have forced me to work up here. Trust me, it would not have been a pretty sight."

Lucy chuckled at her theatrics. "From what I understand, putting you in the public eye is not a good idea."

"Very true. Even my boyfriend knows better." She handed Lucy a couple of charts that were in her other hand then bent down to scratch Domino behind the ears. "He's a cutie. Terriers are smart little guys. Who knows, he might even out-smart your son."

"Just as long as he remembers who took him home," Lucy said. "How long have you worked for Logan?"

Gwen thought back. "A little over eight years now. Dr. Mercer's vet tech was also his wife, so Logan needed some-one new."

"So you scared him into hiring you?" Lucy had already fig-ured Gwen's bite might be as dangerous as her bark.

"He was still pretty new at this even after working for Dr. Mercer. Very trainable though," she confided. "Believe me, it's not easy breaking in a vet to do things your way."

A male voice behind them startled them both. "Don't you mean my training you to *my* methods?"

The two women turned around to find Logan with his shoulder braced against the open doorway. Magnum sat next to him.

Lucy pointedly stared at the dog then looked up at Logan. "The dog trained you to allow him to carry around a cell phone. And you have a parrot who thinks a cat is his pet."

"Beau's a macaw."

She rolled her eyes. "It's a good thing Gwen did all the training where you're concerned. Who knows what would have happened here next."

He shook his head. "And here I thought you'd be on my side." With a long-suffering sigh, he straightened up and walked back down the hallway.

"Gwen." Lucy stopped the tech from following Logan. "The appointment book doesn't say what kind of animal is coming in. Just the owner's name and pet's name. If it's a snake or something scary, I don't have to touch it, do I?"

"We treat some iguanas along with snakes, turtles and tor-toises. Don't worry, all you have to do is direct the patient to the proper room," she assured her.

She felt relieved. "That I can do."

LOGAN WAS GRATEFUL the afternoon ran smoothly under Lucy's direction. It was near closing time when he checked the front. He found Lucy at the front desk talking to a scowling Lou Walker. He could tell that the man's scowl wasn't directed at Lucy but at a man seated on the bench—his father, Frank Kincaid. Logan muttered a curse as he realized he hadn't warned Lucy that some appointments couldn't be made together.

"I'll tell Cathy about Brenda," Lou said, deliberately ignoring Frank.

"Will it be much longer, Mrs. Donner?" Frank spoke up, not caring he was interrupting.

"He just has one more patient ahead of you, Judge Kincaid." While Lucy's tone was polite, there was a frosty edge to it.

The judge glared at Lou as he realized just who that last patient was.

"Hi, Lou," Logan said as he entered the reception area. He looked over to add, "Dad, I'll be with you soon." He picked up the chart with Lou's name typed neatly along the edge and gestured for Lou to go ahead of him. Lou called his German shepherd, who followed him.

"Lucy said that Brenda had her baby yesterday," Lou said. "And that she'll be helping out here for a while."

"Yes, she is."

"You were lucky to get qualified help so quickly."

"She more or less took charge and I'm grateful to her." He began his examination of the German shepherd. "Jasmine, my love, your ear infection appears to have cleared up nicely."

"Cathy said that Lucy's been a little restless since she finished with her house and grounds. She's quite a homemaker, you know. But I have to say her house is meant for more than just her and Nick." Lou watched him closely.

"What's wrong, Lou? Running out of kids to marry off?" Logan asked dryly. "There's still Nikki."

"My daughter is in medical school and won't be thinking about men for some time if I have anything to say about it," the older man stated. "I'm just saying that Lucy's not one of those good-time girls."

Logan chuckled at the other man's old-fashioned phrasing. "I get the idea, Lou. Lucy's here to work, nothing more. I won't be putting any moves on her. And if you're worried about her single status, I'm sure you can find someone for her."

"If you weren't so stubborn about remarrying, I'd say you were pretty darn perfect for her."

Logan shook his head. "No thanks. Once burned and so on."

"How does Nick feel about his mother working here?"

He didn't miss Lou's deliberate change of subject. He was grateful for it, too. "How would you feel if you were his age and learned your mother was working where you were?" Logan asked.

Lou grimaced. "As much as I love my mother, I wouldn't have wanted her anywhere in the vicinity. Even now I cringe when she comes in the garage. She always wants to rearrange my tools."

"Then you have an idea how Nick feels. I told him not to worry. I'd keep her busy enough she won't have time to check on him." Logan jotted down some notes in Jasmine's chart. "She looks good, Lou."

"That's a relief." Lou picked up Jasmine's leash.

"What are you working on now?"

The older man's eyes lit up. "A nice little 1930 Ford Coupe. Poor thing needs a lot of work, but that's what I do best."

"I'll have to come by and take a look." Logan walked Lou out to where Lucy took over. He looked to the remaining patient, deliberately turned away so as not to have to acknowledge Logan. "Hello, Farley," Logan greeted the dog sitting by his father's legs.

The judge rose and gently urged an elderly yellow Labrador to his feet.

"How did Mrs. Donner end up working the front desk?' the judge asked once they were in the examination room. "Or did she manage to persuade you she could handle Brenda's job so she could remain close to the boy? She seems to have a smothering effect on him. He needs to have more outside activities without her interference."

"From what I heard, Nick has more than enough outside activities between basketball and baseball along with some of the school clubs. A lot of them had to be put on hold because of his working here," Logan commented. "As for Lucy, she sort of took over when all hell broke loose this morning. It would have been a disaster if she hadn't sorted things out. How's Farley's arthritis doing?" He carefully picked up the dog and set him on the examination table. His touch was gentle as his hands moved over the dog's hindquarters.

"With the weather cooling off he's moving slower," the judge replied. "He's enjoying the heated bed I got him."

Logan nodded as he checked the dog's vitals. The Lab turned his head and licked Logan's face. He grinned.

"You're a forgiving guy, Farley," he told the dog.

"How is the boy working out?" the judge asked.

"Just fine, which I'm sure you already know from my last report." Logan glanced at him. "Why, did you want to talk to him? Did you want to make sure I wasn't overworking him or he wasn't trying to con me?"

"Of course not," he said gruffly, frowning at his son. "I just wonder if it's a good idea for Mrs. Donner to work here. I noticed in court that day that her attitude toward her son is a little possessive," the judge said. "Not exactly a good thing for a growing boy who needs positive role models in his life. Luckily, she appears stable otherwise."

"I would think that the Walker men are positive role models for Nick, along with his uncle."

The judge's snort wasn't in keeping with his usually formal manner.

"Louis Walker doesn't have one reliable bone in his body," he rumbled.

"Dad." The one word was warning enough.

Farley whined and stretched out a paw to his master. The judge's stern demeanor relaxed in a smile as he took his dog's paw.

"You want to talk about someone needing a woman in his life, let's talk about you," Logan said.

"Farley and I are happy being a pair of old bachelors." He narrowed his gaze at his son. "You're a different story. Anything else I need to know about Farley?"

Logan knew his father didn't want to discuss his own single status even if he was only too happy to talk about Logan's.

"Keep him on those supplements. It will make it a little easier for him. At least you live in a one-story house so there's no stairs for him to struggle up." He clapped his father on the back. "Come on, I'll help you get Farley into your car."

Logan noticed Lucy was filing charts as he walked his father to the front door.

"There's no charge for this visit," he told her as they passed by.

"Mrs. Donner." The judge nodded in her direction.

"Judge Kincaid." She was just as formal.

Logan followed his father outside glancing over his shoulder at Lucy, certain that he heard her murmur "old fogy" under her breath.

"I heard that Nancy Glenn is back in the area," the judge mentioned as Logan carefully hoisted the elderly dog into the back seat and adjusted the harness for him that was attached to the seat belt. "You should give her a call."

"Only if I win big at Lotto and plan to die in the next week. She likes them rich and at death's door." Logan closed the car door. "I mean it, Dad. If you try to set me up, I'll do the same to you. There are plenty of widows in the area who'd jump at the chance to date you."

Judge Kincaid threw up his hands. "Just remember a bunch of dogs can't comfort you in your old age."

Logan looked at Farley. "I don't know. You seem to be doing just fine."

The judge scowled at him. "Dinner Friday night?"

"I'll be there." Logan remained outside until his father drove off. When he walked back into the clinic, he found Lucy coaxing Beau into his cage.

"I hate to tell you this, but my dad would have loved being called an old fogy," he told her.

"I'll have to start studying the dictionary and come up with some new descriptions then."

THE MUTED SOUND of cannon fire alerted him that he had a new e-mail. Nick quickly clicked on the proper icon and brought it up.

Plan appears to be working well, but we cannot let down our guard. They need to be reminded now and then. That is up to you.

"No problem there," he said softly as he deleted the e-mail.

Chapter Five

"I can't believe you got a dog." Cathy chuckled as the puppy tried to scramble up into her lap. She took pity on his frantic jumps and reached down to pick him up. He happily licked her chin.

Lucy, Nick and Domino had joined the Walkers for a family barbecue. The puppy was happy to have so much attention lavished on him until Gail and Brian's young daughter, Jennifer, pulled his tail a few too many times. After that, he headed back to Lucy and safety.

"I very rarely make impulsive decisions," Lucy admitted. "The last time I made one I set up Ginna and Zach."

"Which ended up very nicely," the older woman said. "Thank you for three more beautiful grandchildren."

Lucy smiled at Cathy for generously including Nick in that number.

"And then there's your working for Logan," Cathy said. "How do you like it?"

"Very different from the travel business. I'm not sure which is more interesting. The humans or the animals."

"Are you talking about the ones visiting the clinic or the ones inhabiting it?"

Lucy threw up a hand, waving it back and forth in a languid motion.

"I'd say it's a toss-up. He has a macaw who thinks a cat is

his pet and a dog who carries a cell phone around in his mouth. So far, the oddest one coming in is a toy poodle and her owner who wear matching sweaters."

Cathy nodded. "Myra Robinson. The dog also has the most exquisite little crocheted blankets and booties to keep her feet warm during the winter. Myra's husband also has a large wardrobe of hand-knitted sweaters."

"Talk about taking a hobby too far." Lucy watched as Nick was pulled into a volleyball game. When they'd left the house she hadn't realized how short his T-shirt was on him. She wondered how a boy could grow three inches overnight.

"Every new baby in the area receives a blanket from Myra. She claims knitting and crocheting is something she can do while her husband fishes." She cast Lucy a sideways glance. "How is Logan as a boss?"

"Give him enough coffee and he's tolerable." *Warm, funny, too tempting at times.*

"And here I thought I was downright charming."

Lucy turned around so fast her chair would have tipped over if Logan hadn't quickly grasped the back and kept it upright.

"What are you doing here?" She was so surprised to see him she hadn't realized how rude her question sounded.

"I have an open invitation." He dropped a kiss on Cathy's cheek. She looked up and smiled at him as she patted his cheek.

"Which you never take enough advantage of," Cathy scolded him. "How's your father doing?"

Logan pretended to look about in fright. "You are one brave woman to ask that when your husband could be in earshot."

"My husband and your father are two old fools who need to put the past behind them," Cathy said, gesturing toward the end of the patio where Lou stood guard over the barbecue pit while conversing with several men.

"But their feud makes it more fun for the rest of us." Logan grinned.

Cathy scoffed, "That stupid feud. High school was a long time ago. More years than I like to think about. They competed all through school and I swear they've never stopped. Frank should have realized long ago I wasn't the right woman for him. One day I am going to take both of them by the scruffs of their necks and force them to sit down and talk."

"I don't think I'll be the only one who will want to be there for that." Logan looked down at Lucy. "How come you're not over there playing volleyball?"

"I prefer being a spectator," she explained. "It's more fun to watch the men get all hot and sweaty than for me to get all hot and sweaty." She regretted her provocative words the moment they passed her lips.

The wicked light in Logan's eyes told her he hadn't missed them.

"I'm not very athletic," she amended, knowing it was too late to salvage the moment.

"She's right on that," said a breathless Zach as he ran up to them. "Lucy was famous for her excuses to get out of gym class. Logan, Mark wants to sit out for a while. Want to take his place?"

"Sure." Logan reached down and pulled his T-shirt up and over his head. He grinned and dropped it in Lucy's lap. "Keep an eye on that for me, will you?" He moved off with Zach.

Lucy felt her mouth grow dry as she stared at a very nice expanse of bare tanned skin lightly dusted with golden hair. If Logan was still surfing on his off days, that was definitely the sport to take up to keep the chest looking that impressive. His jean shorts hung low on his narrow hips.

This was a man who didn't worry about the exterior. And why should he when women only had to take one look at him and start to drool?

Without thinking, she swiped at her chin with her fingers. Luckily, they came away dry.

She knew she was going to take control of herself before she did something foolish—like throw herself at the man.

She really had been without a man for too long.

"Domino, sweetie, here's something just for you," Lucy cooed to her dog, picking him up and setting him on her lap.

"For someone who's said in the past she isn't interested, you're giving off some very powerful signals," Cathy said.

"Who's giving off signals?" Ginna asked her mother as she took a free chair.

"Shouldn't you be cheering your husband on to victory?" Lucy asked her sister-in-law.

Ginna twisted in the chair. "Great spike, sweetheart!" she shouted, clapping her hands. "Keep it up!"

"Always do, darlin'," he called back with a hot grin.

Ginna sat back, looking the picture of a well-satisfied woman. "He's so damn cute when he thinks he's being macho."

"You're still in the honeymoon phase, I see," Lucy commented.

Ginna glanced over at the volleyball game then back to her friend. "You should try it."

"Oh no!" She put up her hands in a back-off gesture. "That kind of matchmaking stays within your family and I'm just enough of an in-law to be immune to the disease."

"Now, Lucy, I need to repay you for all you did for me," Ginna insisted. Laughter danced in the brilliant blue eyes that were a Walker trademark. "If Logan's not your type, I'm sure we can find someone who is."

"Oh, Logan's her type," Cathy said. "She just refuses to admit it."

Ginna twisted back around. "Girls, we have some dirt to dish!" she called out to her three sisters-in-law.

Lucy wasn't sure whether to glare at Cathy first or Ginna. She settled for slumping down in her chair.

One Walker was bad enough, but five of them concentrating on her single status were downright dangerous.

LOGAN HAD TROUBLE concentrating on the game when Lucy was in his line of sight.

All he could see was her long, slim legs revealed by a pair of short-shorts. He even noticed a gold toe ring on her right foot and her pink-polished toenails. A turquoise leather sandal dangled from one foot as she sat with her legs crossed.

He wasn't sure what the women were talking about, but judging by the intense expressions on the feminine portion of the Walker women's faces and the pained one on Lucy's, the conversation must have to do with her.

He grunted when the volleyball hit him between the shoulder blades.

"You here to play or ogle the women, Kincaid?" Jeff Walker hooted from behind him.

"They're plotting against you, buddy." Brian came over and slapped Logan on the back. "What you see over there is a dangerous group. So far they've had a perfect record."

"Then I guess it's time they lose one." Logan moved back to take the corner to serve. He tossed up the ball and punched it with a little more force than necessary. It easily sailed over the net and eluded the other team.

"Nothing like the fear of a woman to get those winning points!" Jeff cheered.

Logan glanced in the direction of the women who were now watching the game with great interest.

"If I didn't know any better I'd swear they're planning the wedding already," Brian said.

"They can plan all they want. That doesn't mean I'll stand still long enough to get hooked the way you dummies did," Logan said.

It wasn't until he faced the team on the opposite side of the net that he realized Nick Donner had heard every word he said.

"Don't worry, Logan," the boy called out. "Mom's not looking for a guy. I don't know, maybe you're not her type."

Logan ignored the laughter around him. *Not her type?* He

was every woman's type. He was considered a good catch. He'd had his share of women chasing after him and he prided himself on escaping them all.

And she was telling her son that Logan wasn't her type? No matter that he was pretty much stating the same thing. It was the principle of the thing.

"Always good to hear since I came to my senses and realized she isn't my type either," he said in a raised voice.

"Not his type?" Lucy muttered. She was positive he'd made sure she heard the entire conversation. "For three months the man tried everything under the sun to persuade me to go out with him. Now all of a sudden he's decided I'm not his type."

"Defense mechanism," Abby pronounced. "That way he doesn't feel as if you rejected him, but that he turned you down."

"Well, he knows what he can do with his damn defense mechanism." Lucy glared at the man in question.

By the time Lou called out that the food was ready, Nick's team had won by two points.

"From now on you're on my team," Logan told the boy as they walked back to the patio. "All that height is to our advantage."

"I'm on the basketball team at school," Nick replied, proud to be a part of the winning team.

"Brains, looks and brawn. The kid has it made," Zach said, the picture of the proud uncle.

With the intention of retrieving his T-shirt, Logan walked toward Lucy.

"Too bad you lost," she said, not sounding the least bit sympathetic.

"It happens." Logan looked at his shirt; Domino was curled up on it. He suddenly had a bad feeling.

"Oh." She looked as if she realized what he was looking at. "You want your shirt, don't you? Come on, sweetheart," she murmured to the puppy as she gently pulled the shirt out from under him. "Oh, look what happened. Bad puppy," she said without the least bit of censure. She held up the shirt now sporting a couple of holes. Her expression was properly remorseful. "I'm so sorry. Puppies tend to chew anything they come in contact with. But then, as a veterinarian you know that, don't you?" She held up the shirt to him. "Of course, I'll replace the shirt."

"Don't worry about it," he assured her as he pulled it on over his head. "I've had much worse done at the clinic." He reached down and picked up the glass of iced tea sitting in front of Lucy. He drained half the glass before he set it back down. Smiling, he made a mocking bow to the rest of the group. "Ladies." He walked off.

"Why is it so sexy when a man drinks out of your glass, but if he makes even a hint of a move toward your toothbrush…" Nora shuddered. The other women made the appropriate noises for her remark.

"I can see this is going to be fun," Abby murmured, glancing around the circle of women.

"I don't want to go out with Logan," Lucy firmly stated.

The women looked at her with knowing expressions and pity.

"It won't fly here, honey," Abby told her. "We've all been there and we've all let the men catch us even if they were the ones doing the running. Letting Domino chew on Logan's shirt was a nice touch."

"And to think I despaired of my boys finding women who could put up with them." Cathy chuckled as she pushed herself out of her chair. "Ladies, it looks like it's time to bring out the rest of the food."

Lucy should have known that Logan would make sure she couldn't ignore him.

"I brought a few extra burgers in case Domino gets hungry," he said, taking the seat next to hers as he set a plate loaded with hamburgers in front of her.

Her eyes widened at the pile. "I can't eat all of these."

"Don't worry, I'll take care of what you and Domino can't." He picked up the puppy sitting on the bench next to her and deposited him on the ground. "Sorry, fella, you'll get your share later."

"Nick is sitting there," she said.

He looked over his shoulder to where Nick was seated with several teenagers.

"Well, Mom, it looks like your baby boy has deserted you." He put one of the hamburgers on her plate then two on his. "So I guess it's just us."

"Guess again, sweetheart," Abby said, sitting down across from them with Jeff following her. Gail and Brian soon followed along with Nora and Mark.

"You haven't changed since high school, Ab. You're still a pain in the ass," Logan said.

She smiled, not the least bit insulted. "We went out once," she explained to Lucy. "For a while, I thought I'd ruined him for other women."

"Ruined is right. No offense to Abby, but once was enough." Logan turned to Jeff. "You should be nominated for sainthood, Jeff. Abby is one of a kind."

"It took her a while, but she realized a good thing when she had it." Jeff grinned.

"More like the other way around," Abby corrected.

As the conversation flowed around them, Lucy was aware of Logan's leg resting lightly against hers. Some would say it was accidental, but she knew better. The man looked at her the way a starving person looked at a hamburger.

If only he didn't affect her so much! She'd vowed not to get involved with anyone. So why did Logan Kincaid prompt her to rethink that vow?

When Lucy had accepted Cathy's invitation to attend their barbecue, she hadn't realized that Cathy had also invited Logan. She should have known better since she was aware that Logan had grown up with the Walker siblings and remained friends with the family. But he hadn't shown up every time she attended. She'd relaxed her guard when she was here.

Then again, she might be making too much of it.

Except he had left his T-shirt with her. And he had flirted with her.

And his leg was pressing a little too closely against hers.

Lucy looked across the table and straight into Abby's eyes. When the blond woman smiled at her as if she read her mind, another thought came to Lucy's mind. She smiled back and easily shifted her leg. His leg seemed to follow hers way too easily.

"Something wrong, Logan?" Abby asked with just the proper show of innocence that didn't fool anyone seated at the table.

He seemed to choke on his mouthful of hamburger then swallowed.

"Not a thing." He reached for his can of soda and drank thirstily.

The other men watched him with genuine sympathy, all of them having been in the same position themselves.

Logan eyed everyone at the table, keeping his stare longest on the men.

If he didn't know better he'd swear there was a conspiracy going on. But why would the men be in on it?

Men stuck together, dammit! All for one and so on.

But then he looked at the women again. The area between his shoulder blades itched like crazy. Had someone painted a target on his back?

He decided he was just feeling paranoid. It had nothing to do with the smug smiles on the women's faces or the sympathetic ones on the men's.

To display his disregard for whatever crazy thoughts were going through their heads, Logan bit down hard into his hamburger and practically tore the meat and bun away. The bite was too large and he was in danger of choking, but he managed to swallow without any harm.

It wasn't until then he realized that Lucy was giving a sales pitch for Adoption Day.

"Maybe you all need puppies," she told the three couples.

"What about yours?" Abby asked. "Doesn't your dog need a playmate?"

"Domino is still dealing with Luther."

"Don't you mean Luther is still dealing with Domino?" Abby teased. She turned to Logan. "Have you met that cat yet?"

Logan shook his head. "But I've heard stories."

"Stories don't do it," Abby said. "This cat is worthy of a Disney villain."

Lucy came to her pet's defense. "If he was a dog he'd be the equivalent of one hundred and five years old. You don't think you'd be cranky if you were that age? I don't want you scaring Logan off. Luther's ears have been bothering him and I'll have to bring him in for treatment next week."

"Wear really heavy gloves," Abby advised.

"A Kevlar vest would help, too," Jeff interjected.

Logan was intrigued. "Now I really have to meet that cat." He turned to Lucy. "Bring him in Monday morning."

It wasn't long before everyone was clearing off the tables under Abby's direction. She didn't allow the men to sneak off and rest after their big meal as she handed them large trash bags and told them to get to work.

"How many people here have adopted animals from you?" Lucy asked as she loaded trash into a bag Logan held.

He thought for a moment. "Just about everyone. They've become pretty much a tapped-out market. I told the brothers they either need to move to another station or find all new friends." Once finished, he tied up the bag and added it to the growing pile.

Logan saw her keeping an eye on Nick. The boy was walking toward the garage with Lou.

"He's old enough not to be watched twenty-four-seven, you know," Logan said, noticing the direction of her gaze.

"I know, but I still worry."

"Because of what happened at his school?"

"He's been the model kid since then," she said.

"Before you know it he'll be in college chasing cheerleaders."

Lucy shuddered. "Please, I have enough trouble thinking of him as a teenager." A high-pitched yip caught her attention. Domino sat by her feet, his head cocked to one side, one ear up and one ear down.

Logan chuckled and bent down to pick up the puppy. The dog licked his face with enthusiasm.

"You have no idea how lucky you are," he told the puppy. "Mrs. Crenshaw would have turned you into a designer dog with all the cute outfits and doggie furniture."

"The poor baby!" Lucy took the dog out of his arms and cuddled him against her breasts. "You could have had all that luxury and instead, you have to sleep with me."

Logan stared at the dog who he swore was giving him a canine version of a smirk.

"As I said before, lucky dog." He picked up another trash bag and carried it over to the Dumpster.

"How did we end up with so much trash?" he asked.

"Think about thirty adults and half that number of kids," Lucy replied.

LUCY SMILED as she walked up to the house. Cathy and a few of the women were in the kitchen putting leftovers in containers.

"I'd forgotten just how much fun flirting was," Lucy announced.

"You once told me you wanted to be wild and wicked," Nora reminded her.

"And then I chickened out, which was very easy to do when the man I thought to be wild with was more mouse than lion." She scratched the dog behind his ears. He closed his eyes in bliss.

"It's about time," Ginna said, as she rinsed off dishes.

"The man isn't looking for long-term and neither am I," Lucy said.

"So said we all," Abby said. "At least Logan's house-broken. Otherwise, we'd suggest you look for a new pet elsewhere."

"Maybe that's the problem," Lucy mused aloud. "If we looked at men the same way we look at dogs and cats, we might be better off." She set Domino on the floor where the puppy promptly circulated in hopes of handouts.

"Scratch him behind the ear. Rubbing his belly. It's all the same." Gail grinned, and the women all laughed at the mental picture.

They went back to work and had the kitchen clean in minutes.

Ginna walked up to Lucy carrying two glasses filled with wine. "Come on." She nudged her friend with her elbow then walked outside.

Lucy followed. She had a feeling her friend meant to have a heart-to-heart talk whether Lucy wanted one or not.

Ginna chose a small round table near the side of the house, away from the men who'd relaxed either on the grass or in patio chairs around the swimming pool.

"It never fails. The women do the dishes while the men take naps." Ginna grinned, setting one of the glasses in front of Lucy.

"If you're intending to set me up with one of the guys, please spare me," Lucy pleaded, deciding it was best to speak first.

Ginna shook her head.

For the first time in Lucy's memory, she saw her friend looking serious.

"Remember the night of my bachelorette party?" Ginna asked.

"That night you and I went out on the beach to watch the sunrise because we were so wired we couldn't sleep. I talked about my excitement in marrying Zach. And you talked about the excitement you'd had before your marriage and then you talked about your disappointment when it didn't work." Her brilliant blue eyes were shadowed. "You told me how Ross wanted to be a husband but not a father. That he could never take responsibility for anything. How you hadn't seen that weak side of him until after the marriage. But that I never needed to worry about my marriage turning out like that because Zach could take on the responsibility for ten men, he would love me with every ounce of his being and he would always be there for the twins and me. You wanted me to know I had a very special man. Lucy, I knew that already, but hearing you reaffirm what I felt told me how true it was. Here I am, a woman who told herself no way was she going to do the home and hearth bit and now I'm doing it all and loving it."

"And you're telling me this because…"

"Because you can kick and scream all you want, but it's your turn, m'dear. Your life has taken some pretty wild turns in the past year what with that jet turning your house into a load of broken lumber and stucco. Then you moved out here where you've pretty much started a new life. It's time for that next step."

"If this is about Logan Kincaid."

"I've known Logan all my life. He had a nasty divorce while yours was coldly civilized," Ginna stated. "You both claim you aren't looking for a commitment for various reasons, but I think you're both just afraid of getting hurt again. I had a lousy first marriage, Lucy. My second one is pretty darn perfect—as long as Zach picks up his dirty clothes." She grinned. "We've all taken a chance and it's worked out."

"So you think I can somehow have that same luck?" Lucy was amused by her friend's confidence.

"Call it more like fulfillment. Nick's growing up. What will you do when he's gone on to college?"

"Go on cruises like my parents."

"You get seasick just looking at a rowboat. We won't even mention what happened when we saw *Titanic*."

Lucy reflexively pressed her hand against her stomach; it had started rolling at the mere mention of the movie. "All the more reason not to get involved with someone who practically worships surfing."

Ginna made a point of looking around. "Beautiful weather, surfs up, yet the man is here and there's no surfboard in sight. Do yourself a favor, Lucy. The next time the man asks you out, just say yes."

"What makes you think he'll ask me out again after all the times I've turned him down?"

"Logan's dad raised him with the intention he would go into the law. When Logan informed him he intended to be a veterinarian he was told there would be no money for school. Logan worked two jobs and saved every penny he could for veterinary school. Trust me, he'll ask you again."

Lucy shook her head. "First Nick ends up working at his clinic, then I do. Now you're sitting out here telling me what I need to do is date the man. I'm surprised you're not already planning the wedding." She narrowed her eyes at her friend. "Which you better not be. I swear, if I didn't know better I'd think someone was plotting against us."

Chapter Six

"Mom. Mom."

Lucy rolled over and groaned. "Can't it wait until morning?"

"Not really," Nick said urgently, sitting down on the edge of the bed.

"What time is it?" She tried to force herself to move past the thick fog of sleep.

"A little after two."

She pushed her hair away from her face. "What's wrong?"

"Luther's sick. He threw up in my bathroom." He wrinkled his nose. "I tried to get him to drink some water, but he threw that up, too."

Lucy tried to sit up, but she found herself effectively trapped under the covers with Nick sitting on the side of the bed. She gently pushed her son off the bed. As she pushed the covers back, chilly night air hit her with a vengeance. It would have been so easy for her to slide back under the warm covers. She gritted her teeth and reached for her robe, but that was also trapped. This time under Domino's body. The puppy sat up and yipped.

"Let's see what's going on." She retrieved her robe and slipped it on. "Is he still in your bathroom?"

Nick nodded. "I put him in the bathtub in case he throws up again."

Lucy set Domino on the floor and loosely tied the sash of her robe as they walked to Nick's bathroom.

A pitiful yowl reached their ears as they neared the room.

"That's definitely not Luther," she murmured. "He disdains sounding pathetic."

Inside Nick's bathroom, the sound of the cat's misery seemed to bounce off the tile. She swallowed her sigh of dismay as she discovered Nick had used all of his towels to cover the soiled floor. But it was her cat, huddled in a corner of the bathtub, that caught her attention.

"Oh, Luther, did you eat something bad when you were out tonight?" She dropped down to her knees and reached over the side of the tub to stroke the cat's back.

His answer was another pain-filled yowl. Her stomach clenched in sympathy. She couldn't remember the last time her cat was sick. She used to joke he was too ornery to get sick.

"I'll call Logan," Nick said.

Lucy then noticed he held the phone in one hand.

"He's always available for emergencies," he explained, waiting as the line on the other end rang. "Logan? It's Nick Donner." He paused. "Uh, no, she's fine." He cast a quick glance in Lucy's direction. "It's Luther. He's throwing up a lot." He nodded as he listened. "Okay." After giving directions to their house, he hung up. "He said he'll be here in about ten minutes."

"That fast?" Luther's plaintive meow brought her back to attention. "Don't worry, baby," she murmured to her cat. "The doctor will be here soon and will make you feel better." She looked up at her son. "You better finish wiping up the floor before Logan arrives."

"Me?"

"If you can clean up after all those dogs and cats at the clinic, you can clean up after your sick cat," she said firmly.

Nick muttered under his breath as he quickly wiped up the floor with his towels then wadded them in a bundle.

"Put them in the washer, not in the hamper," Lucy instructed.

She continued to stroke the cat, afraid to pick him up in case the motion only made him more ill. She was so engrossed with reassuring her cat everything would be all right, that she didn't hear Logan's arrival until he walked into the bathroom.

"So this is the infamous Luther."

Lucy looked up. If Logan had been awakened from a sound sleep he didn't look it. His brown eyes looked alert behind his glasses, even if his dark-blond hair was mussed.

Her worries about her cat dissolved as Logan crouched down next to her and leaned over the side of the tub. His words to the feline were soft and reassuring. Luther looked at the stranger with a wary gaze but allowed Logan to touch him.

"With him throwing up like this, putting him in the tub was a good idea," he said.

"Nick did that," she replied.

"Good thinking," he told the boy.

"More like training," Nick said, pleased with the compliment. "I fell off my bed and split my head open when I was younger. Mom took me into the bathroom to check it out. She said it was easier to clean up tile."

"Very true." Logan gently examined the cat and took his temperature.

Lucy knew her pet had to have been feeling wretched since he didn't give Logan any trouble. Not once did his claws appear to take an angry swipe at an unwary veterinarian.

"Has he been outside lately?" Logan asked.

"He was out for a while tonight. He's not much of an outdoor cat, but he likes to do some roaming at night."

"He'd make a good snack for a hungry coyote," Logan commented.

"The coyotes are afraid of him," Nick said.

"Probably for a good reason." Logan continued his medical assessment. "When he's been out lately, has he caught any-thing?"

"We've found some lizards and a couple of gophers that he left by the patio door," Lucy replied.

"At first glance, I'd say he picked up something that didn't agree with him," Logan said, sitting back on his heels. "It some-times happens where they come across a dead animal that's too good to resist. I brought something to help settle his stomach. He's probably already gotten rid of most of what made him sick."

"Tell me about it." Nick wrinkled his nose. "I had to clean it all up."

"Cats are usually choosey about what they eat, but some-times they're tempted."

"Probably because I changed Luther's food over to a for-mula for senior overweight cats," Lucy said. "He hasn't been happy with me since then."

Logan rummaged through his case and filled a hypoder-mic. "He'll be sleepy once this takes effect."

"I'll fix him up a bed in here." Lucy stood up and left the bathroom.

Nick watched over Logan's shoulder. "She was really wor-ried about him," he said.

"The sad part about animals is that they can't tell you where it hurts." Logan deftly injected the medication.

"She's also glad you came out here in the middle of the night," Nick added.

"No problem there." Logan lightly ran his hands along the cat's back.

"Here's one of Luther's favorite blankets." Lucy walked into the bathroom carrying a fleece throw. She folded it sev-eral times and placed it in a corner of the bathtub. Logan gen-tly picked up the cat and placed him on his soft bed.

"His bed is a shredded blanket with puppies on it?" he commented. "Does Domino feel as if he has a target painted on his back?"

"Luckily, Luther's too fat to chase him and Domino already knows it isn't a good idea to tease him," she said.

Logan settled down on the floor, crossing his legs in front of him while Lucy leaned back against the side of the tub and stretched her legs in front of her.

"You know that saying about pharaohs worshipping cats as gods and cats never forgetting that? Well, that's Luther in a nutshell. Even as a kitten, he wanted to be revered. Here was this tiny kitten I could hold in the palm of my hand and he had such an arrogant attitude." She chuckled.

"And the name?"

"I have no idea," Lucy admitted. "From the beginning I realized calling him Fluffy wasn't going to work, but the name Luther did. He even responded to it right away."

"Lex Luther was Superman's archenemy. Names make an animal unique."

"Like Magnum."

"Like Magnum," he agreed.

"If you guys don't mind, I'm going back to bed," Nick called out from the hallway. "I put the towels in the washer, Mom. And, yes, I turned it on and added soap."

"Thank you and good night," she called back. "Wow, he actually figured out how to turn on the washer."

"Good night, Nick," Logan echoed.

"I'm taking Domino with me," Nick told them.

A moment later they heard a door close.

Lucy looked down at her legs and cringed at the sight before her. "Oh my God," she murmured, forgetting her human audience.

Logan looked at her curiously. "What's wrong?"

She wasn't about to admit she was appalled to realize that due to the chilly night she was wearing a pair of flannel pajamas Nick had given her the previous Christmas. Chocolate cookies and glasses of milk danced across the blue background and the cozy pajamas had quickly become her favorite nightwear. They weren't the ideal clothing to be seen in by a member of the opposite sex.

For a moment she wasn't sure whether to scream with embarrassment or laugh.

She wanted to put the man off, didn't she? What better way than for him to see the real her, baggy pajamas and all? All she needed was her hair done up in rollers and a colorful night masque covering her face.

She lifted a stealthy hand to her head. Along with the pajamas she sported a definite case of bed head.

"You look kinda cute in a rumpled sort of way," Logan said, as if he read her mind.

"I haven't carried off this look since I was sixteen," Lucy muttered. "And at sixteen I wouldn't have been caught dead looking like this."

"Which shows how much you care for your cat," he said. "You'd be amazed what I've seen when I've gotten a middle-of-the-night call."

"Silk and diamonds?" she teased.

"More like Frederick's of Hollywood."

"The women consider you that hot, do they?" Lucy chuckled, worries about her own appearance now forgotten.

"More like a few who are bored and think that calling me to come over to look at their so-called sick dog or cat will relieve that boredom. They even dress that way when they bring their animals into the clinic in the middle of the night."

"And then I impress you with my cookies-and-milk pajamas and Tweety Bird slippers." She plucked at the heavy flannel as she pointed one foot covered with a yellow fuzzy cartoon bird.

"Even if Nick hadn't been the one to make the call, I would have known your call was genuine," he said. "Even when it hurts, you've been upfront with me."

Lucy thought back to what Ginna had told her the previous afternoon.

"Such as saying 'not in this lifetime,'" she murmured. "You are a glutton for punishment, aren't you?"

"Keeps me humble."

"I doubt you've ever been humble." Lucy glanced over her shoulder and noticed Luther was now lying on his back fast asleep. His rounded tummy rose and fell with his heavy breathing.

Logan turned around and checked the cat. "I'd say the worst is over."

"I'm sorry Nick called you," she apologized.

"It never hurts to make sure it isn't something serious. Especially in a cat of his advanced age," he said.

"Luther believes in being served only the best," Lucy said. "But every so often it's as if he goes into the great kitty hunter mode and looks for the most disgusting thing he can find. Since we've moved out here, he's been in rodent heaven. He was the laziest cat in the world before and while he's still pretty lazy he'll rouse himself for a good hunt. I do appreciate you coming out."

"No problem." He stood up then reached down to pull her to her feet. His hands lingered alongside hers.

Lucy had always thought that Nick's bathroom was good-sized until now. She felt as if she was standing inside the close confines of a closet.

"Are you okay?" Logan asked.

"Yes." *No.* There was a definite unsettling sensation in her stomach. She detected the faint scent of fabric softener from his T-shirt and a muskier scent from his skin. She was in big trouble.

Logan turned away and packed up his case.

"I'd offer you coffee, but I guess the last thing you want is something that will keep you up," Lucy said brightly. She mentally thumped herself upside the head as she realized how it sounded. Where was her ability to say the right thing at the right time? "I guess you want to go to bed."

"While your invitation is tempting, I think I'd better head for home," Logan said with a straight face while wicked amusement danced in his eyes. There was no mistaking how he'd taken her words or how much he enjoyed her plight.

"Let me see you to the door," Lucy said swiftly, sidestepping her way around him and walking out of the bathroom.

Logan's SUV was parked near the front of the house.

"I haven't seen the house since before you moved in," he commented, when they walked outside. "But what I can see looks great."

"Thank you." His praise warmed her. "I couldn't believe I was so lucky in getting the property. And I love the sprawling layout of the house, so that we each have our own space."

"It's a good place for a family," he agreed, walking around to the rear of his Jeep and stowing his case away.

"Thank you again," she said, following him. "I'm sure Luther also appreciates your coming out."

Logan slapped the rear door shut. He turned around and leaned against it.

Before Lucy could realize what he was dong, he pulled her into his arms. Her lips were parted in a surprise when his mouth covered hers.

She couldn't remember the last time a man had kissed her, but she did know that no man, not even her ex-husband, had ever kissed her the way Logan was kissing her at that moment.

The air around them was chilly, but the man holding her was warm and his kiss intoxicating as he alternately nibbled and stroked her lips apart. If she hadn't been holding on to his arms she would have easily melted into a puddle of pure sensation.

The kiss could have lasted five seconds or it could have been five hours. She lost all track of time as the hot temptation of his mouth painted in her mind sensual pictures that had to be illegal. She had no idea when her arms ended up looped around his neck or how her body molded itself against his until nothing could have gotten between them.

Lucy forgot everything but the heated feel of the man wrapped around her. The man who had her feeling as if they had all night to do just this.

When did kissing become this erotic? A hazy part of her brain acknowledged he was truly gifted. He tasted of midnight fantasies all wrapped up in silk and chocolate. She tipped her head to one side and nipped his jaw just because it seemed like a good idea. Judging by the hardened feel of his body against hers, it was an excellent idea.

Logan Kincaid was good enough to eat!

Lucy felt as if she was floating until she realized that Logan was holding her up off the ground.

Logan leaned back a little and stared down at her. The moonlight shone on his face, starkly detailing his arousal.

"Lady, you pack one hell of a punch." His voice was raspy with the same searing desire that engulfed her.

"Ditto." She felt so dazed, it was a miracle she could say anything at all.

Logan carefully set her back down on her feet.

"I've got to get home." His voice hadn't recovered its usual deep timbre.

"Why?" She had trouble catching her breath. Even her knees felt wobbly. The idea of dragging him back into the house and having her way with him was very appealing. If she stopped to think about what she was considering, she'd swear she'd lost her mind. If Ginna and the others ever heard about their kissing, they'd never let her forget it. If they sensed what had just run through her mind, they'd be out ordering the wedding invitations.

Logan took a deep breath. He looked away, dragging his hand through his hair. "I only meant to kiss you. To throw you off guard a little. I didn't expect—" He shook his head, unable to say more. Or just plain not willing to. He turned back to her. His expression was fierce and could have appeared frightening to anyone who didn't know him. "Go inside,

Lucy. Go back inside and check on your cat and look in on your son and your puppy and then go to bed. Alone. Do all this before I completely lose my mind and convince you to go home with me."

She raised her chin. The fire in her eyes dared him to argue with her. "Who says I'd allow you to convince me?"

Logan revealed that actions spoke volumes over words. All it took was one hard, fierce kiss to have her melting again. He lifted her up by her forearms and carried her back to the steps that led to the front door.

"Good night, Lucy." He pivoted on his heel and got into his truck. Five seconds later all she saw were the red taillights of his truck as it moved down the driveway. Away from her.

She gently touched lips that still tingled from his kisses and muttered, "Now that's what I call a house call."

HE'D KISSED the woman until they were both senseless and all day she acted as if nothing more than a platonic handshake had happened between them.

Logan hadn't wanted to leave Lucy that night. He had been so hard with arousal, he thought he'd explode. But he was also aware her son was in the house and spending the night making love to the boy's mother might not be a good idea. Not to mention he was convinced she was dangerous.

From the moment Lucy stepped into the clinic until she returned that afternoon with Nick, she'd treated Logan as a, well, as nothing more than her employer.

Her smile never left her lips, and she'd even joked with him and Gwen about a new patient, a woman whose hair was tinted the same apricot shade as her miniature poodle's.

Logan had to admit that the practice ran smoother under Hurricane Lucy, as he liked to call her than it had under Brenda. Files were always in easy reach, they were kept updated and even the dog and cat treats jars were kept filled.

When Nick walked in, Logan noticed he was holding a

large cat carrier. The angry yowls emitting from it warned him Nick was carrying Luther.

"I stopped home to check on him and discovered he'd thrown up again," Lucy explained.

"Why don't you bring him on back and we'll see what's going on," he suggested.

"So this is the cat from hell." Gwen took the carrier from Nick. "I've heard so much about him, I can't wait to see the real thing. So he was sick over the weekend?" she asked Lucy.

"Most of Saturday night. Logan came over and took care of him."

"Really?" A wealth of information was injected in that one word as the tech's gaze moved from Lucy to Logan and back to Lucy.

Lucy prayed she wasn't blushing. She compared Gwen's powers of observation to Ginna's. And neither woman refused to be put off. She'd gotten to know Gwen over the weeks of working at the clinic and enjoyed the talks she shared with the sharp-tongued vet tech.

"Gwen, you want to check his vitals? I'll be in there in a minute," Logan said.

"He doesn't like being examined," Lucy warned Gwen, following her into the examination room.

"No problem. He'll soon realize I'm more evil than he is."

Lucy stood back and watched Gwen skillfully extract the angry cat from the carrier. Luther snarled and tried to swipe at the woman with unsheathed claws but she easily avoided injury.

"Oh, honey, nastier critters than you have tried," she chuckled, wielding a thermometer.

"We wouldn't be too fond of that process either," Logan said, walking in. "Over the weekend, Luther found something that didn't agree with him. I hope that didn't happen again."

"He stayed in the rest of the weekend and demanded full pampering," Lucy replied.

The large cat's head swiveled around in Logan's direction. His nose scrunched up as he hissed.

"This is definitely a cat meant for Halloween." Gwen looked impressed with the feline's temper.

Logan was more cautious as he examined the cat. "Let's draw some blood, make sure there are no parasites lurking about." He looked up when they heard the front door open.

"Thanks." Lucy smiled at them then slipped out of the room.

Gwen didn't wait much longer before she said, "Let's see if I've got this right. You kissed her, but you didn't stay the night."

Logan's head snapped up.

"The way she avoids looking at you directly says a lot while you practically stand on your head to get her to look at you. If you two had had sex, you'd probably make sure to stay out of her way." She picked up the cat who by now recognized he had met his match. He remained docile in her grasp. "Don't hide from Nick, boss. That will be a telltale sign to the kid." She waltzed out of the room.

Logan pressed his hands against the side of the metal examination table.

"Spare me from women who are intent on making me crazy."

He knew kissing Lucy could land him in trouble. Not with her, but with himself. Since his divorce he'd trod carefully around women, not wanting anyone he dated to think she would have the chance to become the next Mrs. Logan Kincaid.

His ex-wife taught him a lesson about relationships that he'd never forget. He thought he'd married the love of his life, instead, he'd married a woman who thought he would change his way of life to what she wanted. He enjoyed the quieter more rural life. She wanted bright lights and the busy city. To this day he couldn't understand how he was first attracted to someone so much his opposite. But back then he wasn't thinking entirely with his brain.

He'd thought he could keep it light with Lucy. Light flirting, maybe some dinners out, and if they ended up in bed together, he wouldn't complain. Except Lucy didn't make it easy for him. He indicated his interest. She shot it down. He asked her out. She rejected him. His ego was more than a little bruised and even he couldn't understand why, like an idiot, he continued to pursue her.

Then her son ended up performing community service in his clinic and she took over his front desk on a full-time basis.

If he didn't know better, he'd think fate had thought up the ultimate practical joke by throwing them together.

Chapter Seven

"He is so adorable that I want to just cuddle up with him," Lucy chattered away, each word easily heard by Logan as he exited one of the examination rooms.

He could hear the faint sound of another woman's voice, but he couldn't hear it clearly enough for him to make an identification. He inched his way down the hallway in an attempt to find out.

"This is all new for me and I have to admit I'm really enjoying it," Lucy went on.

He stealthily made his way farther down the hallway, so he would have a better chance at finding out to whom she was talking.

Lucy's laughter floated back toward him. "Having that warm body under the covers on cold nights is a definite plus. He's like sleeping with my very own personal furnace."

Logan didn't think she was dating anyone. When had that changed? Who was she dating and how come he hadn't heard anything about this before?

He racked his memory through past conversations, but he swore she hadn't said a thing about seeing anyone. He would have heard something. Gwen and Kristi excelled in dissecting everyone else's social life. He'd overheard enough of their discussions to make sure he kept his private life exactly that—private.

"What are you doing?"

Logan jumped at the unexpected intrusion. He spun around with his hand flat against his chest. Yep, his heart was still beating. He glared at Gwen who looked at him with mock innocence.

"I swear I'll put a bell around your neck someday," he whispered fiercely.

She merely arched an eyebrow at him then tilted her head up as she heard Lucy's voice.

"The kisses get pretty wild," Lucy said, oblivious to the two eavesdroppers. "But sometimes that's the best part."

Logan swore that Gwen's expression radiated pure feminine evil. He countered it with his best innocent look, but she wasn't buying it.

"You little dickens," she whispered with a wicked smile. "You've been fooling around with the help."

"Have not," he stoutly denied, secure in the knowledge he hadn't fooled around with Lucy the way he'd like to.

She looked as if she didn't believe him. "You try anything with me, you will get smacked upside your head," she threatened before walking down the hall toward the front of the building.

Logan knew Gwen well enough to know her threats were as secure as Fort Knox. He hurried to catch up with her. When he reached the front he slid to a stop. Lucy was partially leaning over the counter as she talked energetically to Ginna whose white shepherd, Casper, was sitting quietly by her feet.

"There's nothing like a furry bed warmer." Ginna chuckled as Logan walked out.

That was when he noticed that Domino was sprawled on the counter surface. Lucy's new lover.

"He crawls under the covers and stretches out beside me at night," Lucy said as she adjusted the wiggling puppy.

Stifling a smile, Gwen shot Logan an amused look. Then she picked up a chart on the counter and turned to Ginna. "Do you want bring Casper back?"

As Ginna walked past the desk, she glanced at Lucy then at Logan then back to Lucy. She turned to Gwen as they walked back down the hallway.

"It must be getting mighty interesting around here," Logan heard her say to the assistant.

"More interesting by the minute," Gwen replied.

"Did you need something, Logan?" Lucy put Domino inside the multi-colored fenced enclosure set up behind the counter to keep him from wandering around the clinic. Unfortunately, it was short enough that he could climb over it, but so far, he was happy enough staying in there. The puppy immediately pounced on one of his toys.

"Yes." He moved toward her.

She turned around to ask what he needed, but the pressure of his mouth against hers immediately silenced her words.

His kiss was swift and hard and spoke volumes. When he lifted his head, she appeared dazed.

"Who knew that listening to someone talk about their dog cuddling up with them could turn a guy on," he murmured as he turned and walked away.

Gwen was writing in the chart when Logan entered the examination room. The smile on her lips warned him the two women shouldn't have been left alone.

"Here you go," Gwen said, said handing him the chart. "I'll get the hypodermics ready."

"Thanks." He checked the information she had written down. "How's Casper doing with having kids around all the time?" he asked.

"He loves them. I think it has to do with all the treats they slip him. And they learned he hates peas just as much as they do." Ginna chuckled. "How are you doing?"

"Busy as always." He concentrated on the dog since he knew just how skilled Ginna was in extracting information. He remembered how she had watched him at the barbecue. He always considered newly married women to be one of the most dangerous species on the planet. They always wanted to see their friends married and didn't care what they had to do to accomplish that task. He wasn't about to dredge up old memories by reminding Ginna he'd been married and most of that time hadn't been happy. He knew she'd only point out that it was time he had some happiness. It wasn't happiness he was afraid of. It was fear of getting hurt that kept him cautious.

Lucy had tempted him more than enough already, but so far he'd kept his wits about him. At least he thought he had.

Damn. He hoped he had.

He was relieved when Gwen returned with the hypodermics and the dog was soon brought up to date on vaccinations.

"All done, Gin," he pronounced.

"Thanks." She smiled broadly as she passed by him with the dog. She stopped before she reached the door. "Oh, by the way, while Canyon Rose is a great color on Lucy, it really doesn't do all that much for you." Her smile grew even wider. "'Bye, Logan."

He spun around to stare into the shiny metal surface of the paper-towel dispenser. A smudge of pink smeared his lip. Cursing under his breath, he pulled a paper towel down and wiped his mouth. He crushed the damp paper towel until the damning evidence was hidden from the casual eye and tossed it into the trash.

He walked to the rear of the building and entered the shelter area. Kristi was busy setting kittens down in an enclosed area for exercise so she could clean their cages.

"Where's Nick?"

Her head snapped up; apparently she was surprised by his abrupt tone.

"He's outside exercising Jake. Although you'd think that it's more like Jake's exercising him," she said with a grin. "That dog's energy level is two speeds—fast and faster."

"He needs a home with lots of kids to keep up with him," Logan said, heading for the rear door.

"I'm sure he'll get one."

When he walked outside, he heard Nick calling the dog's name. Logan stood at the fence and watched the boy running back and forth with a black-and-white Australian shepherd. He was impressed that Nick did his best to keep up with the energetic dog. Smears of dirt on the kid's T-shirt and grass stains on his jeans revealed Nick did more than just run with the dog. Logan wondered what Lucy thought of all the dirt Nick brought home each day.

"I'd have a better chance if I had four legs like him," Nick panted, as he walked over to the fence while the dog paused to investigate a corner of the enclosure.

"You and Jake seem to have hit it off," Logan commented.

"He's pretty cool," the boy agreed. "I think he's tried to herd me a few times." He grinned.

"There's some sheep herds still around here, so he could have come from one of them. Just a shame he wasn't wearing a collar and tags."

Nick laughed when the dog walked up and nudged him in the back as if to say "We're not through playing yet." "Boy, you're pushy. Just like Mom."

"Speaking of your mom." Logan took a deep breath. "Would it bother you if I dated your mom?"

Nick's head snapped up. "Excuse me?"

"I asked you if it would bother you if I dated your mom."

"That's what I thought you said." Nick took a deep breath as he looked off into the distance. He kept his hand resting on Jake's head. The dog stood quietly by his side as if content with the contact. "Mom doesn't date much."

"So she's said." Logan couldn't remember ever feeling so awkward with a conversation. But then he'd never asked a teenage boy for permission to date his mother before either.

"So she said she'd go out with you?" He sounded surprised.

"Not yet, but I thought if she knew you were all right with the idea, she wouldn't give me as much grief," he admitted. "Do you have any suggestions on how I can wear her down?"

Nick considered his question. "Forget sending her flowers. She thinks that's dorky. Or trying to impress her with fancy restaurants. When I was eight she went out with this guy named Stuart. He owned an art gallery in Capistrano. I didn't think the paintings he had there made any sense, but they sold for lots of money. He always took Mom to fancy restaurants and plays and concerts. He called me Nicholas." The dark expression on his face said what he thought about that. "And he kept telling Mom I should expand my artistic side."

"I don't see anything wrong with that," Logan commented. "He was probably trying to find a common bond with you. While a single mother is raising you, a single father raised me. Some of the women my dad dated tried to act like a mother toward me, others tried to be a friend."

"I couldn't stand the guy," Nick confessed. "See, he bought me all these paints and told me to paint my feelings. So I painted words on him. Mom took away TV and video games for two months. He told her I obviously had psychological problems and recommended she take me to his psychiatrist whom he'd been seeing for a real long time. Mom told him to take it up with his psychiatrist."

Logan breathed a silent sigh of relief that he wouldn't have to compete with the memory of a wealthy art dealer.

"Got it. As long as I don't call you Nicholas or suggest you take up art, I'm safe."

Nick scratched Jake behind his ears. When the dog dropped to the ground and rolled over displaying his belly, Nick crouched down and began rubbing.

"So far, Mom's turned you down. If you convince her to take her out, more power to you."

"That's good enough for me." Pleased with their little talk, Logan walked back to the building.

"Excuse me, Dr. Kincaid, but did you happen to forget you have patients waiting?" Gwen asked him the minute he stepped inside. "This is an animal clinic, remember?"

He didn't break stride. "The barking was my first clue."

She followed him down the hallway. "Glad to see you got the lipstick off."

"Yeah, I might have told everyone it was yours." Logan's grin grew wicked.

Gwen got off a parting shot as she entered an exam room. "Until they looked at Lucy and realized she was wearing the same color."

Logan remained in the hallway for a moment, listening to Lucy talk to Beau. The macaw's raspy reply told him the large bird was as captivated by her as Logan was.

He walked into the examination room, feeling more relaxed and lighthearted than he had in some time.

He'd kissed Lucy Donner exactly twice. He hadn't realized those two times would only whet his appetite for more. Shannon hadn't affected him this way the first few times he'd kissed her. He hadn't realized that his memory had been playing tricks on him since his ex-wife had actively pursued him and had initiated that first kiss.

But it was the memory of Lucy's kisses that kept Logan going all through the afternoon. He cheerfully ignored Gwen's questioning looks and Lucy's curious expressions. For once, he felt in control.

He wondered what Lucy would say if she knew her son had given him permission to date her. Of course, now the challenge would be to convince her to go out with him.

It was a good thing Logan enjoyed challenges.

THANKS TO a slow afternoon, Lucy was able to catch up on housekeeping chores. As she straightened up the supply cabinet, she was aware of a piercing gaze centered on a point between her shoulder blades.

"Do you honestly think you can mentally coerce me into giving you what you want?" she asked, not bothering to turn around. "I can be as stubborn as you are." She continued with her task. Ten minutes later, the prickling sensation was still there. She heaved a pretend sigh. "Oh, all right, but just one." She pushed items aside as she dug into the back of the cabinet and pulled out a large bone-shaped dog biscuit. She casually tossed it over her shoulder. She heard the clatter of plastic hitting the floor then the snap of powerful jaws and a crunching sound. She turned around but by then the cell phone was back between Magnum's jaws. There was no sign of the dog biscuit. The dog bowed his head in a regal motion before he rose to his feet in a graceful play of muscles and walked away.

"He's got you trained," Logan said.

"I figure if I keep him well fed he won't have that hungry look in his eye when he looks at me," she replied, returning to her desk and sitting down.

"I think that dog could eat a Tyrannosaurus Rex and still ask for seconds." Logan wandered around the area.

Lucy watched him. She wondered why he appeared so restless. Logan was always such a focused person, she couldn't imagine him acting like this.

"Would you like to go out to dinner tonight?" he asked abruptly. "Nick's even invited."

"Well," she murmured, amused by the invitation issued so bluntly, "it does save me having to cook."

Logan winced. "I didn't say that very well, did I?"

"You've done better, but perhaps you thought if you changed your technique you'd have a better chance," she said kindly.

"So did it?" he asked. "Work, that is."

Lucy appeared to consider his question. "I'm not exactly a fun date," she warned him.

"Says who?"

"I have references," she said gravely.

"Then you need to change who you go out with." He braced his hands on the edge of the desk as he leaned over her. "Come on, Lucy. Take a chance," he softly coaxed.

She looked up at him, bemused by the dusting of gold in his brown eyes. The minuscule bits of light seemed to make them gleam.

The man really was too handsome for his own good. But he wasn't someone who was obsessed with his looks. Free time at the beach had given him tiny lines around his eyes and the lean musculature of a swimmer.

Then there was that smile of his. Talk about dangerous! Logan's smile held a hint of wickedness along with the temptation of the forbidden fruit. Forget the apple. Logan Kincaid was more than enough to entice any woman to go astray.

She reminded herself what had happened the last time she'd gone astray. The divorce may have been civilized but it had still been traumatic for her.

"I eat pretty much anything. Nick is the same except that he won't eat sushi," she said. "I have to take Domino home first and make sure Luther is all right."

"He's improved his eating habits?"

"He's stuck to his senior low-fat kitty food," Lucy said. "He hates it, but he knows he won't be getting anything else."

"How about I pick the two of you up at seven?"

"Fine."

Logan drummed his knuckles on the desk surface then walked away.

Lucy felt a stir in her stomach as if she was free-falling from a great height.

"It's only dinner and Nick will be with us," she whispered to herself.

"WHY DO I have to go with you guys?" Nick asked, when Lucy informed him of their dinner plans with Logan.

"Because you were invited and I'm not leaving you home alone."

"I'm old enough to stay by myself for a couple hours and there's no way Logan would want his date's son along," he argued. "No offense, Mom, but that's really gross."

"You're invited, you're going," she said firmly. "So go put on a clean shirt."

As she turned to go to her room and dress, she tossed him another mandate over her shoulder. "Do me a favor and take Domino out," she instructed. "We haven't had an accident in more than a week and I'd like to keep it that way."

Nick got up from the floor and headed out of the bedroom with the puppy running behind him.

With one eye on the clock, Lucy changed her clothes and applied makeup. She couldn't even recall the last time she'd been out on a date.

"Consider this a test run," she told her mirrored self. "Dating was never good for you. Maybe now things will change."

There was that insurance broker who'd come into the clinic with his black lab last week, she recalled. He'd learned she was single and wanted to get to know her better. He'd suggested they get together for coffee sometime. So why didn't she take him up on his offer? Because he had a habit of not looking at my face, she reminded herself. She'd felt as if he could see all the way to the label on her bra.

Or maybe she just imagined he acted like that. Wasn't it easier to put a man in the wrong before she got hurt? What would she end up doing next? Was she going to turn into one of those mothers who hung on to their children for as long as possible? That was a picture she didn't want to consider. At this rate the world would be telling her to get a life.

Lucy quickly shook the thoughts out of her head. "Self-analysis never gets you anywhere," she said, then returned to her bedroom to dress.

NICK WAS in the front yard when Logan drove up.

"Cool car!" Nick gazed with covetous eyes at the red BMW convertible.

"It has a lot less dog hair in it than my truck does," Logan confided, reaching down to pet Domino as the puppy ran to him.

"You really don't have to worry about me coming along and ruining your night," Nick said as Logan picked up the puppy. "I can stay home."

"I think he's afraid we'll embarrass him," Lucy said, coming out of the house.

Logan looked up and froze. A light left on inside the house sent sparkles through the etched-glass panels in the double front doors, surrounding her with a magical aura of light.

She wore a flirty-looking skirt and her hair had been styled in loose curls that were swept back behind her ears. The only makeup he'd ever noticed her wear at the clinic was a tinted lipgloss. Tonight her eyes were highlighted with a taupe eye shadow and dark mascara and blush brought out her cheekbones. Her shimmery warm red lipstick brought his gaze to her lips then down to her bare toes sporting the same color. He suddenly had a vision of her wearing that lipstick and nothing else.

Good enough to eat.

Logan shifted uneasily. Not exactly the best thoughts to cross your mind when you were standing next to your date's kid.

"How does Mexican food sound to you two?" he asked quickly.

"All the guacamole I can eat?" Nick asked hopefully.

"Until you turn green."

Nick whooped with joy and ran into the house with Domino. He was back outside in moments.

"There's a reason why I'm afraid to take him to an all-you-can-eat buffet," Lucy told Logan.

Nick climbed into the back seat and settled back.

"Have you been to the Hacienda Inn?" Logan asked as he started up the car.

"No, but I've heard good things about it."

"I want my food to burn the roof of my mouth off." Nick draped himself over the top of the front seat.

"What do you think you're doing? You do not take off your seatbelt," Lucy scolded her son.

He grinned at her as he sat back and pulled his seatbelt across his chest and clicked it in.

"You'll really like this restaurant, Nick," Logan said. "Their salsa is hot enough to start a fire."

"Cool!" Nick's enthusiasm was infectious.

"One thing he'll never be is the blasé teenager," Lucy told Logan.

"Yes, I've noticed." He grinned.

As Logan had hoped, Lucy was suitably impressed with the restaurant, which was designed to resemble an old California mission. They were seated at a table on the patio surrounded by cactus and exotic flowering plants.

Nick started to reach for the bowl of salsa and companion bowl of warm tortilla chips but quickly subsided when his mother shot him a warning look.

"So I guess this means no margarita for me?"

"Not for another eight years," she told him.

"Trust me, they would have carded you," Logan confided to Nick out of the corner of his mouth.

Lucy was grateful for her margarita to cool the heat generated not only by the fiery salsa but by her nerves. No matter how much she told herself not to be, she was nervous about this evening. How many men were willing to take a woman's son along with them on a date? None of the men she had dated in the past—not that there were all that many—had asked Nick to come along with them. In fact, many of them had offered to pay for a baby-sitter.

Logan Kincaid, the man she considered a player, was the

one who included her son. He'd treated Nick as an equal from the beginning.

Under the cover of lowered lashes she watched Logan as she sipped her drink. The patio lights shone down on him, turning his hair into a golden aura. She imagined she could even see the sparks of gold in his brown eyes that held warmth and laughter as he joked with Nick.

When their appetizer of chips with melted cheese and guacamole came out, they dug in with relish. The plate was clean when it was replaced with their meals.

"That looks good." Logan eyed Lucy's fajitas with a hungry eye.

"Back off, buster." She waved her fork at him.

"You never get between Mom and food," Nick chortled.

"Same here." Logan easily blocked Nick's covert movement to sneak a tacquito from his own loaded plate. "You try it again, kid, there will be no dessert for you."

"Ha! I looked at the menu and no offense, but flan isn't one of my favorites." Nick returned to his heavily loaded chicken burrito and spooned a good portion of the fiery salsa onto it.

"You're a chili fan, aren't you?" Logan asked.

"I'm a growing boy," Nick said around a mouthful of food. He winced when he caught the look of censure on his mother's face that clearly said "Do not speak with your mouth full!" He quickly swallowed. "Sorry."

She wasn't surprised to see him not only finish his burrito but polish off the last of her fajitas.

"You're right, he'd clean out an all-you-can-eat buffet," Logan said.

"That's my boy." Lucy beamed. "The reason my grocery bills equal the National Debt."

"And here I thought the dogs ate a lot." Logan met Lucy's eyes. "Maybe that means he won't want dessert."

"Yeah, I want dessert. Just not flan," Nick confessed.

"Then you're in luck. We're going to the kind of place that caters to everyone's sweet tooth," Logan confided.

"Mom's got one of those," Nick said. "We won't talk about how she is once a month." He ducked as she pretended to swat him.

Logan's surprise turned out to be a large old-fashioned ice cream parlor complete with a soda fountain and jukebox playing rock-and-roll music.

When Nick spied some of his classmates, he asked permission to join them. He was gone before the word *yes* had barely passed Lucy's lips.

"We'll have your sundae sent over there," Logan told his departing figure then turned to Lucy. He grinned at her. "Alone at last."

She made a point of looking around her. "Bright lights, loud music, kids running all around. You're right, we're in a regular haven of solitude."

"Does that bother you?"

"No." *Yes, it did.* He'd kissed her a few times. She'd like to try it again, but there was no way it was going to happen here.

Lucy had a sudden mental picture of Logan stretched out on the counter with scoops of ice cream surrounding him. Bite-size pieces of fudge brownie were scattered across the ice cream then topped with thick super-rich hot fudge sauce, a coating of real whipped cream, a sprinkling of chopped nuts and a nice red maraschino cherry on top.

She could feel herself salivating and not just for the edibles.

"Lucy. Earth to Lucy."

Judging by the tone of his voice, he'd said her name more than once. She jerked herself back to the present and found a teenage waitress standing by their table.

"Are you ready to order?" Logan asked.

Lucy's smile spoke volumes as she scanned the menu. "Oh yes," she practically purred.

Logan almost fell off his chair. If he didn't know better he'd swear Lucy meant something entirely different than the fudge brownie sundae she ordered for herself or even the pecan praline sundae she ordered for Nick.

He'd come here before with dates, usually for a post-movie treat. But none had aroused him the way Lucy just did.

The lady was giving him X-rated ideas while they were sitting in a G-rated establishment.

He was never so grateful as when their sundaes arrived. He needed something good and cold to focus his attention on.

Lucy's eyes gleamed as she dipped her spoon into the dish. The sound that escaped her lips as she took her first taste was almost sinful.

"This is the absolute best hot fudge sauce I have ever had." She daintily licked the back of her spoon.

Logan watched the tip of her tongue appear. It was way too easy to imagine her savoring him the way she savored her dessert.

He wondered if Nick could find a ride home later. Much later.

"It's going to melt."

Lucy's comment barely made a dent in his consciousness. "Hm?"

"Your ice cream." She pointed with her spoon. "If you don't eat it at a fairly good speed, it will melt."

"Mom, Sean asked if I could sleep over there tonight." As if Logan's wish came true, Nick appeared at the table. "His mom said it's okay with her if it's okay with you and she'll drive me home in the morning."

Lucy looked over and smiled at Sean's mother, who smiled and waved at her. Then the woman's knowing gaze shifted toward Logan. She nodded and waved back. She knew what the woman was thinking. She'd have to talk to her about the way her mind worked.

"All right."

"Thanks for dinner, Logan," Nick said before taking off.

"At least he remembered his manners without any prompting." Lucy sighed with relief.

Logan grinned. "As I said before, alone at last."

Chapter Eight

When Logan pulled up in front of Lucy's house, motion detector lights flicked on, lighting up the area. When he shut off the engine, they could hear high-pitched barking coming from within.

"We keep Domino crated when we're gone. More to protect him from Luther than to protect the rugs from him," Lucy explained, pulling her key ring out of her purse and activating the garage-door opener. The door glided upward about six inches, froze for a moment and started descending. She uttered an exasperated sound and punched the remote again. Once more the door started up only to go back down again. "Dammit, Luther! Leave those sensors alone!" she yelled.

"Luther?" Logan asked.

She nodded as she jabbed the button again. This time the door was allowed to move up without incidence. "There's a cat door from the kitchen into the garage and another one to the backyard. Luther likes to trip the garage-door opener sensors. He'll do the same when we're leaving so the door keeps going down. He only does it when he knows we're running late." She led the way through the garage. The sound of the cat door told them where the devious feline had escaped.

"Are you sure he's not a troll in cat fur?" Logan asked as he followed her into the kitchen.

"I'm pretty sure the day will come when he'll end up a fur

pillow," she muttered, noting the bowl that was filled with kitty kibble before she'd left was now scattered across the floor. She swore under her breath. "His special kibble. Can you tell he hates it?"

"I gathered that." Logan grabbed a broom sitting by a counter and started sweeping the kibble into a pile. Lucy scooped it up and tossed it back in Luther's bowl. "Another battle of wills?"

"And one more he'll probably win, but not without a fight on my part. I have to keep Domino's food practically locked up or Luther eats it."

"At least he's staying away from whatever gave him a bellyache that night," Logan said.

"He hasn't stopped his hunting. I still find dead gophers by the patio door." She opened a cabinet and brought out a bottle of chardonnay. "Would you like a glass of wine?"

"Sure." He put the broom back. "Here, I'll do that for you." He took the corkscrew from her and easily extracted the cork.

She poured the wine and handed him one of the glasses. A pitiful whine then a howl sounded from the back of the house. Lucy chuckled.

"Let me go rescue him. It's a nice enough evening if you'd like to sit outside." She nodded toward the patio door before walking toward the hallway. "Mommy's coming, baby!" she called out.

Logan flipped a switch by the patio door and watched twinkle lights surrounding the patio cover come on. He picked up his and Lucy's glasses and carried them outside. A throaty rumble to his left warned him Luther was lurking nearby.

"There's plenty of field mice out there," he called out to the cat as he settled on a cushioned bench and stretched his legs out in front of him.

An ear-splitting yowl was his reply.

Logan relaxed in the cool night air, inhaling the fresh scent from the lemon and tangerine trees planted along the back of the property. Twinkling lights like the ones on the patio cover also covered the roof of a gazebo set in one corner. Through the opening, he could see a small round table and two chairs. In the other corner was a windmill he gauged to be about six feet tall. The evening breeze moved the blades in a lazy circle. He couldn't be sure, but he swore the blades had designs painted on them.

A swimming pool with a slide was the main focus, and a spa on the side, both set against a wall of rocks. It looked as if someone could climb up and jump off from the top if they wished. He sensed Nick had done just that more than once. He knew he would have at that age. Even the nearby barbecue appeared to be built out of rock in keeping with the pool and spa.

Lucy had done everything to make her house a home where a man could relax.

He was right. She was dangerous.

He turned his head when he heard the patio door slide open then closed. He looked back around when he heard the sound of trickling water. Multicolored lights flickered on inside the pool and spa while a fountain spouted up from the middle of the pool.

"Very nice," he commented.

"I call it magic," Lucy said walking over to him. "It's supposed to inspire relaxation. Probably why I spend a lot of time out here."

An excited Domino ran over to him and tried to leap into his lap, but his short legs wouldn't allow it. Logan picked him up, but the puppy soon had other things on his mind and tried to leap down until finally Logan took pity on him and set him down. He immediately ran toward the grass.

"He's doing great with housebreaking, but we still have some issues with chewing things that don't belong to him," Lucy explained, sitting down next to Logan. She turned sideways to face him and tucked one leg up under her as she leaned against the side of the bench.

He noticed she was now barefoot. He handed her her glass.

"Thank you." She sipped her wine. "And thank you for dinner and dessert."

"You're welcome." He looked across the yard. "Your cat is stalking your dog."

"Yes, he does that." She heaved a sigh. "Luther doesn't understand that Domino's still too young to know fear, but it doesn't stop him from doing his best."

"I hate to think what that cat does for laughs."

"That *is* what he does for laughs."

"When did Nick become interested in that little blond girl?"

Lucy whipped around so fast she almost fell off the glider. *"What?"*

Logan swiftly leaned over and grabbed her wineglass before it fell from her fingers. He was amused by her reaction.

"The little blonde in the group of kids he was with. The whole time we were there he couldn't keep his eyes off her. Trust me, I know these things."

Her mouth opened and closed but no sound came out. "That's Brooke Taylor, Sean's sister. Sean's his best friend. Nick's too young to look at girls."

"He's thirteen, Lucy," Logan said gently, seeing the shock written on her face. "Before you know it Nick will be in high school and dating."

"I told him he can't date until he's forty," she whispered. "He isn't all that interested in dating anyway. He hasn't wanted to attend the dances they've had at school."

"He was looking at her as if she was as good as, if not better, than the sundae he was eating," he told her.

That was the last thing Lucy wanted to hear. Memories of the vision she'd had of an ice-cream-covered Logan were still too strong in her mind. She almost gulped the rest of her wine down.

"I'm not ready for him to date," she croaked.

"I doubt he'll be asking to borrow the car anytime soon,"

Logan teased her. "I only noticed that Nick watched her with more interest than a kid normally has in a member of the opposite sex."

"Which are things you would know about."

"As a guy, yes. One day we tell the world that girls are evil, the next we realize they're not so bad after all."

"At least it's Brooke." She accepted the inevitable. "She's very sweet and not boy-crazy the way a lot of the girls their age are. There are some girls in his school who put my teeth on edge. Too many of them are thirteen going on thirty."

"He's working a job that will weed the real ones out," he said. "Girls first think that working around dogs and cats sounds cute until they realize that means cleaning out a lot of kennels. That doesn't give them a very romantic picture."

Lucy shuddered. "I really don't like to think of the word *romantic* in conjunction with my son."

"So what do you think of in conjunction with *romantic?*" He set his glass on the ground and picked up her foot then tugged her other one until her feet rested in his lap. He wrapped his hands around her toes, running his forefinger over the gold ring.

Lucy giggled and tried to jerk her feet out of his grip but he refused to release them.

"Ticklish, are we?" he murmured.

"I can't even have a pedicure without going crazy," she admitted, trying not to laugh as he gently manipulated her toes. A giggle escaped her lips and she pressed her fingertips against her mouth to hold it in.

The tiny lights framing the patio cover gave him enough illumination to see the helpless laughter dancing in her eyes.

"So where else are you ticklish, Lucy Donner?" he murmured, wrapping a hand around her ankle.

"I'll never tell."

Logan rubbed his thumb against the soft skin along the inside of her ankle. She didn't try to pull away, but there was a tension in her body that told him it wouldn't be difficult to find her other ticklish spots. He was eager to discover everything about her. He wanted to know how responsive she could be if he found just the right spot. The idea of searching for those spots was intriguing.

He kept his hand wrapped around her leg as he trailed it up to her knee. His fingers rubbed lightly against the sensitive area in the back. A soft, indrawn breath escaping her lips was his first alert.

"I guess you're not ticklish there," he murmured, looking up at her.

"No," she whispered, keeping her eyes on his face.

"Or here." He moved his fingers up another inch.

Lucy said nothing. She lowered her gaze to his hands. One rested warm against her thigh while the other was still wrapped around her toes.

"Maybe being ticklish is like the hiccups," he murmured. "If you try shock treatment, it stops."

Logan tried to gauge her expression. The faint light finally revealed the glint in her eyes.

He leaned over, grasped her around the waist and before she could utter anything more than a squeak of surprise, turned her around so that she was settled back against his chest. He wrapped his arms around her.

"There, that's better," he said in a low voice filled with contentment.

"It is nice," she agreed.

Logan freed one hand long enough to reach down to grasp Lucy's wineglass and bring it back up. He gently bumped it against her hand and she curled her fingers around the stem.

"You've got quite a setup out here," he said.

"Thank you. I wanted Nick to have a kid-friendly place for his friends."

"Yep, kids just love gazebos and windmills."

Her shoulders shook with soft laughter. "No, those are for me just as the trees are."

"Trees but no flowers?" Logan asked.

Lucy groaned loudly. "Oh, I had lots of flowers out here. There was only one problem. Luther thinks all flowers are a delicacy. When we moved in, I spent all afternoon planting flowers. By the time I finished, my back felt as if it was broken and I wasn't sure I could ever walk upright again. The next morning I looked out the kitchen window to admire my efforts and screamed. Luther was in the middle of the flowerbed. By then he'd eaten more than half of the flowers. Tempting him with his favorite treats didn't get him away from the flowers, neither did threats. So far, the trees have been safe. I guess they're not as tasty as the flowers were."

"The gazebo is a nice touch," he remarked.

"It is, isn't it?" She sounded proud of the small building. "It's something I've always wanted. Our last yard wasn't big enough to have one. I thought it would be nice to have a quiet place for reflection. You can't see it from here, but a bench is attached along the inside wall. It's perfect for stretching out."

"Sounds like a great place to take an afternoon nap." He rested his chin on top of her head. Strands of her hair teased by the evening breeze tickled his nostrils. A subtle powdery scent he guessed was expensive surrounded him.

Gossip in the area said that, thanks to settlements from the airline and the company that manufactured the airplane, along with the sale of her house, Lucy had been able to pay cash for this house. She'd wasted no time in landscaping the property. He knew the school Nick attended wasn't cheap. And he understood that Lucy had put most of the balance of the settlement in the hands of a financial expert. He'd bet that even if Nick wouldn't be eligible for scholarships to just about every university in the country, she had his college tuition put away. But Lucy didn't act like someone who had come into a tidy fortune.

Logan made a nice living, but he knew that while his clinic

and the property it sat on looked just fine on paper, his bank balance rarely did. It never mattered to him since he didn't require a lot of money except to care for the shelter inhabitants. Donations and adoption fees helped pay for their upkeep.

At one time his business had almost been destroyed because his ex-wife wanted him to suffer. And he had suffered. It had taken him a while to recover. After that, he'd sworn he'd be a love-'em-and-leave-'em kind of guy. His own nature hadn't allowed him to be that callous, but he still walked warily where the opposite sex was concerned.

Then he'd met Lucy Donner at a party, and he almost fell over his own two feet. She wasn't beautiful in classical terms, and the first few times they were together weren't stellar since she let him know she wasn't interested. But there was a vibrancy about her that attracted her to him.

Tonight, he was content for the two of them just to sit here and enjoy the evening.

Well, almost content.

Logan grasped Lucy about the waist and turned her around. She squealed in surprise and would have dropped her glass if he hadn't taken it from her and set it on the ground.

"I just realized that there's no reason to let a pretty night like this go to waste," he drawled.

She was wide-eyed. "There isn't?"

"Nope," he said almost cheerfully and then proved his point by bringing her down to him. He could taste the wine on her lips as he explored her mouth thoroughly.

Lucy gripped his shoulders for balance while Logan kept his hands at her waist. He'd already discovered the woman packed quite a wallop with her kisses, so he wanted to take it as slow as he could.

The minute her lips touched his he knew he was in trouble.

Lucy was all woman. The kind every red-blooded man

dreamed about. Except his dream was very real and very desirable.

She whispered his name and softened her grip on his shoulders, allowing her body to align itself with his. He moved one hand along her waist and up until his fingertips reached the lacy edge of her bra.

"Are you trying for first base?" she whispered, laughter lighting up her voice.

He grinned, thinking of a time when baseball terms gauged how far a boy got with a girl.

"Do I have a chance?"

She closed her eyes as she considered his question then opened them again. She wiggled her hips just enough to get his attention. "Maybe."

Logan inched his fingers just under the lace edge and traced the rounded curve of her breast.

"Why, Doctor, what a gentle touch you have," Lucy murmured, pressing butterfly kisses along his jaw line and up to his ear.

"Tames the savage beast."

"I thought it was music that tamed the savage breast."

Logan smiled at her tongue-in-cheek remark. "I was trying to be a gentleman."

She fingered his shirt collar then ran her hand down his chest to his belt before lightly skating farther down then back up to flick her fingertip against his chin. "Gentlemen don't let their attentions be known so blatantly."

"I'm too busy figuring if I dare try for second base."

Lucy shook her head in mock exasperation. "You men and your sports analogies." She shifted a bit and framed his face with her hands. "This is what helps you get to second base."

And then she kissed him in a way guaranteed to make him forget everything including his name, rank and serial number.

If he didn't know any better he'd swear she'd said something about hot fudge sauce.

Logan didn't think any woman had kissed him the way Lucy was kissing him.

He slid down the length of the glider until he lay flat against the cushions with Lucy a pleasurable weight on him. With one foot planted on the ground, she was able to fit very nicely in the cradle of his hips.

Fingers mapped out curves and angles. Mouths followed, sliding over bare skin to discover the spots that had one of them murmuring with pleasure. Logan's shirt ended up on the ground with Lucy's sweater drifting down after it.

"You're not cold, are you?" he murmured against the hollow of her throat.

"Not at all." Her words seemed to be imprinted on his skin.

The atmosphere was made for romance and seduction with the starry night overhead, the sensual sound of trickling water from the fountain and the feel of their bodies against each other.

Logan's hand was warm against Lucy's bare thigh when something that didn't seem quite right asserted itself.

"Lucy?" He was having trouble thinking as she nibbled on his ear.

"Hmm?" Her soft voice vibrated pleasurably against the sensitive skin just behind his ear.

"Domino's chewing a lot?"

She leaned back her head. "Uh." It took a second for her to comprehend his question. "Yes."

"I thought so. He's working on my shoe."

Logan groaned as Lucy shifted her body against his aroused one so she could lean over the side of the glider. "Domino, no! That's not yours!" A soft whine told them the puppy took the scolding personally. Lucy turned back to Logan. Embarrassment covered her face instead of the desire that previously captured it. "I owe you a pair of shoes. Lately, he's been convinced that any shoe he comes across is his. We have to make sure the closet doors are closed. I guess all his toys aren't enough for him."

"Just one of the hazards of dog ownership." He started to rise up but she pushed him back down. She pulled one of the cushions away from the back and adjusted it behind his head and shoulders. "There. Isn't that better?" She leaned back over and brought up one of the wineglasses. She glanced to one side. "Domino, go get one of your babies. We call his toys his babies," she explained to Logan. Then her shoulders started shaking, not with cold but with amusement.

"Who needs a cold shower when you've got a dog?" Logan said.

"I'm sorry." Her apology fell short with her laughter. "But if you could have seen his face when he realized he was caught…" She buried her face against his shoulder.

"Better him than Luther. Who knows what that devil cat would have done with his claws." He winced as he imagined what could have happened.

Logan's mirth joined hers. He wrapped his arms around her and gently rocked her against him.

Lucy finally raised her head then straightened up. "Our chaperone was making sure you didn't go too far."

"Better the dog than your son," Logan said wryly.

Lucy picked up the other glass and handed it to Logan. She tapped his glass with hers.

"To our conscience."

Logan lifted his glass to her and drank. "I'll have my vengeance." He grinned at the look of alarm crossing her face. "When you bring him in for his *operation*."

"Don't give away the surprise," she playfully warned.

He stood up, grasped her hand and pulled her to her feet.

"Time for me to say good-night." He kept one arm around her waist as they walked to the patio door with Domino following behind them.

They walked through the darkened house to the front door. Lucy flipped a switch to turn on the carriage lights set on either side of the door and walked with him to his car.

"I had a wonderful evening," she told him as they stood by the driver's door.

"I did, too." He smiled. "I'd like to do it again." He locked his hands at the small of her back.

"You wouldn't have to feed Nick next time."

"Or we could let him loose at an all-you-can-eat buffet."

"A good way to test their promise," she joked.

Logan's smile softened as he looked down at her.

"I'm glad you were willing to give me a chance."

"There's something irresistible about a man beloved by kids and animals. Besides, I was starting to weaken," she confessed.

"Whatever it was, I'm glad." He kissed the tip of her nose. "Good night, gorgeous."

"Good night." She stood back so he could get into his car.

"Go inside and lock the door," he ordered, kissing her again, this time on the lips.

"You forget." She glanced down at the bundle of fur sitting on her feet. "I have a ferocious guard dog."

"Even when he's adult size he won't be ferocious. Good night, Lucy." He was reluctant to drive away, but he knew it wasn't the right time to think about spending the night even though her son wasn't there.

He was relieved when she smiled and walked back to the front door. But she remained in the doorway with Domino cradled in her arms.

He drove off with the sight of Lucy reflected in his rear-view mirror.

"Maybe I'll bring Magnum next time. He should be able to handle both the pup and the devil cat with one paw tied behind his back."

For a minute he was tempted to turn the car around and return to Lucy's arms and perhaps an invitation to stay the night.

It took every ounce of self-control to stay on the road back to the clinic where an arrogant Malamute instead of a lovely woman would greet him.

It just wasn't going to be the same.

Chapter Nine

It's going to be our best reunion yet, fellow Rangers!
Join us for dinner and dancing at the Sunset Canyon
Clubhouse. Don't be left out!

"Please leave me out," Logan muttered, tossing the invitation
toward his wastebasket just as Lucy walked into his tiny office. It fluttered to the floor instead. She stooped down and
picked it up, not missing the bold lettering as she smoothed
out the rumpled paper.

"Your high-school reunion. How neat!" she said. "You're
going, aren't you?"

"I'll seriously think about it when they hold the fiftieth
reunion."

Still holding on to the invitation, she took the chair opposite him. "Why wait that long? I went to my reunion and had
so much fun. Our class hunk didn't do well once he was out
of high school," she confided with a saucy grin. "And gym
class."

"High school wasn't exactly a fun time for me," Logan admitted. "I was the loner who lived for weekends and vacations
and high surf."

"There must be people you might want to see."

"I see the ones who matter to me."

"I bet there are others you're curious to see," she said

after studying him for several long minutes. "That's why you won't go. Tell you what: I'll make you an offer you can't resist. I'll go with you," she offered. "I will even get all tarted up if you want. I could speak with an accent and look exotic. Just don't ask me to wear a dress that's more Spandex than fabric. I have this thing about needing to breathe."

Logan shook his head. "Why would you offer to do this?"

"Because you pretty much live in this clinic. You need to get out more. Or—" she paused for devilish effect "—I could talk to Abby and tell her you need to go."

"I went to school with Brian, not Jeff."

"And Abby," she reminded him.

He made a face. "You'd actually sic her on me?"

"In a heartbeat."

"You'll have to call Abby, Lucy." Gwen stood in the office doorway. "He won't go."

He sat back in his chair with his crossed feet propped on the desktop. He stared at Lucy, looking as if he was seriously considering her proposition.

"No spandex, huh? How about wearing a dress cut down to here with a hem up to there or lots of sequins?"

"Cut down to here will only work with a good push-up bra. I'll do what I can if it means you'll go."

Gwen looked from one to the other with great interest. "I'll want pictures," she stated.

Logan kept his gaze locked on Lucy's. She didn't bat an eyelash under his regard.

"Why are you trying to organize my social life?" he asked.

"You can't organize something that doesn't exist. I told you. Besides, this way I can see if all reunions are alike. The old cliques banding together again, some of the jocks talking about their glory days and many of the nerds now million-aires." She reached for the phone. "Or I can call Abby."

Logan was faster in grabbing it. "Fine, I'm calling your bluff. Get out the red lipstick and high heels."

Lucy snatched up the invitation. "I'll just phone in your RSVP. I'd hate to think you'd forget to do it." She sailed out of the office.

Logan caught a knowing expression on Gwen's face. "What?"

She grinned and shook her head. "Oh no, this is way too much fun to watch."

"What?" he insisted, still not understanding her amusement.

Gwen laughed. "I just love watching the way she plays you. I think I could even learn from her." She turned and walked away.

"Ha! You know enough to unnerve most of the single guys in this county," he called after her departing figure.

"What can I say? It's a gift," she called back.

Logan sat back. He could hear the muted sound of Lucy's voice along with a crowing sound coming from Max. If only he hadn't taken in that rooster a couple of weeks ago. The macaw not only had picked up the bird's verbal salute to dawn, but he enjoyed crowing at all hours of the day. It wouldn't have been so bad, but Magnum seemed to think he should howl in accompaniment.

Right now Logan felt like doing a little howling of his own.

He hadn't planned on attending his high-school reunion. He hadn't *wanted* to attend his high-school reunion. He didn't hold that many good memories from that time.

But the idea of going in there with Lucy on his arm was appealing.

He had an idea it could end up being a night he'd never forget.

"Uh, Mom, is that what you're going to wear?"

Lucy turned to face her son who sat cross-legged in the

middle of her bed. She hadn't seen him look this horrified since he was five and she'd arrived at his kindergarten Halloween party dressed as a pixie. He later swore it would scar him for life.

Tonight she definitely wasn't dressed like a pixie.

"Yes, this is what I'm wearing. Why, what's wrong with it?"

"You don't wear stuff like that very much."

"Clothes?" She looked amused.

"Ha, ha, very funny. It's that you don't wear stuff like that." He inclined his head toward her.

Lucy looked down at the dress she'd paid a small fortune for. Instead of opting for the little black dress, she'd bought a strapless one in a deep coral silk that moved with every curve. The front draped across her breasts and the back dipped down. The short skirt showed off her legs to perfection, right down to the high-heeled sandals with tiny straps that looked too flimsy for walking. Ginna had fixed her hair that morning in a knot of curls high up at the back of her head. After her bath, she'd applied a shimmery scented lotion to her shoulders and arms that gave her skin an extra golden sheen. She thought she looked pretty damn good and even sexy for the mother of a teenager.

Anticipation for the night built up inside her like the first swirl of a tornado.

Nick kept up his scrutiny. "You don't look like a mom. Not that you don't look nice," he hastened to add. "You look really pretty. You don't dress up very much, so maybe it's more that I'm not used to you looking like this." He looked embarrassed.

Lucy thought back to the too few times she'd dated in the past. She knew she'd dressed up for other men, but she'd never splurged on a dress this sexy. She hoped it would literally bring Logan to his knees.

"Sorry, my darling son, but there are times when moms like to look hot."

Nick made a face. "You do realize it's statements like that that will put me in therapy when I get older?"

Lucy smiled. She was used to her son coming up with dramatic statements.

"So I guess he has to dress up, too," he said glumly.

"I wouldn't be surprised if he shows up wearing a tie," she said. "Do you have your clothes packed for your overnight at Cathy and Lou's?" She was grateful the older couple had asked if Nick would like to spend the night with them since Lucy didn't know what time they would be returning from the reunion.

His head bobbed up and down as he continued to stare at his mother with horrified fascination.

"Don't worry, Cinderella will turn back into a pumpkin after midnight," Lucy teased.

Nick slid off the bed. She winced as she saw her beloved comforter slid right with him. He noticed her expression and quickly turned around to straighten it.

"Don't forget to take Domino's dinosaur." She mentioned the squeak toy that the puppy had adopted as his green latex baby and now slept with.

"It's packed."

Lucy noticed her son's squirming. "Now what?"

He looked uncomfortable. "It's just that you, well…" He grimaced. "Mom, you look good." His face growing redder by the second, he made his escape with Domino hot on his heels.

"Poor baby, he hates the idea of having a mom who might be considered attractive to the opposite sex," she said under her breath as she applied coral lipstick. "I must remember to truly embarrass him when he starts dating."

"Mom! Grandma Cathy and Grandpa Lou are here!" Nick's shout was easily heard from the front of the house.

"Yes, dear, thank you. I'm sure the entire state of California heard you," she muttered.

Lucy walked into the living room, finding Cathy holding an enthusiastic Domino in her arms while Nick shifted his canvas bag from one hand to the other. He looked excited at the prospect of spending the night at his surrogate grandparents' house. Lucy guessed it meant an evening of movies and junk food since Cathy and Lou firmly believed in spoiling the kids in their family.

"Don't worry about picking Nick up early, dear," Cathy said. "Come over anytime. I'll have waffles ready."

"Waffles?" Nick perked up.

Lucy easily read the knowing glint in the older woman's eyes. She clearly expected Lucy to be occupied come morning.

"I'll be sure to show up before Nick has a chance to eat his weight in waffles."

Cathy smiled. "No hurry."

"You should be ashamed of yourself," she mouthed to the older woman.

Cathy merely kept smiling.

When the doorbell rang, Lou, who was closest to the door, leaned over and opened it.

Logan grinned at Nick who stood beyond Lou. "Hey, Mr. Donner, I'm here to pick up your mother."

"You better behave with her," Nick said straight-faced. "I have a large dog with big teeth and an even bigger appetite."

"We're taking Nick for the night," Cathy said brightly.

"Cheapest kid care in the county," Lou said to Logan. "You two have fun. As for my crew, time to roll."

"When did you get the fire truck?" Logan asked the older man.

"You got a fire truck?" Nick spun around. "Cool!" He ran outside. "Awesome!"

"A firefighter association hired me to restore it," Lou explained. "A small town in Illinois used it until the late 1930s. It was discovered in a barn and now it's with me for some tender loving care."

"There will be no using the siren," Cathy warned as Lou walked outside. "Have fun, dear." She kissed Lucy's cheek.

"Can we turn on the siren?" Nick could be heard.

"No siren!" Cathy ordered, following them out.

"How far down the road do you think they'll get before we hear the siren?" Logan asked Lucy.

"By the end of the driveway," she guessed.

It seemed the rumble of the big truck had barely faded away when it was replaced by a brief burst of the siren.

"I knew Lou would let Nick try the siren," she said, a grin on her face.

"I would like to say you look incredible," he told her.

"Thank you," she said demurely. "You look pretty good yourself."

He slowly turned in a full circle. "Sticky tape is great for getting off the dog hair."

She'd always thought he was good-looking but in a charcoal suit instead of scrub shirt and jeans, he was devastating.

"Magnum probably thought he was going to be your date," she said.

"He is a party animal," he agreed.

Lucy glanced at the small gold clock set on a nearby table. "I'll just be a minute."

While waiting, Logan walked around the living room. He stared, fascinated, at the small clock on the table, noticing the pendulum swinging one way, while the clock face swung the other. He lightly fingered the pendulum then swore under his breath when it swung a little too hard and separated from the piece holding the clock face. He fumbled to put it together and breathed a sigh of relief when it was swinging freely again.

"Doctor with so-called delicate hands destroys a clock," he muttered to himself.

He studied the large room, noting the mauve and blue sofa and love seat that seemed made for comfort as well as looks.

He could see that what was usually considered a more formal room was still people-friendly and comfortable enough to relax in. He noticed a night-light plugged in near the couch was a smiling sun wearing sunglasses. He walked farther in and sniffed one of the scented pillar candles on the mantel then looked at the painting hanging over the fireplace. Colors echoed throughout the room were slashed across the canvas.

"Whatever happened to seascapes and pictures of deserts?" he muttered.

A hissing sound brought him spinning around.

A wild-eyed Luther stood in the door leading to the living room. The cat's back was arched, his fangs in sight.

"You're safe, Luther," he assured the outraged cat.

The angry feline hissed his version of the last word before he stalked away, his tail held high as a banner of victory.

"I see Luther came out to greet you," Lucy said as she entered the room. She now wore a cream-colored cashmere wrap draped around her shoulders.

"I got the equivalent of a cat curse," Logan said. "'Eat a furball and die.'"

"Luther never forgives and never forgets." She lowered her voice for effect. "He's never forgotten his operation."

"We males are like that." He waited while she set the house alarm and locked the door.

"You seem more relaxed about tonight than you've been all week," Lucy commented as he helped her into his car.

"Resigned is more like it. Brian Walker called tonight and suggested we all go together. I told him you were making sure I'd be there."

"You can look up your old girlfriends and see how they've changed," she suggested.

"Did you do that with your old boyfriends at your reunion?"

"Definitely. The one I thought wouldn't amount to anything is now a multimillionaire in a dot-com business." Her shoulders lifted and rose as she uttered a heavy sigh.

"I told you. My free hours were spent on a surfboard."

"Then we'll show the women what they missed out on," she decreed.

Logan shook his head. He was still trying to figure out how Lucy had talked him into attending his reunion when it was the last place he wanted to be.

"Have you always been this bossy?" he asked.

"It's my nature. Some follow. I barge in. I'm the one who organizes."

"The clinic can attest to that." The powerful car reacted to the light touch of his foot. He would have preferred taking his time getting there. Maybe even find a nice out-of-the-way restaurant for a quiet dinner then find a club for dancing. Too bad he had to mentally shoot down the thought.

"I still can't believe you want to do this," he said. He hoped she might suggest they change their plans.

"Everyone should attend their class reunion at least once." She fiddled with the ends of her shawl. "I think it would be fun to attend a fiftieth reunion. Assuming I'm still mobile by then."

Logan chuckled. "My dad's getting up to that age. Maybe you can persuade him to take you with him."

"Ah, yes, the trophy date. Hard to visualize that grumpy man walking around with a sweet young thing on his arm," she said glibly. "I'll wait for my own fiftieth reunion, thank you."

Logan visualized a silver-haired Lucy circulating through a crowd with vintage music playing in the background.

"You were the Prom Queen, weren't you?"

"No, third runner-up. Evelyne Warner wore the crown. She didn't need to pad her bra," Lucy explained.

"Yeah, teenage guys do tend to look for the obvious," he

said, steering the car onto the freeway and easily merging with the evening traffic. "It's all that testosterone racing through our bodies."

"That's something my brother Zach would say. Back then Zach offered to ask Evelyne for a date then stand her up so she'd feel humiliated."

"Did he?"

"He asked her out, she said yes, but he somehow managed to forget to stand her up." She laughed. "Did you miss not having brothers and sisters?" Lucy asked curiously.

"Sometimes, but you forget I grew up with Brian, so I had his brothers and sisters."

"Your father didn't mind you being around the Walker family even though he doesn't like Lou?"

He shook his head. "His beef is and always was with Lou only."

"So your father used to date Cathy, but she chose Lou."

"Cathy was one hot item back then," he chuckled. "I saw her picture in one of Dad's yearbooks."

"So all your father ever told you was that he fell for Cathy and she turned him down? Don't you want all the juicy details?" she teased.

"Wanting all the details is a girl thing," he teased back. "And what I do know came from Cathy. My dad never talked about it and Lou only muttered things about stupid men. She said they're both hard-headed old fools who are too stubborn for their own good."

"I still find it interesting that while your father sees Lou as his enemy he still allowed you to be friends with Brian and the rest of the family," she said.

Logan nodded. "He believed if he ordered me to stay away from the Walkers, I'd do the opposite. He was right. I was pretty rebellious. You forget, my dad's a judge. He has to be fair even if it kills him." He flipped the turn signal when he saw their exit coming up.

It wasn't long before they saw a lighted sign announcing the Sunset Canyon High-School Reunion.

Logan pulled up in front and turned his car over to the parking valet.

As they walked in, he realized that while he felt some apprehension about the evening ahead of them, he wasn't as uptight as he'd thought he would be. He was even able to smile naturally as they approached the registration table. And it all had to do with the woman walking beside him.

"Here you are," Lucy said, picking up a name badge that had a small picture attached to it. Her lips twitched with a badly suppressed grin as she pinned the badge to his lapel.

"I told you, I was a surfer back then," he muttered, wincing at the visual reminder of his past in his graduation picture. "My dad was not happy I didn't get a haircut before the pictures were taken."

"Which accounts for the long shaggy sun-bleached blond hair, but what about that line across your nose?" she asked as she wrote her name in an elaborate script on a blank badge.

"It's called surfboard connects with nose," he said.

Logan was more interested in seeing where she was going to attach her badge. When she draped her shawl over one arm and stuck the sticky paper against the front of her dress, he knew he'd be spending the evening scowling at a lot of men for staring at her breasts.

"Just take a breath and smile," she said under her breath as they walked through the double doors and into a ballroom filled with people milling about. A band set up at the front of the large room was playing energetically. "No one will bite and if they do, you've had your shots."

"Were you always this much of a smartass?"

"Not until I turned thirty." She looked around with interest. "So your school colors are maroon and gold. Ours are red and black. The Cougars."

"Head cheerleader?"

"I told you Evelyne Warner was the class hottie. There's Brian and Gail. And Abby and Jeff," she said, pointing to a round table with eight chairs placed around it. Gail turned and saw them. Her delicate face broke into a broad smile and she waved at them.

"Yeah," Logan said. He noticed the men had a hint of grim determination on their faces that he was sure was echoed on his own, while the women sparkled the way Lucy did.

The women complimented each other's dresses and the men escaped to get drinks.

"How did you talk Logan into showing up?" Abby asked. "He swore he'd never come to a reunion."

"I bribed him with my body."

The two women practically howled with laughter then abruptly stilled as if they thought there was a chance she was serious.

"Just how much of your body did you bribe him with?" Gail asked curiously.

"All of it," Lucy said. "I told him how much fun I had at my reunion and that he needed to go to his. And if he agreed to attend, I would come along as his eye candy."

Abby grinned. "I'd say you're doing a good job of it."

"Maybe the three of us are doing a good job of making the men look great." Lucy's lips curved in a broad smile.

Logan, Brian and Jeff arrived at the table and set the drinks down in front of the women.

"Something tells me there was some plotting going on while we were gone," Logan said to the other two men.

"Something tells me that can only mean trouble," Brian predicted.

"Something tells me we'll only learn what they want us to know," Jeff said with the air of one who knew his wife only too well.

Abby took a sip of her wine and set her glass down. "Come

on, sexy, I want to dance." She stood up and dragged Jeff to the dance floor. Gail did the same to Brian.

By then, Logan didn't need any hints from Lucy. He rose to his feet and made a dramatic bow.

"Madam, would you care to dance?"

"I would love to." She matched his melodramatic tone.

As the music shifted to a sultry song made popular by the Righteous Brothers, Lucy moved into Logan's arms.

"Let's see. I told you how gorgeous you are. How about that you smell as great as you look?" he murmured in her ear.

"Thank you," she said demurely.

"So tell me something, gorgeous, how soon can we get out of here so I can relive other episodes from my teenage years?" His breath was warm against her cheek.

"Are we talking baseball analogies again?"

"Mmm, maybe, although we haven't finished the first inning yet. I don't even think we've reached third base," he murmured in her ear.

Lucy arched an eyebrow. "My mother warned me about guys like you."

"That's okay. My dad warned me I'd come up against a girl who'd give me a run for my money. That's something you've done since day one."

Lucy could have said the feeling was mutual, but she was speechless as she looked up at his face. She saw an intensity in his expression that literally took her breath away. She knew she was in trouble.

The idea didn't bother her one bit.

Chapter Ten

Lucy decided that trouble was Logan's first and last name. Not that she would tell Logan that. The man already knew what he was. She looped her arms around his neck as they moved around the dance floor in a lazy circle.

"I have a thought." Logan locked his hands at the base of her spine.

Lucy looked cautious. "Why do I feel that might be a dangerous statement?"

He flashed her a give-me-a-minute look. "There's this hotel up in the hills near La Jolla that believes in pampering their guests."

She knew exactly where he was going with his thought. The question was, would she agree to it. It wasn't as if she had to get home by a certain hour. Nick and Domino were spending the night at the Walkers'. Luther had plenty of water and kibble.

"Pampering, huh?" She refused to make it easy for him. "Something tells me you and I might have different takes on the word. You might consider it pampering if they wax your surfboard for you, while I might want something a little more indulgent. Even if it's something as little as room service."

"They have twenty-four-hour room service," he said slowly. His gaze was watchful. Even hopeful. "Including spa services. They'll come to your room to give massages and facials."

Lucy could feel the tension tightening his muscles as he waited for her answer. She was tempted to make him sweat. Did he honestly think she would automatically jump at the chance to spend the night with him? Who was she kidding? She wanted to say yes and be alone with Logan.

That still didn't mean she would make it easy for him.

"The absolute first thing I need in the morning is coffee. Trust me, I'm not a pretty sight when I haven't had my caffeine fix."

She swore at that moment the world around them was much brighter because of his smile; it widened with every word she spoke.

"Maybe you haven't tried the right wake-up methods," he said modestly.

"Why do I feel as if you had this all planned?" She couldn't believe they were having this conversation in the middle of the dance floor.

"There was no advance planning. Well, maybe it was there in the back of my mind," he conceded. "But it wasn't complete until I looked into your beautiful eyes. That's when I knew I didn't want this evening to end."

"I don't want it to end either," she whispered.

"Hey, kids, the music's stopped and the band announced a break, so I don't think you want to stand out here." Brian tapped Logan on the shoulder. Gail stood in the circle of one arm. "Logan, I just saw Carly."

"Carly?" Lucy's interest was piqued. Even more so when she saw the expression on Logan's face. She silently vowed to find out more about the unknown woman.

The two couples walked back to their table.

"They dated during our junior and most of our senior year," Brian said. "Then Carly dumped Logan for a college sophomore with a cooler car and his own apartment."

"Thanks for the update, Brian," Logan growled. "I only hope I can do the same for you."

Lucy fixed Logan with a cool gaze. "Really? And here you practically inferred you lived like a surfer monk all through high school."

Abby walked up to them with Jeff in tow. "Logan, I just ran into Carly in the ladies' room. She said she hopes she'll get a chance to say hi."

Logan looked past Abby's shoulder to see a pained expression on Jeff's face. The man was trying to communicate something to him, but Logan couldn't figure it out.

He knew he should be dancing Lucy right out of the room and to his car.

"Logan!"

He turned to face his first love.

The Carly Edwards who Logan remembered had been tall and athletic with the fresh-faced look of the typical girl next door. She had been one of the stars on the girl's track team.

That wasn't the Carly that faced him now.

Time faded Carly's freckles and her bright-red curly hair had softened to auburn with the tight curls in submission. The girl had grown into a drop-dead gorgeous woman.

"Hi, Carly, it's been a while." He smiled.

In high school he'd only had to look at her to experience that free-falling sensation in the pit of his stomach. His life had been driven by hormones back then and Carly had been a big part of it.

Now when he looked at her he felt nothing other than mild admiration for the woman. Then he looked down at Lucy who stood quietly by his side. That free-falling sensation hit him hard.

"Give me a hug!" Carly enveloped him in an embrace that he belatedly remembered to return. "You look great. Abby said you now own Dr. Mercer's clinic. You always did enjoy taking care of animals, so I'm not surprised you became a veterinarian."

"That's me," he agreed. "Lucy, this is Carly Edwards.

Carly, Lucy Donner." He watched the two women smile and say all the right things.

He looked at Lucy and Carly and saw no comparison between the two. Carly might look as if she'd just stepped out of *Vogue*, but it was Lucy who captured his heart.

The realization hit him like a ton of bricks. The world around him receded until only Lucy appeared in clear relief.

Oh, man, he was well and truly sunk.

"I'll be in town for a couple of weeks. I hope we can have a chance to catch up," Carly said with an expectant smile.

"The clinic number is listed," he said, reining in his impatience. He suddenly wanted to be alone with Lucy. "Sorry if we seem rushed, but we were just on our way out. It's good to see you again." He grabbed hold of Lucy's hand and headed for the entrance.

"Real subtle, Kincaid," Brian muttered as they passed the two couples.

Lucy barely had a chance to snatch up her shawl and purse as they passed the table.

"What is with the caveman routine?" she demanded, as she tried to keep up with his ground-eating stride.

"Call it a light bulb going off inside my head." He paused when they left the room then headed down the hallway that led to the lobby.

"Logan!" Lucy tugged on her imprisoned hand to no avail. "We can't just leave like this."

"Sure we can."

She sighed when she saw the determined expression on his face. She'd seen that look on his face before. When he wore it there was no budging him. Or, in this case, stopping him.

"For one thing, it's rude," she gasped. "Can you imagine what they're thinking back there after you just dragged me out like some Neanderthal?"

She uttered a protest as he suddenly veered right and walked down a darkened hallway. Before she could ask him his intentions, he had her backed against a wall, his hands braced on either side of her shoulders.

"They're probably thinking this," he murmured, lowering his head.

Lucy barely had a chance to take a breath before Logan's mouth captured hers in a kiss that was so blistering she felt scorched all the way down to her toes.

The only part of his body that touched her was his mouth. It was more than enough to send her pulse rate rocketing.

She moaned under the primitive onslaught that sent her spinning. The hard feel of his mouth against hers had her reeling as if she had been thrown into a swirling vortex of pure sensation. Every nerve ending was singing.

His tongue thrust into her mouth, mimicking what he planned to do to her once they were truly alone. She arched up, silently asking for more.

Her soft moans encouraged him more. His body, now pressed against hers, imprinted his arousal against her in a brand she doubted would ever fade.

She lifted her arms to slide them around his neck. She suddenly wanted all their clothing gone. A primal part of her being hungered to rip them off until there was nothing left between them.

Her tongue curled around his then returned the gesture by sweeping through his mouth. She could taste the Scotch he'd drunk earlier. But what spurred her was the pure taste of him.

Lucy rarely gave in to temptation like this. She liked to think things over. Make sure she was making the right choice. Yet here she was, standing in a dark hallway making out like a hormone-driven teenager.

"Hey, Kincaid, haven't you heard about self-control?"

Even with the familiar voice intruding on their private moment, both Lucy and Logan found it difficult to step apart. They turned as one to find Jeff standing at the end of the hallway. With his stern expression and arms crossed in front of him, he could have been a school official.

"A good thing ol' Miss Curtis didn't come this way. She'd have a heart attack if she'd caught the two of you." The wicked sparkle in his eyes betrayed just how much he was enjoying this.

Logan's reply was decidedly profane.

"Sorry, bub, but you're not my type," Jeff said a little too cheerfully. "My advice for you two is to get a room."

Logan threaded his fingers through Lucy's. He was relieved she didn't retreat from him. "What a good idea!" he said, starting to move toward Jeff.

As they walked past him, Lucy said, "I can't wait until the girls are old enough to date, Jeff. Then you'll have something new to worry about every time they go out." She blew him a saucy kiss.

"That was good," Logan complimented her as they walked swiftly through the lobby.

"Believe me, it'll be even better once he realizes exactly what it means," Lucy said with relish. She threw her head back and laughed.

Logan grinned as he listened to the pure, unrestrained sound of joy.

"I have never done anything like this before," she confessed as they ran out of the building. "When we left the ballroom, they could only guess, but now that Jeff saw us, well…" Heat stole across her cheeks.

The parking valet politely ignored their disheveled appearances as he loped off to retrieve Logan's car.

As the chilly night air hit her, Lucy wrapped her shawl tightly around her. Logan noticed her shivering and shrugged off his jacket, draping it around her. As he drew the edges together, he pulled her toward him for a brief kiss.

"If they're thinking *that,* then they have dirty minds," he whispered against her lips.

She laughed softly. "You know very well *that* is exactly what they're thinking."

Once they were in the car, Logan turned on the heater and adjusted the vents so the warm air was directed at Lucy.

"My reason for getting us out of there so fast wasn't because I saw an old girlfriend," he explained. "This was our evening and I wanted it to be just for us."

"She's very beautiful." There was no envy or jealousy in her tone, just a calm statement of fact.

"Yes, she is," he said honestly. "But she doesn't have what you have."

"You?" She couldn't resist teasing.

He didn't smile at her joke. "What she doesn't have is that special inner self that I see every time I'm with you." He took an extra moment at the stop sign to lean over and kiss her. Their lips clung. "But you're right. She also doesn't have me," he murmured against her mouth.

A blaring horn from behind tore them apart.

Logan swore under his breath as he started up. "With our luck, that's either Jeff or Brian."

"I do not care how much they beg, they cannot join us at the hotel," Lucy said firmly. "They will just have to find their own."

He was surprised by her words, especially after what had happened so far. He wasn't used to feeling like a teenager caught necking with his date.

"Do you still want to go?"

She held out her hand, her fingers wiggling in a "gimme" gesture. "Your cell phone, please."

"It's in the inside pocket." He nodded toward his jacket she still wore.

She did a quick search and pulled out his cell phone.

"Cute." She held it up, showing the picture of the phone-carrying Magnum as a background on the display. She quickly punched in a series of numbers and waited. She didn't look away from Logan. "Cathy, hi, it's Lucy. Listen, I called to say that I don't think I'll make it over there in time for brunch in the morning. I hope you won't mind if I don't show up until later in the day." Her lips twitched as she listened to the older woman. "Yes, I'm sure I will. Good night." She disconnected and handed the phone to Logan. "She said you better remember to feed me breakfast. Now, shouldn't you call Magnum and tell him you'll be very late getting home?"

"Jeremy's spending the night. Not because I thought ahead," he added quickly. "We had some patients who need to be under observation."

He leaned across the console and opened one side of the jacket, carefully sliding the phone back into the pocket. "There's just one thing. I might think like a hormone-crazy teenager, but I'm not prepared like one."

She understood his meaning. She appreciated his honesty and that he didn't have a box of condoms stashed away in the car's glove compartment.

"I'm on the patch," she told him. "And I'm much too embarrassed to admit how long it's been since I've been with anyone."

"Same here." He looked at her expectantly.

"Then I say we don't need to worry about a thing. You know, I really like this jacket." Lucy stroked the lapel. "I might not want to give it back."

"Wear the jacket and nothing else and it's yours."

She smiled at his suggestion. "My, my, how tempting."

Lucy felt very wicked.

She was the woman who always put the top back on the toothpaste tube. Who never tore off one of those "Do not remove by penalty of law" tags found on pillows and mattresses. Who once drove ten miles out of her way to return a dollar she was overpaid. Who studied all the consumer reports before making a major purchase.

No man was ever invited to spend the night under her

roof. Few of them met Nick because Lucy didn't want him to think the man might become his stepfather. Truthfully, she didn't think most of them could have understood her son with his never-ending imagination and penchant for trouble. She had also convinced herself that a second marriage wasn't for her. The last thing she wanted was to endure the emotional pain she'd gone through with her first marriage. Yet there was no doubt what she was planning to do with a man she'd once declared the last man on earth she would ever date.

There had been a time when Lucy flirted with the idea of becoming a wild and wicked woman. In the end, she settled for blond highlights in her hair and a toe ring.

Now she was traveling through the night to an unknown destination with the express intention of making love with this man.

Not only that, but she would leave a hotel in the morning wearing the same clothing she wore when she arrived.

"You look like the cat just after he ate the canary," Logan said, glancing at her face reflected in the light from the passing streetlights.

She wrinkled her nose. She found she couldn't stop smiling. "I feel very wicked."

"Are we talking good wicked or bad wicked?"

"Definitely good wicked," she said without hesitation. "And all I have to say is this hotel better know their pampering."

"How about warm cookies and milk available all night? Does that count?"

"That's a good beginning."

Lucy had more questions for him about the hotel, but he refused to answer them. He told her to use her imagination. She didn't dare tell him if he knew what was running through her mind, he'd run for the hills. Then again, he might not.

Lucy straightened up when Logan exited the freeway and

drove up into the hills. The car soon passed through large iron gates with a discreet bronze plaque set in the side wall announcing Mañana.

"Tomorrow." She translated the word.

"Sort of along the lines of escape the real world today, it will still be there tomorrow," Logan said.

"The real world staying out here is just right."

Even with old-fashioned street lamps stationed along the drive, Lucy couldn't see much of the long, rambling hotel. She could see that it was an adobe-style building that appeared to be a perfect fit in its remote setting.

The reality of what was going to happen set in.

"If you'd rather, we can head back."

She realized she must have radiated the uncertainty that crossed her mind.

"You would honestly do that if I'd told you I changed my mind?"

"Of course."

Lucy saw that Logan meant what he said. He was allowing her to lead.

"Or we can even get separate rooms," he said.

"Wicked women check into a hotel without even a toothbrush and they don't ask for separate rooms," she said.

Logan got out of the car and walked around to the passenger door. The late-night breeze took her by surprise. She was glad for the extra protection Logan's jacket gave her as they headed for the large glass double doors.

"Then let's get this wicked woman inside before she turns into a Popsicle," he said.

Due to the late hour, the lobby was deserted except for a few employees.

Lucy kept her expression blank as Logan murmured something about their feeling too tired to drive home after a party.

"Trying to save my reputation?" she murmured as a bellman escorted them to their room.

"Are you kidding? It's mine I need to worry about," he said straight-faced.

Lucy's eyes widened as she entered a large sitting room. The bellman turned on the lamp in the bedroom and pointed out the amenities before pocketing the tip Logan slipped him and leaving the room.

"This is what makes it all worthwhile." Logan walked over to the sliding glass door that opened onto a private patio and slid it open.

Lucy joined him and inhaled the brisk scent of salt and the sea as she listened to the rumbling sound that she knew was ocean waves crashing on rocks.

"The hotel is set on a rocky cliff that overlooks the ocean," he explained. "Late at night you can hear the waves crashing down there and it sounds as if it's right outside the door."

She smiled, picking up on what he really meant.

"Wild?"

She swore the gold dust in his dark eyes twinkled with light that warmed her from within.

"Definitely."

Lucy sensed that Logan was deliberately holding back. He was allowing her to set the pace between them. While she appreciated his thoughtfulness, right now she wanted the man who kissed her with such abandon that he made her forget where she was. The man who kissed her with such sheer intensity that she forgot her own name.

She looked down as she ran her fingers along the lapels of his jacket. She slowly slipped it off, folded it neatly and carefully laid it over the back of a nearby chair. Her shawl received the same care. Still not looking at him, she kicked off her shoes and took off her earrings.

"No, please," she said when he started to slide the door shut. "I like hearing the ocean." She walked over to him. "It makes me think of us."

Logan traced the curving neckline of Lucy's dress with his

fingertip. The combination of cool silk and warm skin was arousing. He used his other hand to search out the pins holding up Lucy's hair. He smiled when the heavy strands fell down around her shoulders.

"This is the Lucy I'm familiar with." He tunneled his fingers through her hair. "The wicked woman."

Lucy smiled back as she wrapped Logan's tie around her fist and pulled him toward her.

"And the wild man."

"There's something to be said for taking things slow and easy." He rested his hands against her waist as he dipped his head.

Instead of the raw hunger he'd shown her at the club, Logan's kiss was soft and gentle as he seduced her mouth with bare touches that tempted her to rise up on her toes to keep the contact.

Lucy wanted to coax out the wild man. She stroked his lower lip with her tongue then nibbled a corner of his mouth. When that didn't work, she moved in closer and slid her arms around his neck. She even shimmied her hips for emphasis.

"We can't dance without music," he murmured with a thread of amusement in his voice.

"Actually, I wasn't thinking about that kind of dancing. Unless you know how to dance the tango."

Logan's answer was to deepen their kiss. His hands roamed over her back, paused then moved in a circular motion against her spine.

"Just one question," he said against her lips. "Where's the damn zipper in this dress?"

Laughter bubbled upward. She lifted her right arm to show the zipper along the side seam.

Logan muttered curses on dress designers who had to make it difficult as he ran the zipper down and peeled Lucy out of her dress. One look at her in a cream-colored bustier stopped his train of thought and shot his arousal sky-high.

He swallowed as he fingered the dainty bow centered between her breasts. "If I'd known you were wearing this under that dress we would have ended up here a hell of a lot sooner." Abandoning the bow, he skimmed his fingers across her bare shoulders and down her sides, acquainting himself with her curves.

"I'm glad you're impressed. Uh-uh-uh." She wagged her finger back and forth at him. "I do not intend to be the only one standing around in my undies."

"Yeah, well, yours are a lot more interesting than mine."

"Let me be the judge of that." She loosened his tie and pulled it over his head then worked on his shirt. Logan's patience was further tried when Lucy took her time by pressing a kiss against each inch of bare flesh revealed with each opened button. "Now we come to that burning question," she whispered against his navel. "Boxers or briefs."

Her question was soon answered when she discovered dark-blue boxers. But there was more. Lucy learned that there was a light dusting of dark-blond hair on sun-bronzed skin that arrowed down to his waistband. She found out that there was a great deal more to the wild man than she'd ever imagined.

She had no idea how they ended up in the bedroom, but she wasn't about to complain. With one hand still around her, Logan used the other hand to pull the bedspread down to the end of the bed. He carefully laid her back against the sheets before he followed her down.

Lucy's bustier seemed to disappear along with Logan's boxers. The sensation of skin against skin was electrifying. She hungered for more even if she wasn't entirely sure what she wanted. That she wanted Logan was a certainty, but a part of her blindly searched for even more.

Logan whispered raw words of desire against her skin as he trailed his fingertips across the topmost curve of her breasts. He praised the silken feel of her skin and told her how beautiful she was.

Each touch was a trail of fire across her nerve endings that almost exploded when his mouth moved down to cover her nipple, drawing it into the heated wet interior of his mouth. The suckling motion seemed to send an electric shock through her body.

"You're like a dream," he murmured as he brought the dark rose-colored nipple to a taut point.

"Exquisite." He admired the delicate contours of her ear.

"Silk." His mouth moved over her jawline. "What?" He felt her smile without even seeing it.

"I like feeling wicked." She circled her fingertip in his navel then did a little exploring of her own. "*Very* wicked."

"Wicked is always good." Logan started a path of kisses down the center of her chest. When he reached her waist, he dipped his tongue into the delicate hollow of her navel then continued downward. He dropped a kiss just above the soft brown hair before delving below.

Lucy's eyes widened as she figured out Logan's destination.

"I—" was all she managed to get out before Logan's mouth covered her core. She felt herself spinning out of control. She wanted to move her hips, but he'd grasped them so she could only take in all he gave. In desperation, she tried to reach for his shoulders to pull him upward, but soon she forgot everything but how he was making her feel. She was past caring that the world around her no longer existed. All that mattered was Logan and what he was doing to her. She gasped as her body tightened into an unbearable knot of sheer sensation before the explosions went off inside her. She quickly learned that was only the beginning.

"My wicked woman," he said as he moved up over her and thrust inside.

She pulled his face down to hers and kissed him deeply. She wanted him to feel the primitive emotions boiling inside her.

She didn't need to worry. He was sharing the chaos she felt.

Logan quickly realized Lucy was a perfect fit for him. As he moved within her, he felt the connection as if they were truly one. He gritted his teeth against the pleasurable pain as her inner muscles contracted around him, pulling him even deeper.

He looked down at her face. Her hair was fanned out over the white pillow in glorious disarray. She looked like the poster child for perfect sex. The smile curving her lips rivaled the sun, but it was the expression in her eyes that hit him like that ton of bricks again. He swore the words that raced through his brain were broadcast loud and clear to the entire planet.

So this is what happens when you fall in love.

Chapter Eleven

"So this is what they mean about being ravaged." Lucy rolled onto her side and propped her head up on her hand. "Who knew?"

Logan opened one eye and slowly turned his head to one side to look at her. He was still in the process of trying to find the rest of his brain, not to mention his body, while lying next to him was a ball of energy. He was beginning to think he was the one who'd been ravaged.

"I'm glad to hear that milady approves," he said lazily.

"Oh yes, milady approves very much." Her purr stroked across him like a silk scarf trailing across sensitized bare skin. She rolled over onto her stomach and rested her chin on her laced fingers which were propped on his chest. Her smile of satisfaction was echoed in his own grin. "Didn't you say something about room service offering milk and cookies?"

He grabbed the phone off the nearby table. "I'll see if they'll do a little substitution for the milk."

A half hour later, Logan, wearing a thick terrycloth robe provided by the hotel, accepted a small trolley from a waiter who only stayed long enough to open a bottle of champagne and pour it into two champagne flutes.

"Cookies and champagne! I love it!" Lucy looked delighted at the late-night treat. Wearing an identical robe, she picked up a cookie and nibbled on it while Logan poured the champagne into two glasses. They carried their snack back to the bedroom.

"White chocolate chip and macadamia nut," she announced, holding up her cookie. "Still warm and chewy. Now, this is service."

Logan leaned over to take a bite out of her cookie, but she laughed and held it out of reach. She relented and broke off a bite and held it out. He nibbled his way through the cookie so he could do the same to her fingers. He repaid the favor by holding up another cookie.

"Chocolate chip, still warm and chewy." He waved it under her nose. She closed her eyes and inhaled the rich chocolate aroma before closing her lips over the cookie edge. She bit down and chewed.

"My, my, you do know how to pamper a lady, Dr. Kincaid." Logan held up his glass. "Here's to the wicked woman."

She held up her own. "And to the wild man." They clinked glasses and drank to make their toast official. "Long may we reign." She leaned over for a kiss, which he obliged with a great deal of enthusiasm. It was some time before they parted.

"You don't need the rest of those cookies right now, do you?" He took the glass out of her hand and set it to one side.

"I don't know. They're still warm." She arched an eyebrow. "Are you planning on ravaging me again?"

"Yep."

"And then I can ravage you?"

"If I'm still alive by then." He kept moving forward, which meant she had to lie back. Exactly the position he wanted her in.

"I really like this hotel!" Lucy laughed as Logan shrugged off his robe and divested Lucy of hers.

She wasn't thinking of cookies anymore.

LOGAN COULDN'T REMEMBER ever experiencing a night like this: lovemaking that was so powerful he felt as if he'd been turned inside out, shared laughter that made the experience that much more special.

But all in all, it still came down to Lucy. He hadn't expected her enthusiasm.

Even now, with her hair disheveled, not a speck of makeup on her face and eyes dreamy from their lovemaking, she was still the most beautiful woman he'd ever seen.

A voice deep down warned him this was also one very dangerous woman. He didn't want to fall in love. He didn't want commitment. Just because Lucy enjoyed the more rural area of Sunset Canyon now didn't mean the day wouldn't come when she'd prefer moving back to Orange County with its faster pace and more glamorous lifestyle.

"I really like you," he said quietly without thinking twice about what he was revealing.

Lucy looked surprised by his statement.

He went on. "I feel as if there are all these layers to you and I keep discovering something new. With everything I learn I like you even more."

Smiling broadly, Lucy, who had been kneeling on the bed, moved across the rumpled sheets and settled herself on his lap.

"Guess what, hot stuff, I like you, too," she confessed.

He wiggled his eyebrows and prompted, "Because…"

"Because," she said, drawing the word out, "you also have all these layers. Peeling them away shows much more than this aging surfer image you sometimes like to show."

"Aging surfer?" Logan winced. "Go ahead, say what you mean, Lucille. I can take it." He tightened his grip around her waist as she leaned back, obviously confident he wouldn't let her fall backward. He wondered if she realized how much her complete trust in him touched him.

Lucy looped her arms around his neck. "Actually, my full name is Lucinda Jeanette Stone Donner. My mother was under the influence of a lot of drugs at the time and she wanted a name that flowed."

"Lucinda Jeanette." He rolled it around in his mouth. "It sounds like you."

"No, it doesn't. All through school I was asked if I was really in love with Schroeder." She mentioned the piano-playing character pursued by the bossy little Lucy in the "Peanuts" comic strip. "But let's get back to you. I could have gone into a deep depression after meeting your drop-dead gorgeous high-school girlfriend."

He groaned at her reminder. "I knew I should have stayed away from my reunion."

"Oh, I don't know. We gave people something to talk about when you dragged me out of there," she pointed out.

"I'm usually a lot more civilized, but there's something about you that brings out the beast in me."

"I can tell." She wiggled in his lap. "Unless you're too tired, that is."

He lifted her up onto his erection. "What do you think?"

THE SUN SHONE brightly across Logan's face, urging him to open his eyes.

He had no idea what time they'd finally fallen asleep. They'd made love, talked lazily and finished the champagne, then made love again.

He felt more relaxed than he had in a long time. And it all had to do with the fetching woman in his arms.

Hmm, wait a minute. With eyes still closed, he mentally took inventory. He was in bed but he was alone.

"Wake up, sleepyhead."

Logan opened his eyes and viewed a picture he knew he'd never forget.

Wearing Logan's suit coat, Lucy stood at the end of the bed. Even with all the buttons fastened, the neckline revealed a good deal of cleavage and the hem revealed even more bare leg. The sleeves hung down to cover her hands and only showed the tips of her fingers. He was positive she wasn't wearing anything under it.

"Good morning, Dr. Kincaid," she said in a husky voice that felt like rough velvet against his skin. "This is your wake-up call."

"Nice jacket." His voice was raspy from sleep and arousal.

"Thanks." She pirouetted to better show it off.

"Take it off."

Two seconds passed before the jacket hit the floor and a nude Lucy was kneeling on the bed and pulling back the sheet.

"Just as long as you remember you said I could have it," she murmured, prepared to take her time exploring his body.

"TELL ME about Carly."

Lucy and Logan had chosen to have their breakfast on the patio. As he'd said the night before, the sounds of the ocean were softer, punctuated by the shrill call of the seagulls flying overhead.

"We dated."

"Cute, Kincaid." She playfully punched his arm.

"That's me."

"Give me more than a brief synopsis. Was she your first serious girlfriend?" Lucy still wore Logan's suit coat. He'd settled on wearing the slacks.

They sat side by side on a lounger with the table in front of them. To be on the safe side, Logan had requested two carafes of coffee.

Lucy shared her Belgian waffle topped with strawberries while Logan fed her bites from his omelet.

"Yes, she was," he admitted reluctantly, suddenly finding his toast interesting.

"Did you two lose your virginity together?" She took the toast out of his hand, liberally spread blackberry preserves on it and handed it back to him.

"Damn, woman!" He barked a short laugh. "Is there nothing sacred with you?"

"Which means you did." Lucy's voice softened.

"Carly and I dated, we did all the idiot stuff kids our age did and thought we'd love each other forever. Then a couple months into our senior year, she met a guy in college who said all the right things, so she broke up with me. At the time I was pretty hurt, but I got over it."

"And now she's come back and thinks you're a good prospect again," she said.

"She's from a long time ago. I have no desire to relive old times. Thanks to you I don't have the energy to do anything," he muttered with a devilish glance in her direction.

"So what about your ex-wife? Where did she come in?" She munched on her bacon.

"You better be prepared to tell your part," he said.

"I already told you about Ross."

"You coasted through the subject," Logan reminded her. "There has to be more to it."

Lucy's smile dimmed. Logan hated seeing that happen. She'd been pure sunlight before. How much had that bastard hurt her?

"I met Ross in college. I was the starry-eyed freshman, he was the serious senior. He had plans to make it big in the real estate market and actually accomplished his goal. He owns a great deal of property in the Seattle area. We were married seven months after we met. I quit school and we moved up to Seattle. It was as if he had the Midas touch with property and he did very well from the beginning. I didn't enroll in school up there. I wanted to help him realize his dream." She nodded when she saw Logan's expression. "Yes, we're talking the usual story of a young woman giving up her dreams because she thought she was working toward a mutual future."

"But…"

"But it wasn't long before I became pregnant. It was a surprise. I thought it was wonderful even if unplanned. Ross told me it was a mistake."

"Hadn't you ever discussed having a family?" Logan asked.

Lucy nodded. "Except I heard his 'let's wait awhile' for just that, while he really meant never. He didn't want the baby. I did. He wasted no time in filing for divorce."

Logan felt a burning sensation deep in his gut. "He ran out on you."

"In a way, he did me a favor," she corrected. "In his own way, Ross believed in doing the right thing. I moved back down to California where I had family. He made sure my medical expenses were covered and even paid the tuition for me to return to school after Nick was born. I had plenty of emotional support from Zach and our parents. Every month Ross arranges for money for Nick's support to be deposited into my checking account. The amount has even been increased every year. Ross doesn't send any cards or presents, nor has he ever asked to meet Nick or requested a school picture." She looked off into space. "Ross is the one who lost out. Thanks to Zach, Nick has had a positive male role model in his life."

"What about Ross's parents? Didn't they want to know their grandson?" Logan asked, thinking of the number of times his father mentioned the need for grandchildren in hopes he would have a Supreme Court justice in the family.

"His parents weren't married and his mother gave him up at birth. He was one of the lucky ones and was adopted. I don't think he ever bonded with his adoptive parents or even cared to." She took a deep breath. "I thought Ross was quiet and reserved. I had no idea he was distant."

Logan couldn't imagine any man being standoffish with Lucy or walking away from her without a backward glance, content with giving her money every month instead of having contact with his son. His own dad was a cranky SOB at times, but he was always there for Logan.

His marriage to Shannon had been tumultuous but their time together was never bloodless the way Lucy's had turned out.

"Hey." Lucy touched his arm. "We turned out fine. Maybe even better. If you knew Ross you'd know Nick is much better off without him."

"Did he ever remarry?"

"His fourth wife is a former model who's pretty much a copy of wives number two and three. She prefers keeping her figure to having babies, which is just fine with him. I've now told mine, so you have to tell me yours."

Logan took her coffee cup out of her hand, drank some then handed it back to her.

"I had recently purchased Dr. Mercer's practice and felt pretty good about having my own clinic. Shannon came in with her mother's sick cat. She asked me out and swept me off my feet," he said wryly. "Before I knew it we were driving to Las Vegas to get married."

"And…" She prompted him the way he had prompted her.

"And she didn't like living in the house behind the clinic or even living out here which was definitely more rural back then. She had worked as a loan officer in Beverly Hills. She had this idea I could become a vet to the rich and famous."

"Except that wasn't what you wanted," Lucy guessed, tucking her hand inside his.

"Definitely what I didn't want. It wasn't long before the fights started, and from there, things only got worse. Shannon left, but she wanted to draw blood. She felt she deserved something for giving up her career. She had a good attorney and almost wiped me out."

"But she didn't."

"Only because I was determined not to let her win. I wasn't going to let it ever happen again."

Lucy was silent as she finished her coffee.

"It was for the best," she said finally. "Besides, I don't think Magnum would have accepted her." She laid her head against his shoulder.

"True. I remember when I had to keep a sick iguana in the house overnight," he said. "She stayed at a hotel."

"Understandable, but as long as it was sick and not hungry, I wouldn't go to a hotel."

"You really do know how to look on the bright side." He felt better than he had in a long time where his ex-wife was concerned.

"With Nick I have to look on the bright side. Otherwise, I would have sold him to the gypsies the day he used my makeup to draw a mural on the living room wall when I was having a party. To make it worse he used my hairspray as a sealant."

Logan chuckled. "Did the threat of selling him to gypsies work?"

"Only until he was five, then he wised up. Next I tried threatening to send him off to a military boarding school, but he thought that would be cool. He thought it meant he would fly jets."

"But you survived," he reminded her.

"I survived. And I allowed Nick to live," she said lightly. She picked up her glass of orange juice and held it high. "To Ross and Shannon. May they always get what they truly deserve," she said with just the right touch of drama.

Her toast surprised Logan. "No wishing warts or worse on them?" He tapped his glass against hers.

"No way. That's how karma gets back at you. If I wished that Shannon woke up with a hideous growth on her chin or that Ross's latest wife got around the pre-nup I'm sure he had her sign, I could end up in much worse shape. No, I'll just wish they get what they deserve." She looked up at him under the cover of her lashes.

Logan had seen that expression before. His body tightened with anticipation.

"I like your style, but I'll like you even better when you're naked."

She touched the button of the jacket. "Smart man."

LUCY HADN'T BEEN this nervous since the day Nick went to court. She felt those same combat boot-wearing butterflies stomping through her stomach.

She had always been discreet with her love life.

Yet, she'd spent the night with a man and was bringing him with her while she picked up her son who was old enough to figure things out.

At least she wouldn't show up wearing what she'd worn the night before. Logan had surprised her with shorts and a shirt from the hotel clothing boutique. He did the same for himself. As they sped down the road, she kept glancing down at her feet. A delicate gold chain circled one ankle with breaching dolphin as part of the chain.

"A reminder of the ocean," he'd told her when he'd handed her a gift box.

The hours spent with Logan were magical. She had memories she knew she would always treasure. She wanted herself to never expect more. Logan had no desire to remarry and it wasn't on her list of priorities either. Maybe last night was more their need for a physical closeness.

Just say it, Lucy!

Okay, for sex. Just sex. Nothing emotional involved.

She didn't want to be hurt again and she feared she was already heading down that road. She twisted her hands nervously in her lap.

Logan slowed down and pulled over to the side of the road.

"Would you rather I take you home and you pick Nick up on your own?" he asked her.

"Only if it would bother you to go over there. Nick's old enough to figure things out," she said.

"I'd rather go with you." He pulled back onto the road.

Ten minutes later, Logan parked the car in front of the Walker house. With the convertible top down, they could hear children's screaming coming from the back of the house. Lucy was aware of Logan standing close behind her as she rang the doorbell. A moment later, Cathy opened the door.

"Look at you two!' She hugged Lucy. "Come in, we're all out back."

"No problems?" Lucy asked, following her through the house.

"Of course not. Nick and Lou stayed up half the night watching Freddy Krueger movies." The older woman shuddered. "Abby, Jeff and the kids are here."

Lucy and Logan exchanged glances.

"Abby said while it was nice to see people at the reunion, it got a little boring." Cathy's smile was guileless as she pushed open the patio door.

Sounds of two little girls' screams assaulted their ears as they stepped outside. The cause of their screams was a water fight with Nick who was willing to let the girls jump on him. Their arms, supported with inflatable water wings, flapped around him when he popped up for air.

"Hey, Mom! Hey, Logan!" He waved at them.

"I guess you didn't miss me," Lucy teased, walking over to the side of the pool. She bent down to pick up Domino who'd run over to greet her with high-pitched yips.

"Cute outfit, Lucy," Abby called out from the other side of the pool where she sat in a chair.

"Thanks."

Abby's eyes dropped down to the glint of gold on Lucy's ankle then moved up to flash a quick glance at Logan before returning to Lucy.

"New?" she asked.

"Yes." Lucy knew nothing would irritate Abby more than not offering a bit of information. Abby could be as suspicious as she'd like, but that didn't mean Lucy would volunteer any information.

"Did you kids have lunch?" Cathy asked. "You have time to stay, don't you?"

Lucy looked at Logan who nodded.

"We'd love to."

"Do you think they suspect anything?" Logan whispered as he led her to a chair.

Lucy thought of the looks exchanged by all the adults that spoke loud and clear what they were thinking.

She had a smile which she knew would confirm their suspicions. Still, not even their wildest imaginations could conjure up anything close to what had happened last night and this morning—and what would have happened in the car on the way here if that friendly sheriff's deputy hadn't stopped to ask if they were having car trouble.

Then again, she thought, a smile would have them going a little crazy while they tried to figure out the details…

Lucy released a dazzling smile at Logan that had Abby looking as if she'd been hit by a two-by-four.

"They don't have a clue."

Chapter Twelve

This was new to him. Logan normally didn't date women with children. He considered it to have complications he didn't want to worry about.

Now he knew why he'd always stuck to that self-imposed rule.

The afternoon spent at the Walker house wasn't all that bad. He told himself if he felt uncomfortable it was because he made himself that way. Over lunch, they talked about the reunion in general terms. He wasn't sure what was worse: Abby looking at him in that dissecting way she had or Jeff acting like Lucy's big brother.

Obviously picking up on vibrations emanating between the adults, Nick looked from one to the other. Logan didn't even want to think what was going through that kid's mind.

By the time the day was over, he experienced pure relief as he drove Lucy and Nick home. He was ready to get back to the safety of his little house. Where he could think clearly. He rapidly learned that Lucy's perfume did strange things to his thought processes. Jeremy greeted him with the news that all was fine. Magnum shot Logan a look that said "I know what you did" and went off to do whatever he did when he preferred to be alone.

Logan was more than ready for the weekend to be over. He had too much time on his hands and a mind that wandered in Lucy's direction every time he made a conscious effort not to think about her.

He thought about her wearing his suit coat and nothing else. Then he thought about her wearing nothing at all. He recalled the look of delight that appeared on her face when she had opened the box holding the ankle bracelet. He relived the memory of her wearing that ankle bracelet and nothing else.

Over the weekend Lucy had displayed a new side that intrigued him. Aggressive without overpowering. Seductive with a wealth of femininity.

They'd made love, laughed and talked about everything and anything.

They'd managed to make time stand still when they were at the hotel.

Then she went toe to toe with Abby and for the first time to anyone's knowledge, the mighty Ab backed down.

Damn, Lucy Donner was a loaded weapon.

"YOU DID IT, didn't you?"

Logan took a deep breath and turned around. "Good morning, Gwen. Did you have a good weekend?"

She rolled her eyes. "Please, Logan, no BS, okay? You and Lucy had sex. Why did you screw things up? She keeps all the appointments in order, the records can be found without any effort and we never run low on supplies. If you ruined this set-up by letting *that*—" her eyes wandered downward then back up so her heated gaze could smack him between the eyes "—do your thinking for you, so help me, I will make you sorry you were born."

"No wonder you can't keep a boyfriend," he muttered, walking away quickly before something worse happened to him.

"Trust me, I keep him very happy."

Desiring more amiable company, Logan headed for the front of the clinic but walked into chaos instead.

The tension-filled atmosphere hit him the minute he stepped out there.

A frantic-looking Lucy was holding on to Domino with a death grip while throwing mental flaming daggers at a teen-age boy who looked as if the wild-eyed woman would scale the front counter and throttle him.

Logan sighed. Chad Whitman could only mean one thing. Henry.

"But he's harmless! I swear he is!" Chad told Lucy.

"I don't care if he's made of rubber, find him now," a tight-lipped Lucy ordered.

Chad caught sight of Logan. He looked relieved to see someone who wasn't prepared to kill him.

"Hi, Dr. Kincaid."

"Henry?" Logan asked.

He nodded, looking miserable. "I had the carrier secured. I swear I did. But you know how he is."

"Yeah, I know," Logan said wearily. "Where were you sitting?"

The boy pointed over his shoulder. "She's really ticked off," he whispered. "I think she's afraid of Henry."

"I can hear you!" Lucy snapped.

"Why don't you go on back and have Gwen come out here to help us look," Logan suggested to Lucy.

"There is no way I'm moving from here." She held Domino so tightly the puppy squeaked. She immediately loosened her hold and cooed assurances to the small dog.

"My mom's that way, too," Chad said, loping off to the side of the room Logan directed him to.

"How difficult can it be to find one snake?" Lucy asked.

"Henry's more like an escape artist who likes his freedom. He's also pretty fast," Logan explained. "Gwen! Henry's loose!"

"What is it with that guy? All right, I'll look back here," she called out. "And if I find him he's going to end up as a nice pair of boots!"

"It's not his fault!" Chad argued.

"She's kidding, Chad," Logan assured him. "I think."

"There he is." Chad dropped to the floor and lay prone with his hands extended under Beau's cage. The macaw flapped his wings and screamed his displeasure. The boy sat up with the python wrapped around his arm. "He was looking for a dark place for a nap," he explained.

"Go on back to room three, Chad," Logan instructed.

The boy paused at the counter. "I'm sorry if Henry scared you," he said to Lucy. "He only gets this way when he's looking for a place to sleep or he's hungry."

"Go," she said between bloodless lips.

"Henry is harmless," Logan assured her.

"Harmless? I've watched *Animal Planet.* He could eat Domino as a snack. For all I know he could eat Nick!"

"Henry's only six feet long."

"And Nick isn't!" She glared at him.

Logan leaned over the counter. "I would have protected you," he whispered against her lips.

"I told you I wouldn't touch those things."

"I'll make it up to you," he promised.

"Just make sure that thing doesn't get loose again." Lucy refused to release Domino until Chad and Henry, now securely ensconced in his carrier, were gone.

"Henry's pretty mellow," Logan told Lucy. "It's just that he enjoys his freedom and takes advantage every chance he gets. Chad's had him for about six years."

"And to think his mother still lets him sleep in the house. Or does she?"

"She does, but she insists Chad keep his bedroom door closed when he's not home, so Henry can't wander."

"Turtles are okay, but snakes…" She shook her head. "No, thank you."

"Mom, did you see that python? Isn't he cool? Can I have one?" Nick skidded to a stop in front of his mother. He took one look at her set expression and moved back a step. "I guess not. Um, Logan, Kristi asked if you'd come back and check Lily's ears. She's scratching them a lot."

"Okay, I'll be back there."

Nick looked at them. "Are you guys gonna date each other now?"

Lucy and Logan looked at each other.

"Are we?" Logan asked her. He recalled earlier that day seeing a glint of gold in the vicinity of her ankle when her jeans hem rode up a bit.

"Would it emotionally scar you if we did date?" Lucy asked her son, wincing as she looked at the muddy paw prints decorating the front of Nick's T-shirt.

"Of course not, unless emotional scarring means I can have a python or maybe a dog of my own to make my life more fulfilling," he said hopefully.

"No snake. No dog. You'll just have to suffer. And yes, we're dating."

"And you're okay with that?" Logan asked him.

Nick rolled his eyes. "Logan, Mom gave me 'the talk' a long time ago. But I'll still work on getting a snake or dog."

"Nick, go away," Logan said amiably.

"Huh? Oh, okay." With a cheeky grin, he loped off.

"When he starts dating, you're going to embarrass the hell out of him, aren't you?" Logan asked.

Lucy adopted her most motherly expression. "That's what mothers are for."

"So, since we're dating, how about dinner tonight?" he said. "Anything your gorgeous heart desires."

"Better yet, why don't you come over for dinner?" she suggested. "I have a stew in the slow cooker. Nothing fancy, but I'll send leftovers home with you for Magnum."

"I never turn down stew. What time?"

She told him.

"Now I better go play doctor." He leaned over the counter.

"But I don't think it's going to be as much fun playing doctor with Lily as it was with you."

She gave him a wicked smile. It stayed on her face for the rest of the day.

"MAKE SURE the guest bathroom is clean!" Lucy shouted as she quickly fixed up a green salad. "And pick up today's newspaper in the family room."

"Doesn't he already know housework isn't your favorite activity?" Nick asked, walking past the counter. He dodged her slapping hand as he stole a baby carrot.

"I'm not talking magazine-clean, just cleaner than a toxic level." She used her foot to gently nudge Domino from Luther's food dish. "Don't let Luther catch you over there," she warned the puppy.

Nick rested his forearms on the counter, watching his mother work. He looked at the cookie sheet where white lumps of dough rested.

"You never made biscuits before when you make your stew," he said.

"Don't you have homework?"

"Already did it during my free period." He reached across the counter and snatched a cucumber. He grinned at her look of mock outrage.

"You couldn't have accomplished it all then," Lucy said.

"Sure. I only had history, English and some math." He swiped another cucumber.

"Stop eating the salad while I'm trying to make it! Be useful and set the table, then feed Domino before he gets into Luther's food and Luther catches him." She heard a warning feline growl and knew that her cat had seen the puppy head for his dish.

Nick picked up the puppy, rescuing him from kitty claws. He looked at Lucy.

"I thought it wasn't a good idea to cook for a guy you're

dating. That he'll think you're serious about him. That's what they always say in those chick flicks you like to watch."

So her baby boy was already suspicious of the opposite sex. She was convinced he'd inherited his uncle's charm and realized Logan was right. When she picked Nick up at school that afternoon she'd noticed cute little Brooke looking at Nick as if he was the hottest thing around. And Nick had given her a grin that was pure male.

"I don't think Logan will feel as if I'm fitting him for a wedding ring," she said. "Now why don't you go set the table. And wash your hands before you handle the plates."

"Are you sure you don't want me to take a shower with disinfectant, too?" he muttered, heading for the sink. "Boy, when you change your mind about Logan, you change your mind."

"Compared to what?"

"Compared to months ago when he'd ask you out and you'd say no." Nick finished the tasks assigned to him. "I'll get it," he said, when the doorbell chimed. A moment later, he returned to the kitchen with Logan in tow.

"For you." Logan handed over a bottle of wine along with a liter bottle of cola for Nick. He also revealed a chew toy for Domino and a catnip ball for Luther. "I wanted to cover all my bases." He crouched down and held out the ball to Luther. With a sniff of disdain, the cat accepted his prize while Domino promptly pounced on his rawhide bone and proudly carried it off.

Lucy retrieved a corkscrew and two glasses, handing the corkscrew to Logan. "I'll just put the biscuits in the oven," she said after checking the noodles bubbling in boiling water on the stove.

"It smells good." He poured wine for the two of them.

"Thanks." She drained the noodles. "It's one of Nick's favorites."

Logan looked around, admiring the roomy kitchen that was divided from the adjoining family room, by only a counter.

This way the cook could visit with company and not feel left out. A glass-enclosed breakfast nook held a large round table covered with a soft sage-green tablecloth and three place settings. From the haphazard look of things he guessed Nick had set the table. He grinned when he saw the bubble night-light plugged in by the table was a shocking pink flamingo.

Lucy sighed when she saw the table.

"We're improving. He usually forgets the napkins." She handed Logan a covered bowl filled with rich-smelling stew and carried another bowl filled with noodles. "Nick, dinner!" She added a chilled salad and warm rolls to the meal.

"This all looks great," Logan said, taking a seat. "But then I'm more used to take-out or something out of a can."

"That's the best thing about slow cookers. You throw it in the pot first thing in the morning and by evening you have a meal."

"Mom hasn't poisoned me yet." Nick dug in with the enthusiasm of a growing boy.

Lucy realized this was the first time a man, other than a family member, had sat at their dinner table. Yet Logan sat there as if he always had.

It was an unsettling feeling.

After dinner, Nick volunteered to fill the dishwasher and clean up the kitchen and Lucy happily accepted his offer. She fixed coffee for herself and Logan. Since the evening was too chilly to sit outside, they took their coffee and went into the family room where she turned on the fireplace. They sat on the couch with Domino between them. The pup dropped his face down between his paws and instantly fell asleep, while a wary Luther retreated to his basket in a corner of the room where he could keep one eye on Logan.

"In my line of work it's not unusual for animals not to be happy with me. In their memories I'm usually associated with spaying or neutering," he said, amused by Luther's attitude. "Not for helping them get over an upset tummy."

"Then we won't mention what he did to the vet who neutered him," Lucy said, sotto voce.

Logan rested his head against the back of the couch and turned to look at Lucy who was curled up in a corner. She wore green pants and a sweatshirt that looked downy-soft. His fingers itched to find out if it was. He'd discovered that touching her was addictive. When he glanced down and saw the dolphin anklet, he was pleased.

She sat in a loose-limbed position with her coffee mug cradled between her palms. She glanced at Nick who was being industrious by wiping off the table and all the counters. The soft roar of the dishwasher was their only background noise.

"All done," the boy said cheerfully. "I'm going to my room to do my homework."

"You told me you'd finished it during your free period," Lucy said.

"Oh, I did," Nick replied. "But I have a paper due in a couple weeks for my psychology class. I thought I might as well get started on it tonight. I'll take the pup with me if you want."

She looked down where Domino was settled between them. "He's fine where he is."

"Okay. Good night." He looked at Logan then moved down the hallway.

"Good night, sweetie," Lucy called after him. Her son groaned in reply.

"Boys hate to be called sweetie," Logan pointed out.

"He forgets I could call him worse. When he was little I used to call him my little love bug. When he was seven, I received a polite request—in writing, no less—to stop calling him that."

"Understandable." Logan reached across the sleeping puppy and took her hand in his. He laced his fingers through hers, pressing his palm against hers.

"What?" she asked, noticing an amused expression on his face as he gazed at her.

"I was just thinking back to a talk between my dad and me," he said. "He warned me about girls like you."

"Oh really? What did he say?"

Logan leaned forward. "That's the funny thing. I can't remember one word he said," he murmured just before his mouth settled on hers.

Lucy's head whirled as she felt the heat of his mouth penetrate hers. He'd kissed her with passion and hunger and he'd kissed her with downright lust, but he'd never kissed her like this. He showed a gentleness that warmed her all the way to her bones.

He buried his free hand in her hair, tangling his fingers in the loose curls.

"I always thought that memories were overrated," he murmured. "That reality can never compete with memories. I was right."

"You were?" Her voice was husky with desire.

"Oh, yeah. Reality is much better, but just to make sure…" He lowered his head once more and by the time he moved back they were both breathing heavily.

She thought about pulling him down on the couch and having a repeat of the previous weekend.

If Nick hadn't been in the house she would have followed the desires of her body. She settled for circling her fingers around his wrist with her fingertips pressed lightly against his pulse point. She was gratified to discover it was racing.

Lucy didn't expect arousal to flare up so quickly between them. She should have, since she knew first-hand what could happen between them.

"Too bad it's so cold outside," Logan murmured against her lips.

She had to smile. "Why?"

"You could have shown me your gazebo. Maybe we could have checked out that built-in bench you're so proud of." He angled his head to one side and nibbled on her ear. "You said that you liked to stretch out on it."

"Actually," she said as she reluctantly pulled back, "I need to remind myself that my son is in the house and could walk in on us at any second." She rested her forehead against his.

"He said you gave him 'the talk,'" Logan teased.

"Yes, I did, because his uncle wimped out. When I finished, Nick acted as if I expected him to participate in some strange ritual. I thought he was going to run screaming out of the house."

"You're a good mom, Lucy."

"Thank you," she said softly, touched by his sincerity. "But I don't think your father sees me as Mother of the Year."

"He's of the old school. Women belong in the home and all that. If he could, he'd still hold June Cleaver up as the perfect example."

"But we rarely saw what June did around the house when Ward was at work and the Beaver and Wally were in school. For all we know, she could have been down at the local pool hall."

"Or playing craps out behind the dry cleaners."

Lucy laughed. "No wonder your dad never remarried. He couldn't find a woman who could live up to June Cleaver."

"But we're talking about you, not him," Logan said. "You should have a houseful of kids."

"I don't know if I could have remained sane with more than one Nick in the house," she said through a smile. "I had hoped for three or four munchkins, but that wasn't going to happen."

"I'm surprised you didn't remarry." He found distasteful the concept of her married to someone else. But he wasn't about to volunteer for the job of giving her those little ones she talked about. His dad had talked a lot about his lack of grandchildren. Logan had told him if he wanted grandchildren he'd better think about having some other kids. It didn't shut him up entirely, but it got him off Logan's back for a while.

Lucy answered his question. "As a member of the male sex, you, of all people, should know that most men aren't fond of dating women with kids. Especially a kid who can sometimes run rings around them."

"Is that what Stuart thought?"

"Stuart?" Lucy burst out laughing. "Obviously Nick has been talking. I'll have to have a chat with him about that. Stuart wanted to mold Nick into a mini Stuart. Nick wasn't having any of it."

"What about you and Stuart?" He had no idea why he was asking. He'd never been interested in a woman's past social life before.

"Stuart was a very nice man who didn't talk about play dates and Little League," she said. "But he also had a finicky side that made me crazy." She leaned forward to confide. "The man believed in having everything dry-cleaned, including his underwear."

"And you knew this from personal experience?"

"Heavens no! I knew it because I was with him once when he picked up his dry cleaning and laundry. But if you take a finicky man and pit him against a grubby kid, the kid wins every time."

"So Nick ran him off," Logan said.

Lucy shook her head. "I told him he would be better off with a woman who didn't have children or a cat."

"So I should be grateful Nick likes me."

"He adores you," she stated. "You treat him like an equal, not a kid. And he thinks working with Kristi and Jeremy is great. Although I've had to remind him no piercings or tattoos until he's of age. I'm hoping by then he'll forget all about it."

"Maybe dating's just difficult for anyone our age," Logan said.

"It is when a man thinks I'm looking for a father for Nick, which really doesn't say much for what they think of themselves. Or there are the men who want to play daddy without thinking of the consequences to the child involved. That's why I preferred keeping anyone I dated away from Nick."

He played with her fingers, sliding his own up and down the digits. He shook his head. "Your style isn't hunting for a dad for Nick. You've already proven you can take care of him just fine on your own."

"I think life would have been a little easier for Nick if he'd had siblings. Teachers always wanted to put him in accelerated courses, while I wanted him to be a normal kid. We reached a compromise. I signed him up for after-school activities. He enjoys challenges. When he doesn't get them is when he gets into trouble."

"Like hacking into the school computer?"

"Now, that puzzles me. Nick loves that school. He's never had any problems there and as far as I know, nothing's prompted him to create mischief."

Logan frowned as he assimilated her words. "So there was, what, a trigger, so to speak, when anything happened before?"

Lucy nodded. "This was out of the blue."

"Maybe he was trying to impress someone. That little blonde who likes him."

"Nick never did it to impress anyone. He just always wanted to prove that he could."

"We guys like to impress people." His face moved closer to hers.

"Really? So what do you do to impress a lady?"

"I put her to work washing dogs and overseeing my clinic. That way she sees what a hard-working guy I am."

"A man with his own successful business is always good." Her breath was warm on his lips. "What else would you do?"

"I'd show that I'm great with kids and animals. That I care about the local community." His mouth just barely touched hers. "Then I'd let her see that I have a sense of humor. That

I'm polite, open doors for women, help little old ladies cross the street and have good table manners."

"All excellent signs of a well-rounded man. But there should be more." Her eyelids fluttered downward and his gaze followed. All one of them had to do was move that scant distance and their mouths would touch. He was astonished to find himself more aroused by the small space between them.

"Such as?"

"Does he wear a nicely cut suit coat that I'd want to wear? Does he have good taste in hotels? Does he know just what to say at the right time? And will he attend a function he'd rather not get within a hundred miles of, even if he leaves rather early?"

"It's the leaving-early part that was the best."

Logan saw what was going on between them as a sexy battle of wills. Who would give in first? Who would make that next necessary move? He felt every muscle in his body tense with anticipation and saw the same sense of suspense in Lucy's heavy-lidded gaze.

"How long, Logan?" she murmured.

He cocked an eyebrow, playing coy.

"How long before you give in and kiss me again?"

"Maybe you're the one who will give in first," he countered.

She gave a slight shake of the head and managed not to touch him at the same time.

"I took yoga for four years. It's amazing what that can do for your body. Flexibility, the ability to remain in the same position for long periods of time. I not only can regulate my breathing, but when suitably warmed up I can sit with my ankles behind my neck."

His eyes widened at the picture she was painting. "Lady, you are seriously turning me on."

Her lips curved upward. "Glad I can help."

"Make the first move. That would help more."

"Did I ever mention that I have an incredibly stubborn nature?"

"I'm learning something new about you every day."

They had no idea how long they sat there staring into each other's eyes while Domino happily snoozed between them. Logan was grateful Nick had the sense not to come out here. He would have wondered what the two crazy adults were doing. He wasn't exactly sure what was going on either.

"How about a compromise?" He finally broke the charged silence.

"It depends."

"On the count of three..." His voice fell off as he waited to see if she understood what he meant.

"One," Lucy whispered.

"Two."

The silence between them seemed to go on forever until, in unison, they both mouthed the word *three*.

Earlier, Logan said reality was definitely better than the imagination. Now he set out to prove the validity of his words.

He accomplished it.

WHEN JUDGE KINCAID turned his computer on the next morning he noticed the new mail icon blinking.

He scrolled down and, discovering a missive from icandoit@hotmail.com, clicked on the note.

Matters progressing even better than we anticipated. I guarantee our plan is a great success.

Chapter Thirteen

He was a goner. He took it all, hook, line and sinker. She had woven a web of magic around him that he had no desire to escape.

He was pathetic.

Logan told himself that just about every night. No matter what Lucy said about not wanting to get married again, she still had the word *commitment* tattooed on her forehead. He was positive it was in her genes. If he had a brain in his head, he'd back off before it got too late. Instead he called her just about every night even if only to say good-night. Usually he entertained himself with listening to her voice when she answered the phone and he'd growl, "What are you wearing?" More times than not she'd describe something in silk and lace and nearly melt the phone lines.

Yet, at the office she was the perfect receptionist. Nothing in her manner indicated she was definitely one wicked woman. But then she'd pass him in the hall or hand him a chart and he'd see a glint in her eye or something in the curve of her lips that would remind him of something she'd said the previous night.

"You are so pathetic." Gwen sniffed as she walked past him outside the exam rooms. "If you were a dog you'd be out there biting her neck." She indicated a dog's mating ritual.

"Hey, I'm not the one who comes in with hickeys all over her neck," he defended himself.

"That hasn't happened since I was dating Curry."

"Who names a kid after a spice, anyway?"

"It's a family name." Gwen glared at him. "Go pick on Kristi and Jeremy. They're dating now."

"They are? Since when?"

"For about the last two weeks," Lucy said as she joined them in the hall. Magnum walked beside her. "Where have you been?"

Logan looked at the two women and saw the same amused expression on their faces as if they shared the same secret.

"Why do I feel outnumbered when I'm around you two?"

"Because you are," Gwen said.

Logan glanced at his watch. "Anyone still waiting out there?" he asked Lucy.

She shook her head.

He kept his eyes on her. "Gwen, why don't you go to lunch?"

She didn't miss a beat. "I'm on my way."

Lucy looked around. "Just us and the critters," she said.

"Yep." Logan walked over to the phone. "Barbecue or Chinese?"

"Chinese. And this time don't forget the wonton."

Twenty minutes later they were in Logan's kitchen, Lucy seated cross-legged on the table while Logan sat on the counter closest to her. Magnum and Domino had followed them over to the house and sat patiently, hoping for handouts.

"I've seen bigger closets," Lucy said, digging into her lemon chicken. "Not that your kitchen doesn't have charm," she added hastily. "And it's very clean."

"Probably because I don't spend a lot of time in here." Logan fumbled with his chopsticks. He swore under his breath and tossed them into the sink. He leaned over, dug a fork out of a drawer and returned to his broccoli beef.

"I thought you promised to give the chopsticks a try." She easily used hers to scoop up pork fried rice.

"I did. They sucked."

"Now you sound like Nick."

"You can play with your chopsticks. I'll stick with a fork." Logan picked out a piece of broccoli and tossed it at Magnum who, at the speed of light, dropped the phone, snapped up the treat and had the phone back in his mouth. Logan dug back into the carton for another piece.

"Why do you order the broccoli beef when you don't like broccoli?"

"Because I'm an adult and I don't have to eat the broccoli now." He set the carton to one side and eyed her chicken.

"Don't even think about it." She hugged it to herself protectively. She eyed Domino who hadn't taken his eyes off her. "Do you think he'll always have one ear up and the other down?"

"Probably. Gives him character." He watched her lean down and hand a bit of chicken to the puppy then offer a larger piece to the husky. "How come you never scratch me behind my ears?"

"For the same reason I don't rub your belly to see if I can get your leg to shake. I start doing either and you turn into a sex maniac." She pointed her chopsticks at him.

He grinned. "That was fun."

Lucy couldn't help grinning back because Logan was right. It was fun. During some of their lunch breaks they talked, sometimes they made love and all the time they laughed.

When did things change? she asked herself. When did she start falling in love with Logan?

The words might have been spoken silently, but they still sounded as loud as a shout bouncing around inside her brain. The idea was frightening because she told herself this was an affair, nothing permanent. She didn't want a marriage that ended in sorrow again. This time it was more than her heart in danger. She knew she had to think of Nick also. He admired

Logan a great deal. How would he react when the time came for her and Logan to part? Not to mention how would she react?

That didn't stop her from looking at Logan as if he was the best thing in her life. Maybe she should just take what she could get. Enjoy the moment and not worry about what might happen tomorrow.

If Scarlet O'Hara could do it, so could Lucy.

Due to an emergency at 3:00 a.m., Logan had been working nonstop on very little sleep. His jeans looked as if he'd picked them up off the bedroom floor and his T-shirt was badly wrinkled. He hadn't shaved that morning and his beard looked reddish-blond against his tanned skin, while his hair was as rumpled as his clothing. She wondered what he would think if she told him that he looked pretty darn cute in his glasses. She knew enough to look beyond the exterior to the man who, even with little sleep, was patient with the humans along with the animals.

Lucy put down her container and stood up. She walked over and rose up on her toes so she could loop her arms around his neck.

"You don't really want that fortune cookie, do you?"

He looked at the plastic-wrapped cookie he'd just picked up then back at her. "I don't?"

She shook her head. "I can tell you your fortune."

"Really?"

She nodded solemnly.

"What does Ms. Lucinda Jeanette Stone Donner see in my future?" Logan asked.

Lucy rose up again and whispered in his ear. After she told him his future, Logan didn't waste any time in dropping the cookie in the sink and hopping off the counter.

"Magnum, keep an eye on Domino," he ordered as he swept Lucy up into his arms.

"Let's see whose fortune comes true first," he said, carrying her toward the bedroom.

The insistent pressure of his mouth soon silenced Lucy's giggles. They parted long enough to pull Logan's T-shirt off, then her sweater, before working on each other's jeans.

He exhaled a sigh when he saw her red lacy underwear.

"You really know how to drive a guy crazy," he muttered, tracing the narrow lace band.

"I try," she said modestly, but she had other things on her mind and intended to show Logan just what. "Remember that night at the Mañana?" she whispered in his ear.

"In living color."

"Let's see if we can recreate that, shall we?" She trailed her hand downward until she found his erection. Her fingers were cool as they slipped around the hot skin.

"Just remember I need to be coherent this afternoon for the patients."

Lucy hooked one leg around his calf and pulled him down to her. "Don't worry, I'll be gentle."

"I THINK you crippled me," Logan whispered in Lucy's ear as he brought out medication for an arthritic Siamese cat named Clementine.

She smiled. "And you're complaining because…?"

"Who's complaining? I'm just making a statement of fact. I know it's short notice, but I thought I'd see if you were free for dinner tonight and maybe a movie afterward."

"I'm sure Nick could stay with Cathy and Lou. Unless you'd rather he go with us," she teased.

"I like your idea better." He tapped the prescription bottle on the counter and handed it to her before he returned to the back.

"Logan is a sweet boy," Mrs. Bennett, Clementine's owner, a silver-haired woman in her eighties, confided as she paid the bill. "And single. It must be difficult for you having to raise your boy on your own."

Lucy smiled at the woman's pointed look. "Actually, I think my son does the raising."

"I understand he's doing well working for Logan." She patted Domino's head since the puppy was sprawled asleep on the counter. "It isn't good to be alone in your later years. I should know. My Ian has been gone for twenty-six years. The man irritated the hell out of me with his incessant clearing of the throat, but do you know, after he was gone, I found I missed that." Her lined face, highlighted with a bright pink blush, appeared pensive. "It's an odd thing to miss, isn't it, dear?"

"I'm sure there are other things about him you remember," Lucy said as she handed the prescription bottle to her.

"Well…" Mrs. Bennett leaned over the counter and lowered her voice. "The man was an incredible lover." She smiled and patted Lucy's hand. "Clementine and I have to get home for 'Murder She Wrote.' Remember what I said, dear. Dr. Kincaid looks to be in excellent health, so he should last you." She picked up Clementine's carrier and walked to the door.

Lucy winced as she watched Mrs. Bennett back her ancient Mercedes out of a parking space and barrel out of the lot.

"It's better to get off the road when you see her coming," Gwen said, carrying Beau over to his cage. Beau's cat followed them and settled in his bed. "She's a sweetheart, but I'm afraid they're going to take her driver's license away soon."

"At least she's in a heavy car that will protect her," Logan said. "Last patient?"

"She said you look healthy," Lucy said, scooping Domino up and setting him on the floor. "Someone who will last into his senior years. It seems her Ian didn't."

"She told me that Ian was a wild man in bed," Gwen said.

"No! Do not say any of this!" Logan groaned. "That's like listening to my grandmother talk about her sex life. We're talking word pictures that have now been burned into my brain."

Lucy and Gwen exchanged a look only another woman could decipher.

"Logan, you do realize that your parents had sex at least once," she said.

He threw up his hands and muttered something about sadistic women. "You know there are impressionable kids here." He nodded toward the back.

Gwen snickered. "That's men for you. Doing it is fine, talking about it is scary."

"Nick nearly ran screaming out of the room when I gave him the talk." Lucy started straightening up papers on the counter. "One friend of mine told me her son took notes."

"This is why I don't have children," Gwen announced.

"Only because your species is known to eat their young," Logan said.

They turned when the bell over the door tinkled.

"Hey, guys!" Brenda walked in with a baby carrier in one hand.

"Hey, Brenda." Gwen bounced up and hugged her. She glanced in the carrier. "I'm sorry, Bren, but babies are ugly until they start looking human."

Brenda shook her head. "Good thing I'm used to you, Gwen." She turned to Lucy. "Thanks so much for helping out. Logan tends to leave things until the last minute."

"No problem." Lucy felt a sinking in her stomach that started the moment she saw the young woman walk in. She'd known from the beginning that her work here was temporary, but somewhere along the way she'd forgotten that. She'd found something new that she enjoyed, and even with her doubts about having a relationship with Logan she still saw him in a whole new light. That was what she considered her real perk. Not their shared lunches or what went on after lunch. It was their conversations, the easy way they could talk about almost everything.

She made a point of not looking at his face. For all she

knew, he might be happy to have Brenda back. Lucy wasn't used to feeling uncertain when it came to a man, but she felt unsure with Logan right then.

She kept a smile on her face as she went over to look at the infant. As she held the baby girl, she felt a tug down deep that she hadn't felt in some time.

Talk about proof your biological clock hasn't slowed down.

SHE'S GOT THAT LOOK *women get when they see a baby and think about having one of their own.*

Logan suddenly felt as if all the air had left the room.

Lucy was like him. She wasn't looking for a husband just like he wasn't looking for a wife.

They were living for the moment.

Did you tell her that? asked an inner voice.

Could things change that quickly?

"My mom has offered to watch the baby so I can come back to work," Brenda said.

After that announcement, Logan remembered little. But he didn't miss the looks Gwen shot him. None of them boded well for him.

"I vote to keep Lucy," she muttered after Brenda left.

"Can't be done and you know it."

Probably a good idea, Logan. Those lunches with Lucy were getting a little too cozy.

"Go on home, Gwen. I'll finish up," he said.

She turned around and stared at him. "Do *not* do something stupid," she said under her breath.

He ignored her and continued on to the back of the building.

THE FUNK HE WAS IN lasted through dinner and a movie. She'd even agreed to see an action/adventure film over the latest chick flick. Not that he paid attention to it.

"Cathy said they'll drop Nick off at the clinic in the morning," Lucy was saying as he drove up her driveway and parked in front of the garage. "He made sure he had his Adoption Day T-shirt with him."

"Good," Logan said absently.

"But I told him that he can only find good homes for the crocodiles," she said.

"Yeah."

"I really hope no one adopts the dragon," she continued. "He's so cute even if he breathes fire. Who knows, maybe I'll take him."

"Okay." Then it hit him what she'd said. Logan winced. "I guess I wasn't listening, was I?"

She unbuckled the seat belt and half turned in the seat. "Does that mean I can't adopt the dragon?" she asked, batting her eyes.

"Fill out the paperwork and we'll see." He climbed out of the car and walked around the hood to open her door.

Lucy activated the garage-door opener. It raised barely six inches before it started down again.

"Enough, Luther! No treats for you!" She pressed the button again.

This time the door moved up without hesitation.

"I learned if I threaten him where it hurts most, he'll behave," she said as they walked through the garage. The flap of the cat door batted shut.

"Would you like some Irish coffee?" she asked, flipping on the kitchen light.

"Sounds good." He leaned against the counter and watched her grind coffee beans and set up the coffee maker.

"Would you mind getting the whiskey out of that cabinet over there? It's on the top shelf." Lucy rummaged through the refrigerator and withdrew a can of whipped cream and a small container of shaved chocolate.

A plaintive howl reached their ears.

"Want me to rescue the pup?" Logan asked.

"I'm sure he'd appreciate it. He's in my room," she said.

Logan followed the sounds until he reached the end of the hallway and opened double doors. A lamp burned on a table in one corner.

"Hey, guy," he said in a low voice, walking across the room to the crate and crouching down to loosen the latch. Domino pitched himself into Logan's arms.

Logan straightened up with Domino still in his arms. He looked around; he hadn't been in here before.

He could smell her perfume lingering in the air. The comforter covering the bed was a splash of pale colors. Pillows formed a soft sea at the head of the bed. French doors opened up onto the patio and he could see the pool lights twinkling outside. A man could roll out of bed and dive in for an early-morning swim, he thought.

He had a desire to spend the night in this room.

After Brenda had showed up that afternoon, Logan had had a variety of conflicting emotions roll through his mind.

What if Lucy decided she wanted more than an affair?

Ever since that night at Mañana, the word *love* had sneaked into his mind a couple of times, which was damn scary.

Love meant marriage and marriage had proved to be a bad option. Once was enough for him.

He shut down his thoughts, hefted Domino, who crawled up him to drape himself over Logan's shoulder, and left the room.

"Is he okay?" Lucy asked when Logan walked into the kitchen.

"He's fine." He set Domino on the floor.

Lucy poured the coffee, added a healthy shot of whiskey in both mugs then squirted whipped cream on top and a sprinkling of shaved chocolate.

"Since it isn't real chilly tonight, how about sitting outside?" she suggested.

"It'll go good with the Irish coffee," he said, picking up the two mugs and following her out.

The twinkling lights highlighted the small table and two chairs in the middle of the gazebo.

"You need music out here," Logan said, placing the mugs on the table.

"I do need something out here, don't I?" She looked around. "Nick had talked about a sound system, but I think I've put it off since I know the music he prefers."

"Kristi and Jeremy have introduced him to some new bands."

She made a face. "Tell me about it." She sat down and picked up her mug.

Logan sipped the hot coffee, enjoying the rich brew and the bite of whiskey sliding down his throat. 'Whew, you don't stint on the whiskey, do you?"

"That's the best part." She grinned. "You should see what I can do with hot chocolate and crème de menthe."

He grinned back. "There's that wicked woman again." He almost jumped when he felt a foot braced against the edge of his chair. He dropped his free hand down and circled her ankle in a warm grip. He could feel the delicate chain against his palm. Funny how the ankle bracelet he'd given her had him feeling a little primitive as if the chain showed ownership.

Maybe it was the whiskey in the coffee that had him feeling this way. Even if the woman in question was sitting across from him with a whipped-cream mustache.

The table was small enough so he leaned across and kissed the cream away.

"It tastes better on you," he explained. "Come to think of it, everything tastes better on you."

"Ah, that's just the whiskey talking." She smiled.

"I'm sorry I wasn't the best company at dinner," he apologized.

"Logan, I understand about Brenda," Lucy said. "I was there helping out while she was out with the baby. Now she's ready to come back."

He told himself he should be relieved. Memories of scenes with Shannon still haunted him. But Lucy had never staged a scene the way Shannon had. If Shannon wasn't happy, no one was happy.

"Then you're probably glad to get out of there."

"Only when there's a snake in the waiting room." She drank more of her coffee and leaned her head against the back of the chair. "It's so peaceful out here."

Logan cocked his head to one side as the mournful wail of a coyote sounded in the nearby hills.

"I told you, they're scared of Luther."

"Understandable."

"We could turn on the spa," she suggested.

"Maybe later. It's nice just sitting here where I can look at you."

Lucy looked at him strangely. "Are you all right?"

"As long as I can look at you, I'm fine. So, is Nick with the Walkers for the night?"

Lucy nodded, obviously guessing where this was going.

Logan reached into his back pocket and pulled out a cellophane-wrapped package. "I brought my own toothbrush," he said with a hopeful air. "And you did say something about using the spa. Except, I didn't bring my trunks."

"You know the nice thing about not having any neighbors close by?" She didn't bother waiting for an answer. "When the kid isn't home, you don't need to bother with a bathing suit."

IN NO TIME a naked Logan settled on a bench in the hot tub, steam from the bubbling water surrounding him. He never took his eyes off Lucy as she stripped off her clothes and folded them over a chair.

His hunger for her grew by the day, he realized. Not just for sex but the woman herself.

"You look entirely too serious," Lucy said, walking across

the spa to seat herself in his lap with her arms circling his neck.

He watched the rivulets of water stream down her breasts. All it took was a tip of his head for him to lean forward and catch the drop hovering on her nipple with his tongue. Then he closed his lips over the tip, pulling on it gently.

She closed her eyes and moved suggestively against him.

He grasped her hips and raised her up just enough then lowered her onto him.

When she tried to move against him again, he tightened his grip on her hips to keep her still.

Lucy opened her eyes and looked at him with questions in her gaze.

"A battle of wills," Logan murmured. "So who do you think will win this time?"

Her smile should have warned him what was coming, but he didn't expect her to contract her inner muscles around him. He hissed sharply. She flexed her inner muscles again, massaging him to a sensitivity he had no idea he could experience.

"I'd say there's no reason why we both can't win," Lucy whispered, decorating his face with butterfly kisses as she clenched her muscles again.

Logan had to agree that Lucy was right. They would both win this battle.

Chapter Fourteen

Logan looked around at the people milling about. This could be one of his most successful Adoption Days yet. He was glad, since he had more animals than usual and the shelter was in danger of overflowing. He unhooked his sunglasses from the neckline of his shirt and slipped them on.

He could see Kristi assisting a couple admiring a calico cat while Nick was enthusiastically extolling the virtues of Jake, the Australian shepherd. So far, no one had wanted a dog with Jake's high energy level.

His gaze kept returning to Lucy who sat at a table filling out a form for a couple that had chosen a poodle mix.

He thought of earlier in the day when he'd wakened with her in his arms. Lucy had reminded him she wasn't a morning person, but a few kisses had woken her up almost as well as a cup of coffee did.

He'd enjoyed their shared breakfast duties and the teasing as they ate. Lucy had come with him when he'd returned home to shower and change clothes for the day ahead. Luckily, Kristi and Jeremy didn't say anything when he showed up with Lucy and when Nick was later dropped off by Lou.

When had Lucy become such an important part of his life?

"Please tell me all these critters are adopted out," Jeff said, coming up and clapping Logan on the back.

He nodded toward the tent where Abby and their three children were walking among the cages. "Something that's housebroken if you don't mind."

Logan grinned. "We'll fix you up."

The two men started toward the tent.

"Daddy!" One of the twin girls ran up and grabbed Jeff's hand. "We found a doggy!"

"How do you feel about Great Danes?" Abby asked when the men approached her.

Jeff paled. "They're bigger than the kids!"

"But the kids will grow and the dog won't," she pointed out. "And she has such a pretty face."

"A Great Dane?" Jeff turned to Logan.

"Her name's Becca. She's eighteen months old," he said. "Her owner was transferred out of the country and he wanted to find her a good home. She's well-behaved and has been through obedience training."

"That's the most important part of pet adoption," Logan said. "That they want to go with you." He walked over to a table and picked up a leash. "Let's go get your dog."

Logan unlatched the cage and hooked the leash to the large dog's collar. He then draped a red bandanna around her neck, indicating she'd been adopted. The dog's body wiggled with excitement as the kids practically fell on her.

"I won't even require references," he said gravely as he handed the leash to Jeff. "Nothing's too good for our local firemen." He referred to Jeff and Abby having moved back to the area and Jeff now working at the local fire station.

"Something tells me this dog is going to eat a lot," Jeff mumbled.

"As if you don't." Abby laughed. She turned to Logan. "I notice that Lucy does a little bit of everything around here."

Logan looked over his shoulder and noticed that Lucy was overseeing the six puppies who were eager to make new friends. She crouched down to one little girl's level while holding one of the puppies that was trying to wiggle his way out of her gentle grip. She laughed when the puppy twisted around and bathed her face with kisses.

Since Abby had been present when he'd gone primal and dragged Lucy out of his reunion, he had to try to be noncommittal when he could.

"She's a great help," he said trying to sound noncommittal. "We'll be sorry to lose her next week."

Abby looked up, startled. "Why would you lose her?"

"Brenda, my regular receptionist, comes back from maternity leave," Logan said, not looking at her. "Lucy knew the job was temporary."

"Mommy, Becca's all ours!" Carrie and her twin sister, Cassie, ran up to them. "Her name's Becca Walker now," the little girl informed Logan.

"That's good to hear," he said, crouching down to her level.

"I told Daddy she can sleep in me and Cassie's room."

"Daddy's biggest worry is how he's going to feed her," Jeff muttered, coming up with Seth seated on his shoulders and Becca trotting beside him. "Still, with her around, who's going to bother them when I'm on duty at the firehouse?"

"Who's going to bother them when Abby's around? She's scarier than any dog," Logan joked, then ducked Abby's smack.

"Careful, Logan, don't screw up the best thing you've ever had," she said softly as they left the clinic grounds.

Logan reflexively looked toward Lucy.

"I hate to break it to you, Ab, but I'm not a member of the Walker family," he said lightly.

Her smile had been the undoing of lesser men than him.

"Yes, but you forget something, my dear. Lucy is a member of the Walker family. We're known for taking care of our own." She walked away with two miniatures of herself holding on to her hands.

Logan walked around until he was near Lucy at the cat cages. She was assisting an elderly woman and by the sound of the conversation he shamelessly eavesdropped on, it was clear the woman wanted a cat, but she didn't seem sure which one. Lucy was patient as she pointed out the different personalities of each adult cat. She glanced up, saw him and flashed him a bright smile.

He started to move closer.

So this is what it feels like to fall in love.

Logan stumbled as the words streaked through his mind.

Don't screw up the best thing you've ever had.

He felt his breathing constrict and a heaviness in his chest that threatened to crush him.

If he didn't know better he'd think he was set up.

But Lucy wasn't looking for marriage either. They were merely enjoying each other's company.

It was time for things to change. Nick's community service would be up soon. And Brenda was coming back next week. Maybe this was a sign that he needed to step back before it was too late.

He liked keeping things casual. Keeping his emotions out of it.

So why did just looking at Lucy tug at him? And why did making love with her seem like the closest thing to heaven he'd ever experienced?

"Uh, Logan?"

He turned around. Nick stood nearby with a young girl. Logan recognized her as the girl who'd been with Nick at the ice cream parlor.

"Brooke's mom is letting her get a kitten," Nick said.

"Nick suggested I come to Adoption Day to find one," she said in a soft voice.

"That's great." Logan made sure to keep his expression neutral. He wondered if Nick realized his ears were a bright red and the day wasn't sunny enough to cause a sunburn. "We have several to choose from. Maybe that fluffy gray female with the white spot on her face," he suggested, knowing that particular kitten was one of Nick's favorites. "She has a very sweet nature and she's real playful. Last I looked she was still in the kitten corral."

"I like her," Nick admitted.

Brooke's eyes lit up. "Can I see her?"

"Sure." Nick's head bobbed up and down.

Logan watched them walk off. "Glad I could be of help," he murmured.

"You were right, she's interested in him," Lucy said as she walked up.

"I can't remember ever being that young," he said, watching them as they stood by the enclosure holding the kittens. Nick reached down and picked up the kitten, handing it to Brooke. She smiled at him as the kitten snuggled up against her.

"It's love at first sight," Lucy mused.

"What?" He swore he felt his neck snap as he whipped toward her.

She sighed. "My baby boy is growing up. I'm going to have to come to terms with the idea that it won't be long before he'll be asking for a car and going out on dates. He'll even want to learn how to dance."

"You can handle it."

"Easy for you to say."

They watched Nick step back and gesture for Brooke to choose a collar for the kitten, usually a task for the volunteer. He blushed as the girl smiled warmly at him.

"That's an adoption he'll never forget." Lucy smiled at Logan. "Your luck is running high today."

"Yeah," he murmured as he walked away. "I have luck in everything."

Logan was afraid it would soon be too late if he didn't start to back away now. At this rate, it wouldn't be long before he was ensnared in something he couldn't handle.

Namely one Lucinda Jeanette Stone Donner.

SOMETHING was wrong.

Maybe Mercury was in retrograde or the stars were improperly aligned. Or maybe Logan was in a bad mood.

Lucy didn't know what was going on.

She knew she wasn't the only one who noticed that he was quieter than usual during the Adoption Day pizza feast. Kristi shot Logan a few puzzled looks when he didn't respond to wisecracks she and Jeremy made.

Nick appeared puzzled by Logan's standoffish manner, but then seemed to shrug it off.

Lucy knew something had to be wrong when she saw Magnum look at Logan with what could only be called canine disdain when Logan ignored the dog's pointed glances at his pizza. Lucy tempted the dog over to her with the crust from her pizza.

After they'd finished eating, Lucy and Kristi cleared off the table while Jeremy and Nick took the dogs into the enclosure for some playtime.

"What's wrong with the boss man?" Kristi asked.

"I don't know. Maybe it's just one of those days for him." She didn't want to reveal her worry.

"It's just that he's usually upbeat when we have a lot of adoptions. Today was one of our best days yet." Finished with the cleanup, Kristi took one of the chairs and sat down. "Did you two have a fight?"

"Were we supposed to?" She chose amusement instead of pretending not to understand what Kristi meant. She knew there was no way the others couldn't figure out what was going on between her and Logan even if they never advertised it.

Kristi shrugged. "Maybe he's got PMS. Seems only fair the guys find out what it's like." She stood up and raised her arms over her head in a bone-cracking stretch. "Nick, Jeremy! Want some help putting the kids to bed?"

"We're fine." Jeremy waved back.

"Hey, boss, I'm outta here," she called to Logan who stood by the enclosure watching the dogs race around with Jeremy and Nick. He didn't turn around but waved his arm over his head to indicate he heard her.

"Yep, PMS," she told Lucy. "See you next week."

"No, Brenda will be back," Lucy replied.

Kristi shook her head. "I can't see her staying long. Did you see her face every time she talked about the baby? No, she'd rather stay home."

"New mothers tend to feel like that. I was lucky in that I could work from home when Nick was a baby." Lucy looped Domino's leash around her hand. She suddenly felt very tired. She had no idea why Logan was acting standoffish, and right now she didn't care to find out why. All she wanted to do was go home and soak in a bubble-filled tub.

"Good night, Lucy. I know we'll be seeing you back here." Kristi grinned as she headed for her motorcycle. "And not just to drop off and pick up Nick either."

Lucy watched her ride off.

"We're just getting the dogs put away now, Mom," Nick said as he trotted past.

"Okay."

"I'll help Jeremy, Nick," Logan said as he walked over. "You and your mom had a long day."

Lucy looked at him with surprise. "I don't mind waiting."

He didn't look at her. "No, that's fine."

Nick looked from one to the other.

Lucy wasn't going to argue with Logan in front of Nick and Jeremy. Something was wrong and she had no idea what it was.

"All right. Good night." She didn't look at him either as she urged Domino toward her vehicle. She mentally added a glass of wine to go with her bath. A very long bath and a very tall glass of wine.

She didn't expect him to kiss her in front of them, but she didn't expect him to ignore her either.

"Why did Logan act that way, Mom?" Nick asked as he buckled up. "Did you guys have a fight or something?"

"No, we did not have a fight," she said between teeth that were clenched so tightly they were starting to ache from the pressure.

Nick wisely didn't ask any more questions the entire ride.

ONCE HOME, Lucy told Nick she was taking a bath. He nodded and disappeared into his bedroom.

"Men stink," she muttered, pouring herself a glass of wine and carrying it back to her bedroom. "Except for you, sweetheart," she assured Domino as she filled the tub with hot water and added bubble bath. She powered on her CD player and undressed, sinking into the steaming water.

What went wrong?

In less than six months, Lucy had seen her life take more than a few unexpected twists and turns.

The most unexpected was Logan.

The man's kisses were better than chocolate. Better than her first cup of coffee in the morning, and she considered that more important than air.

Dammit! He made her fall for him! He not only made love to her as if she was the most important woman in the universe, he gave her an ankle bracelet to remember that night at Mañana.

So what happened between this morning when everything was peachy keen and tonight when it seemed nothing was good for them? As the day had worn on, he'd seemed to withdraw until by evening he'd acted as if she was little more than an acquaintance.

There is no way I will ask myself what I did wrong!

She knew for a fact she didn't make mistakes some women did. It's not as if she talked about their going long-term. She didn't suggest he leave a change of clothing at her house or that she leave a few of her things at his house. She didn't refer to them as a couple.

Had it all happened too fast?

Or did Logan desire to move on to someone else?

At the thought, she felt a jolt of bitterness well up in her throat.

Memories long suppressed reasserted themselves with startling clarity.

Ross's anger when she'd told him she was pregnant. His insistence that their marriage didn't include children. That night, he'd slept in the guest room with the assumption she would come to terms with his viewpoint on what would remain in their marriage and what wouldn't.

Since she didn't, he'd filed for divorce the next day. She returned to her family who'd gathered her in but wisely didn't try to cushion her from the grief she needed to work through because her marriage had ended before it had had a chance to start.

It had taken time, but she'd come to realize that Ross was a selfish man who didn't want to share her with anyone else. He wanted to be the center of her life without the distraction a child would have caused.

She couldn't fault him entirely. In hindsight she remembered his saying he had no need to carry on the family name. She naively had thought he would change his mind once they had a baby. It didn't happen and now she knew it was for the best. Ross wouldn't have appreciated having a son whose I.Q. was higher than his own, which he thought was formidable. That was a piece of news she had made sure to convey to her ex-husband. Ross might not have wanted to be a father, but that didn't stop Lucy from announcing Nick's achievements.

She knew her mature self wouldn't have given Ross a second look. She would have seen his small nature for what it was.

But he had given her Nick and she was thankful for that.

Here she'd guarded her heart so carefully and what had happened? Another man who had no desire for hearth and family had swept her off her feet.

"So I lied," she told Domino, who snoozed on the rug by the sink. "I kept saying I didn't want a commitment. That I wasn't looking for marriage. Now I feel like some lovesick teenage girl who's doodling his name intertwined with hearts in my school notebook." Unthinking, she slapped the water's surface then sneezed as the bubbles popped in her face. She slid back down in the water. "Men stink."

LOGAN SAT on the tiny patio behind his house with a bottle of beer and Magnum and Jake for company. When he'd done a last check on the animals in the shelter, he'd taken pity on Jake's forlorn expression and brought the Australian shepherd back to the house with him. The shepherd happily trotted alongside them. After he sniffed every inch of Logan's patio, he settled down by Logan's chair while Magnum lay down on the other side.

"I just might have to keep you, fella," Logan murmured, scratching behind the shepherd's ears.

He shouldn't have been alone tonight. If he hadn't backed off the way he had, he probably would have been invited back to Lucy's house. With Nick there they couldn't have indulged the way they had last night, but he still could have stolen his fair share of kisses when they were alone.

But old fears started to surface. While Lucy never made noises about the future the way women in his past had, he still felt that old noose starting to tighten around his neck.

It didn't help when Abby started talking about matchmaking. He hadn't missed other pointed looks directed at him and Lucy during the day as if it was automatically assumed they were a couple.

Logan didn't want to get married. He didn't want a woman trying to change him the way Shannon had.

Except Shannon had tried some of that changing even before the wedding, he realized. Lucy never did any of that. She even helped out in the shelter, grooming the dogs. She didn't complain that night he had to cancel his dinner date because Mrs. Watson brought in her sick Burmese cat. Shannon would have raised holy hell. In fact, she had—whenever emergencies had come up. She'd told him he should just hire someone to handle any after-hours emergencies.

She also wanted to move back to Beverly Hills where she could resume her old life. In the end, he told her that was a good idea. She should move back to Beverly Hills and resume her old life, which would naturally not include him.

He'd had no idea that Shannon had a mean streak in her until she'd tried to take his practice from him. It had cost him more than it should have to get out of their marriage, but he considered it money well-spent.

After that, he was content with dating a woman who was told up front he wasn't looking for a wife.

Then he'd met Lucy Donner.

He'd learned she was divorced, had a son and wasn't looking to get remarried.

He soon learned she also wasn't interested in going out with him.

But after Nick ended up serving community service at the shelter, he saw Lucy more often. She had cheerfully stepped in when he'd needed someone to handle the front desk.

What had changed her mind about him, he had no clue. He was just glad she had.

He wouldn't have attended his high-school reunion and he especially wouldn't have practically carried her off to Mañana.

His body tightened with the memory of that night. Not just the way her mouth tasted or the way her body felt against him. There was also the sound of her laughter, and even the way she looked wearing his suit coat and nothing else.

She had gone through a bad marriage also. She wasn't looking for anything permanent.

He saw them as a good match even if he normally didn't date women with children. But even Nick was different.

Logan tipped the bottle upward, allowing the cold, yeasty brew to trickle down his throat.

He could hear the faint, mournful howl of coyotes in the distance. Jake's ears pricked up and he lifted his head then laid it back down again. Logan knew the sad sound fitted his mood perfectly.

He'd handled today very badly. He'd realized too many people thought he and Lucy were going to take that next step, and it had scared the hell out of him.

He refused to allow anyone to slide him into a permanent relationship. He'd worked too hard to keep his heart intact after Shannon. He wasn't about to let another woman into his life only to have her mess it, and him, up.

"It's just us, guys," he said out loud. "We're much better off this way."

A soft growl sent chills down Logan's spine. Magnum's eyes flashed silver in the darkness as he stared at Logan.

"Damn dog always thinks he knows better."

Chapter Fifteen

Logan could say that things would be fine, but it wasn't always so.

He'd forgotten how haphazard Brenda's methods were and her tendency to overbook appointments.

Beau remained in his cage pouting as only a macaw could. He refused the walnuts Brenda offered him and treated her with macaw disdain.

Magnum curled his lip every time he crossed paths with the receptionist.

"What is his problem?" she asked Logan.

He shook his head because he didn't want to think of the cause behind Magnum's bad mood.

But then, the humans in the clinic weren't much better.

Gwen could curl her lip as effectively as Magnum. Jeremy acted uneasy and Kristi just glared at him.

The only one who didn't say a word was Nick. He came into the shelter, said hello and applied himself to his work. The only time Logan had seen him smile in the past two weeks was when he learned that Jake was now a part of the clinic family. The dog was content herding three ducks Logan had found on the clinic doorstep a few days ago.

To date, he hadn't talked to Lucy once. He'd only caught glimpses of her when she'd dropped off and picked up Nick. She hadn't come into the clinic except once to brief Brenda on what she'd done while the younger woman was gone. Otherwise, she remained in her vehicle while waiting for Nick.

"You are an idiot," Gwen said in a low voice.

Logan swallowed a sigh. He took off his glasses and rubbed his eyes. "Does that make you feel better?"

"No." She advanced on him. "What would make me feel better is you doing the right thing."

"Stay out of this, Gwen." His glare slid right off her.

"Since you blew off Lucy, you have acted like a total jerk," she stated. "I've seen you date other women and go through break-ups, but you have never acted like this. If you treated me as badly as you treated Lucy, I would take a scalpel to you." Her eyes drifted downward.

Logan forced himself not to cross his legs in self-defense. He didn't look away from her angry gaze.

"This is none of your business, Gwen," he stated.

"Then do the right thing and talk to her. Give her your idiotic reason of just why you dumped her."

"You think you know my reason?"

"Anyone with a brain knows your reason. You're a coward." With that parting salvo, she stalked off.

Logan bit back the curse that hovered on his lips. When he turned around, he found Nick standing nearby. There was no doubt the boy had heard every word of the exchange between him and Gwen.

Nick didn't say a word. He merely turned around and returned to the shelter.

Logan had never felt so low in his life.

Two WEEKS and it would be all over.

Lucy kept that thought in mind as she sat in her car and waited for Nick to finish his work at the clinic.

Two more weeks and Nick's community service would

be finished. Then she'd never have to worry about seeing Logan again.

"It would have been nice if he had told me it was over," she muttered to herself. "The jerk." She tapped the steering wheel with her fingertips. "Slime with testosterone. Scum-sucking rodent," she stopped. "Damn, I'm sounding like Nick when he was eight."

The anger and sorrow she'd felt when Ross had divorced her was nothing compared to the pain she now felt from Logan dumping her. It was the only way she could see it. The man had dumped her, plain and simple.

When Abby had called last weekend to see if she and Logan and Nick wanted to come by, Lucy had just said that she and Logan were no longer together. Abby had guessed by the tone in her voice that pressing for details wouldn't help matters any. Instead, she'd called Logan a few choice names and reminded Lucy that he was the one losing out. An hour later, Ginna had called her to say that obviously Logan didn't know a good thing when he had it. Cathy's call had soon followed with the older woman offering a motherly shoulder if Lucy needed it.

So far, Lucy hadn't cried or racked her brain to figure out what had gone wrong. She'd decided if Logan didn't have the nerve to say anything to her directly, she didn't want him in her life. The next two weeks couldn't go by fast enough.

As if she'd willed it, Nick opened the passenger door and slid onto the seat.

"I could ride my bike over here," he said.

"I don't think so." She started up the engine. "Besides, you only have two more weeks then you'll be free and clear."

"Yeah." He stared out the window.

Lucy sensed that Nick was hurt by Logan's defection, but she didn't ask him. Saying his name hurt too much. If her son brought Logan up, she would talk to him about what he was feeling. Otherwise, she was determined to remain quiet on the subject.

As she pulled into her driveway, she realized she'd forgotten a stop she intended to make on their way home.

"I forgot to stop at the pharmacy and pick up my prescription," she said, activating the garage-door opener. For once, Luther behaved and didn't fool with the sensors. "I'll have to go get it. I should be back in twenty minutes or so."

"Okay." Nick climbed out of the car and walked through the garage.

Lucy looked at his bowed head and slow walk. She silently damned Logan. Nick never seemed to miss having a father. As he got older, he realized that Ross had no desire to be a part of his life and he accepted that. But he and Logan had gotten along so well that she should have known Nick would be hurt when she and Logan parted. All these years she'd sheltered him from making an attachment with the men in her life and this time she'd failed.

NICK STAYED in the kitchen waiting until he heard the garage door close. The minute he heard the thump, he practically ran to his room. He checked the clock as he hurriedly punched out numbers on his phone. He had about twenty minutes before his mother was due back home. The minute he heard a hello he wasted no time in talking.

"I know it looks bad between them, but I think it can be fixed," he said quickly.

"HOW CAN they say they don't have my insurance card on file?" Lucy muttered, walking into the kitchen. She picked up the phone. When she heard Nick's voice she started to set it down quietly, but then she heard a voice she wouldn't have expected to hear speaking to her son.

"I don't think it's going to work, son. It's obvious that for some reason they're not speaking to each other. I don't see how you think you can get them together again."

She recognized the voice. It belonged to Judge Kincaid.

"What if you extend my community service at the shelter?" Nick went on. "Or would I have to do something again? If Mom had to keep taking me over there, they'd have to talk to each other sooner or later, wouldn't they? Logan's really unhappy. I can see he is."

"We can't keep on doing this, Nick. We tried and we thought we were successful, but something happened beyond our control."

It all fell into place for Lucy.

She now understood what people meant when they said they saw red. Right now her entire world blazed a brilliant shade of scarlet.

"Hang up, Nick."

His sharply indrawn breath said he knew he was well and truly busted. "Mom."

"Get off the phone now." She felt light-headed as the anger flowed through her in heavy waves.

"But, Mom—"

"Nicholas Barrington Donner, hang up now." The moment she heard the click, she started in on her son's accomplice. "Judge Kincaid, would you like to tell me what you and my son were plotting?"

"Nick only had your best interests at heart, Mrs. Donner," the man said.

"Really?" Disbelief colored the word. "So it was all some kind of elaborate joke the two of you were playing on Logan and me?"

"Not exactly."

"Was this something Logan knew about?"

"He has no idea about this. It was strictly between Nick and myself."

Lucy looked down and discovered her hands were shaking. For a moment she wasn't sure if she would scream or cry. She might settle for doing both.

"You tell Logan what was really going on," she said

fiercely. "You tell him now because if you don't, I will. Trust me, you don't want me doing it." She hung up. She turned around and gripped the edge of the counter until it dug painfully into her palms. She counted to ten then counted again because her fury hadn't subsided one bit.

Lucy felt frozen as she walked down the hall to Nick's bedroom. She found her son seated on his bed. He jumped to his feet the moment she entered the room.

He looked scared to death. She was glad to see he was worried about his future. While she wouldn't hurt him physically, she'd make damn sure he'd never do something this crazy again.

"Mom—" he began, desperate to explain everything.

She held up her hand to indicate she didn't want to hear him. She looked around his room because, at that moment, she couldn't look at him.

Posters from "X-Files" adorned the walls. A navy corded bedspread hung haphazardly as if he'd made the bed in a hurry that morning.

"What have you done?" she asked. "And tell me everything. Make sure you don't leave anything out."

Nick gulped. "Well, you know Nora and Mark's wedding? I talked to Judge Kincaid at the reception." With a minimum of fits and starts, he related the entire story from his first meeting with the judge to their plan to get Lucy and Logan together and how it had all been accomplished.

Lucy discovered her world was now changing from scarlet to crimson.

She and Logan had been set up!

It took a few minutes for her to regain her speech.

"How dare you." Her voice was hushed but no less intense as it trembled on the brink of volcanic. "Who do you think you are to arbitrarily plan Logan's and my lives?" She paused. "Or does Logan know all about this? Was he in on this scheme since I wouldn't go out with him in the beginning?" she demanded.

"He doesn't know anything about this," Nick said in a low voice. "This was just the judge and me."

"Terrific. My son thinks he has the right to interfere in my life." Scorn dripped from each word.

Nick looked stricken.

"I wanted you to be happy like everyone else."

"I *was* happy!" she shouted, and then fought to regain her calm. "You know what? I don't even think I want to look at you right now." She closed her eyes.

Nick's chin wobbled dangerously, as if he was about to break into tears. He ran out of the room. Moments later Lucy heard the garage door open, and the sound of Nick wheeling his bike out before the door closed. Moving slowly as if she had suddenly aged, she reached for Nick's phone. She took several deep breaths as the phone on the other end of the line rang.

"Cathy? I'm pretty sure Nick is on his way over there." Then she burst into tears.

LOGAN WAS DRIPPING WET by the time he came back from his run with Magnum and Jake. Magnum's tongue lolled as he dropped to the cement floor while Jake prowled the area. The Malamute shot him a look that said "Take someone else next time" and dropped his head back down onto the floor. Jake came over and whined as he nudged Logan.

"If you want to go back out and run, you can do it by yourself. I'm beat," Logan muttered, sitting on the floor with a bottle of water in one hand. He was too tired to open it.

"Logan!"

"Back here. The door's unlocked." He was too tired to get up and open it. He looked up as his father stepped inside. "Hi. What brings you over this way? Is Farley okay?" He knew how his father doted on the elderly golden Lab.

Frank Kincaid smiled. "He's fine." His smile disappeared as quickly as it appeared. "It's something else."

For the first time that he could remember, Logan saw agitation in his father's demeanor.

"You're not in trouble with the law or something, are you?" he joked. His own smile dimmed when he saw how serious his father was.

"Logan." Frank Kincaid hesitated. "We need to talk."

A strange sinking sensation settled in Logan's stomach. He suddenly feared the worst. Had his father seen his doctor lately? The older man looked to be in excellent health. Though Logan treated animals not humans, he still knew looking healthy didn't necessarily mean you *were* healthy.

"What's wrong?" he demanded, suddenly fearing the worst.

As always, the older man was concise as he related the plot he and Nick had concocted.

Logan stared at his father. He couldn't believe what he was hearing, but there was no way the older man would make up a story as crazy as this one.

Nick and his father had come up with this incredible plot. Or was someone else in on it, too?

"Was Lucy in on this, too?" he demanded as he jumped to his feet. His earlier exhaustion from his run was now forgotten.

"She knew nothing about it until a little while ago when she overheard a phone conversation between Nick and me." Frank paused. "Nick had called me because he wants to get you and his mother back together again."

"Why would you do something like this?" Logan's voice cracked with emotion. His dad wasn't the type to hatch some crazy plot. That he'd done something like this, with a kid no less, was more than Nick could handle just then. "It doesn't make any sense, Dad."

"Nick presented what seemed like a sound plan. The more we talked about it, the more we realized you two would be good for each other." The judge perched his hip on the edge of a counter. "Nick had a plan for the two of you to be thrown together for a while. It even seemed to work."

Logan tipped his head back and looked up at the ceiling as he laughed. The sound was harsh to the ears.

Magnum looked at the two men, stood up and walked away. Jake sensed the tension and slunk off.

"Great, just great. First my dad tells me I need a woman in my life. Since I don't do anything about it, he decides to take it into his own hands and team up with a kid. Do they set us up on a blind date? Oh no, that would be too difficult. Let's do something easier, shall we?" He sneered. "Let's fabricate some crime where the kid has to appear before the judge who has the right to order him to do community service. That'll work! Brenda having the baby early just made it better for you two, didn't it?" He spun around in a tight circle with his fingers dug deep into his scalp. "I just can't believe the two of you cooked this up on your own. Are you sure she didn't know about any of this?"

Frank nodded. "Positive. Nick said if his mother ever found out what he wanted to do she'd lock him in his room until he was a hundred years old."

"Yeah, that sounds like her." Logan rubbed his face with his hands. His brain felt as if it was on overload. He couldn't take it all in.

"I still can't believe that Nick is so desperate for a father he'd cook up this crazy scheme." His covering hands muffled his words.

"Nick really likes you," the judge said. "He told me he'd watched you two. He felt you would be a good match. I'd say he was right."

"Except neither of us was looking for a long-term relationship," Logan argued. "We both had bad marriages and didn't want to repeat the experience."

"Yes, Nick told me about his father." Frank's face twisted with distaste. "Did you ever stop to think that you and Mrs.

Donner were with the wrong people before? That the two of you had to go through those bad marriages to reach the point you're at now? Did you stop to think that maybe it's time to go forward? To enrich your life with more?"

"My life is just fine." Logan muttered his lie. He ignored the sharp pain shooting for the vicinity of his heart. He didn't want to think just why he was experiencing this pain.

"We saw you and Mrs. Donner as two people who balance each other. The two halves that make a perfect whole."

"Maybe you saw it like some greeting card, but I didn't," Logan said wearily.

Frank stared at his son.

"I didn't realize that I'd raised a son who would do something so downright stupid," his father said bluntly. "Anyone who watched you two from the beginning could see you were meant for each other." He ignored his son's snort of disbelief. "No matter what Nick and I did, we couldn't force you two into something not meant to be. Why can't you see that?"

Logan experienced a crushing sensation inside his chest. Most men would think they were having a heart attack. But he knew no doctor could help this particular ailment.

Frank straightened up and took one of the chairs. He turned it around and sat down, resting his arms on the back.

"Do you remember Melanie Reynolds?"

Logan was surprised by this abrupt question. He had to search his memory before the image of a soft-spoken brunette came to mind. "Wasn't she that family-law attorney? You two started dating when I was ten. There was a time when I even thought she was going to be my stepmother."

Frank nodded. "She thought that, too, but I told myself that I didn't want to commit myself. I wasn't looking for someone to replace your mother. Plus, you and I were doing fine on our own. Then the night came when Melanie gave me an ultimatum: either I assure her we had a future together or I tell her good-bye."

Logan didn't have to ask him what happened next. "So you told her good-bye."

Frank sighed and shook his head. "I told her that I never thought of marrying again. I said we had a good thing. I'll never forget the look on her face when I said that." His expression portrayed the regret that must have been in his heart all these years. "She said she wanted to look forward, not stay the same. She felt we would have a wonderful life together. I didn't give her the answer she wanted. She wouldn't take my calls after that night."

Logan felt sick at his stomach. "I didn't even tell Lucy why," he murmured. "I think, deep down, I was afraid I'd lock myself into something I didn't want."

"And that way she didn't have a chance to tell you she didn't want a commitment," Frank said. "Maybe because you knew she wouldn't say that. I've seen her face when she's around you, Logan. Maybe she didn't know it, but she truly cared for you. And you had that same expression."

The more the older man talked, the sicker Logan got.

So this is what love feels like.

Had he ever bought another woman a special piece of jewelry so a special night could be remembered?

He remembered so much of their time together.

Lucy smiling her wicked-woman smile as she wore his suit coat and gave him the silent invitation to take it off.

Lucy with all her crazy night-lights throughout her house.

Lucy's smile as she offered him Irish coffee in her gazebo.

A naked Lucy, seductive in the hot tub.

But there was so much more. How she treated Magnum like a big ol' regular guy who just happened to wear a fur coat. Her pure female squeals when a snake got too close to her. Her delighted laughter the first time she saw Beau groom his kitty. The way she stood back and allowed Nick to make his own mistakes because she knew it was the only way he'd learn.

Not once had she ever lamented her life as a single mother or hinted that her son needed a father. She'd never said that Logan would make a wonderful father.

She and Nick were doing just fine.

Just as Logan's dad had thought he and Logan were.

"Damn," he muttered, feeling the pain rip through him with the ferocity of a razor-sharp scalpel.

"Exactly," Frank said quietly, recognizing the look on his son's face.

"I just walked away without a word. With Brenda returning, I saw it as a sign in my favor."

"You mean you used it as a prime excuse."

Logan winced at his dad's candid observation.

"You need to sit down and talk with Mrs. Donner."

"Her name is Lucy." He drew a deep breath. "And I don't think she'd be all that eager to talk to me."

"I can't imagine that would stop you. Maybe Nick could say something on your behalf."

"After what's already happened, I don't think that would be a good idea."

"Tell me what you want, Logan," Frank said.

He lifted his head. "I want Lucy."

LUCY NEVER SUFFERED from headaches, but she'd had more than her share lately.

Just as she thought, Nick had ridden his bicycle over to the Walker house. The moment Cathy had heard her tears she'd told Lucy to hang on, that she would be right over. Cathy made tea and coaxed the story out of her.

Lucy started to relax when Cathy began muttering threats on Frank Kincaid's head for going along with Nick's plan. Then she started crying again.

"Lucy, you and Logan need to talk about this," Cathy urged her. "He's running scared, dear. We've all seen you two together. You make a perfect match."

"That doesn't mean we want to be a perfect match in that way," Lucy said. "We're not looking for marriage."

"Just because you're not looking for it doesn't mean it's not looking for you." Cathy stirred a spoonful of sugar into her tea. "I remember Logan's father once going through something like this years ago and in the process, he lost a lovely woman. I think he's regretted that mistake since. Don't go through life with those same regrets."

"I don't want any regrets, Cathy," Lucy said softly. Her eyes stung with tears. "I just want Logan."

Chapter Sixteen

Nothing was the same.

Lucy prided herself on being the mistress of her life. Of keeping control over what went on in her universe even as it expanded.

And now, thanks to one incredibly stubborn man, her life, as she knew it, was a mess.

It hadn't been easy for her to talk to Nick after she'd discovered what he and Logan's father had done.

Cathy had urged Lucy to allow them to keep Nick that first night. Lucy, feeling raw from her realizations, had packed up a clean set of clothing that Cathy took with her. Lucy had spent the night ranting, raving and crying. By morning, she was red-eyed, her voice was hoarse and she was convinced she'd frightened every coyote in a fifty-mile radius. Nick had returned home quieter than she'd ever seen him. He'd again apologized for what he'd done and promised he would never do anything like that again. Lucy had accepted his apology and grounded him for the next six months. For the remainder of Nick's community service, Lou or Cathy had dropped him off and picked him up at the clinic.

Lucy tagged along when Ginna and Nora looked for space for their hair salon. Logan's name wasn't mentioned once. She was surprised Ginna didn't call him anything other than "bastard scum." She was grateful nothing else was said that day.

She prided herself on knowing none of it was her fault. Logan was the one who'd walked away. She hated that now she knew what she wanted and she couldn't have it.

Then there were days like today when she wanted to stay in bed all day. Maybe she would. Nick was old enough to get his own breakfast. She could shuffle out to the kitchen, fill her big insulated carafe with coffee and shuffle back to the bedroom. Curl up in bed with Domino and Luther, read and take a nap or two.

Seemed like a plan.

Domino had crawled under the covers and now lay like a furry lump against her stomach while Luther had curled up against her back. She thought she heard the doorbell and ignored it.

"Uh, Mom."

"Mom is out at the moment. Please leave a message and she'll get back to you next year," Lucy muttered under the warm comfort of the covers.

"I don't think so." The covers were thrown back, exposing Lucy to the morning chill.

"Don't do that!" She sat up, glaring at Ginna who glared back.

Ginna glanced at Nick. "Sweetie, my parents are picking you up in ten minutes if you're willing to help them keep track of the rest of the kids at Sea World."

Nick looked at Lucy who didn't say a thing then back at Ginna. "I'm gone." Which he was two seconds later.

"He's grounded," Lucy said.

"Trust me, spending the day with five energetic little kids and one baby will be plenty of punishment for him." Ginna opened Lucy's closet door. "It's intervention time for you."

Lucy flopped back and pulled the covers back over herself. "Thank you, good-bye."

Ginna deliberately dropped clothing on Lucy's face. "Get dressed."

"I planned to stay home today," she muttered.

"No man is worth this." Ginna walked around the room, opening the mini blinds to let in the morning light.

"I am not depressed." Lucy reluctantly climbed out of bed and started changing her clothing. She knew Ginna well enough that if Lucy didn't dress herself, Ginna would drag her out of here in her pajamas. "If you all are going for your rah-rah session at the park you can just leave me out of it. I don't need to go out there and whoop and holler at men in running shorts no matter how good they look."

"No, we have something much better planned." Ginna walked over and grabbed a length of Lucy's hair, holding it straight out. She clucked under her tongue. "Very sad. Have you used conditioner at all this week? One more thing to add to the list."

"What list?" Lucy had a bad feeling about this.

Ginna picked up Domino. "Let's give the kid some time outside then we're outta here."

Lucy knew something was definitely up when they walked outside to Abby's SUV and she saw Nora and Gail seated inside. She stopped in her tracks and spun around to confront Ginna.

"Please don't do this," she whispered. She thought she was all cried out, but it looked as if that wasn't true.

Ginna put her arm around her shoulders and guided her to the SUV. "Trust me," she said quietly. "This is exactly what you need."

"And what is that?" She feared she was in for one of those touchy-feely days.

Ginna opened the passenger door and none too gently pushed Lucy inside.

"Call it a cleansing ritual," Abby said, starting up the engine while Nora handed out containers of coffee.

Her fears were coming true. "Please tell me we're not going to go to one of those places where women sit together and expose their inner selves."

"Hell, no!" Abby laughed as she sped down the road. "Honey, we're going to treat our outer selves."

Lucy felt as if she'd been swept up in the same tornado that took Dorothy out of Kansas.

Abby had said it was for their outer selves and that's what it turned out to be.

Elysium Day Spa didn't believe in stinting on pampering. With Ginna and Nora in charge, Lucy was dunked in the warm bubbling mineral pool, massaged until her muscles felt like overcooked spaghetti then had her skin slathered with a red clay substance. She was wrapped in a warming blanket while a bright-blue cream was painted on her face and her hair was covered with a pink color goo and wrapped in another towel.

She would have protested that this was torture at its extreme, except it felt too good.

"Shopping doesn't do for a woman's soul what a day at the spa does," Abby said, reclining in a spa chair while a seaweed mask was applied to her body. "You go home after a manic shopping trip and ask yourself why you bought something so ugly. While after a day at the spa, you tell yourself you're beautiful. No one can feel down after a series of beauty treatments."

"I could easily do this on a regular basis," Gail murmured as a green clay mask covered her face.

"Maybe we should," Nora suggested as she opted for a mineral body mask. "The men go off to the sports games. Why shouldn't we do this?"

"I'm in," Ginna said.

Lucy was ready to snuggle down in the blanket and doze, but before that could happen, she was urged off the table so she could rinse off the mask.

"I feel like some little girl's Barbie doll," she said as she was wrapped in a pale-blue terry spa robe and shuffled off for a pedicure and manicure. Next she was herded to the station that had been Ginna's when she'd worked at the Steppin' Out Hair Salon that was part of the Elysium Day Spa.

"No matter how bad you feel, you don't neglect your hair," Ginna instructed, after Lucy's hair was washed and conditioned again. She picked up scissors. "We're doing a whole new look. Don't worry, nothing radical. Just a feel-good style."

Lucy had to admit that as the day wore on, her spirits did lift to where she felt almost human again. Abby was right. There was nothing like having your entire body worked on to make you feel better.

After the salon makeup artist finished her magic, Lucy looked in the mirror and felt she saw a brand-new woman.

She was surprised when Abby walked out with her trademark shoulder-length hair cut short.

"It was time for a change," Abby said. "Let's eat."

As they sat on the restaurant's patio, Lucy looked at the four women seated with her. They declared calorie and fat-gram counters as the enemy and ate to their hearts' content then went to work on the dessert tray.

After they'd eaten their fill, they sat back to enjoy the evening. Lucy held up her glass of wine.

"When I was little I hated having a brother," she said. "I wanted a sister who'd play dolls with me and learn all that girl stuff with me as we grew older. But now—" She had to stop as she felt her throat close up. "Now I feel as if I have four sisters. The best kind of sisters a woman could have because they're sisters by choice, not by birth. Thank you for everything."

The other four smiled and held up their glasses.

"Sisters by choice," Abby echoed. "Gail's right. We need to do this on a regular basis. Recharge our batteries, so to speak." She sipped her wine.

"Let's share the good with the bad, shall we?" Lucy suggested. "Each of you tell me what makes the man in your life so special."

"You want to wallow in your misery, don't you?" Ginna asked.

Lucy shrugged. "Maybe. Or maybe just remember the good parts." She smiled faintly. She looked at Gail.

"I was one of those quiet, anal types," Gail said softly. She wrinkled her nose at Ginna when she laughed. "And that's an understatement. Brian showed me a whole new world, a whole new me. He completed me in a way I never imagined."

"Mark makes life brighter," Nora admitted.

"Zach made me rethink my life," Ginna said. "That there was a way to have it all."

The women turned to Abby. She rolled her eyes and sighed, "The bonding thing." She chuckled. "Jeff has always been considered the quiet brother. Trust me, he's not. The man can be an animal." She cocked an eyebrow. "I was raised with an in-your-face attitude that pretty much scared off the men. Except it never scared off Jeff. He looked beneath the exterior. He is definitely my soul mate."

Lucy blinked her eyes. "I hope this mascara is waterproof," she murmured. "Logan was just *there*. He has this caring nature that I don't think he's totally aware of. He said he was 'surfer dude' in high school, but there's a lot more to him than that. I mean, who else lets his dog have his cell phone?" She gulped and shook her head in an attempt to compose herself.

The four women looked at each other and nodded in unison. Lucy caught the movement.

"What?"

Ginna reached inside her purse and pulled out a folded newspaper page. She handed it to Lucy.

"We wanted you to have the day just for you before you read this," Ginna said.

"The classified ads?" Lucy looked down and easily found a section circled in red ink.

Two single dogs and macaw with cat seek someone to give them the tender loving care they deserve. Must be

willing to put up with male Homo Sapiens who wants
to make things right. Only someone whose name begins
with *L* need apply. 951/555-9344.

Lucy felt the blood leave her face.

"First he dragged you out of the reunion so he could
make out with you in a hallway, then he takes out an ad,"
Abby said.

"Logan made out with you in a hallway at the reunion?"
Gail's eyes widened.

Lucy nodded. "When the man kisses you, you forget your
own name."

"Someone who kisses like that can't be allowed to run
free," Nora proclaimed. "It isn't safe for him at all. What if
some hussy gets her hooks in him?"

"He took out a newspaper ad?" Lucy said numbly. Only
someone whose name begins with *L* need apply.

"There's nothing like a man admitting it in print," Ginna
pointed out.

Lucy thought of her cell phone tucked away in her purse
on her dresser back at home. She hadn't been allowed to
bring it. When she looked up, she saw four cell phones on the
table in front of her.

She slowly picked one up and punched out the number. Her
stomach tightened when a familiar voice answered.

"Uh, yes, I'm calling about your ad."

LOGAN WANTED to see her.

She had no idea what he wanted to tell her and he'd given
her no hint on the phone. The newspaper ad gave her hope,
but what if it only meant that he wanted to apologize for his
bad behavior? Could she say, "Yes, I just want to be friends,
too," and sound as if she meant it?

Not when she'd changed her mind. She wanted everything

she used to say she didn't want. She wanted it all. And she wanted it with Logan.

Nick looked at her strangely the next morning when she went all out with breakfast, preparing waffles, bacon and even hash-browned potatoes.

"Is this my last meal or something?" He looked at the food on the table.

"I do cook sometimes," she reminded him. She toyed with her mug of coffee. "Logan's coming by this afternoon."

Nick stilled. "And?"

"And I don't know."

He used his fork to draw circles on the tabletop. "So he's not mad at us anymore."

"I don't know that either." She watched him carefully pour a drop of syrup in each crevice of his waffle as he'd done since he was old enough to hold the syrup bottle by himself. She knew he would take one bite of waffle then a bite of bacon then a forkful of hash browns. Her son was a creature of habit.

He was great big-brother material. Even with all his complaining last night, he'd enjoyed the day at Sea World with his cousins.

She should have opened her mind to marriage long ago. Given Nick those brothers and sisters he deserved.

Maybe she would have a chance to make it up to him.

Nick ate slowly. "If you want I can go over to Grandpa Lou and Grandma Cathy's," he offered.

"You don't need to." She picked up a piece of bacon.

He looked up. "Then I think I should stay here."

Lucy thought the clock would move slowly, but instead, it seemed to race. Nick mowed the front and back lawns without being told to and then cleaned the pool and spa. She grew tired just watching him.

Even with her watching the clock, she wasn't aware anyone had arrived until the doorbell chimed. She quickly glanced out the window and saw Logan's Jeep SUV parked in front. It seemed as if the moment the doorbell sounded Nick disappeared into his room.

"Breathe," she ordered herself as she walked toward the door.

Lucy wasn't sure what to expect when she opened it, but the sight of two dogs sitting there, each holding a red rose in his mouth, wasn't it. Each dog wore a red ribbon with a neatly printed sign hanging down. Magnum's sign read I'm Sorry while Jake's declared Please Forgive Me? There was no sign of Logan.

"So you were the one who put in the ad," she said to Magnum. The Malamute's plumed tail waved back and forth like a banner while the Australian shepherd's back end wiggled at a faster beat.

"Turn them over." Logan's voice sounded off to the side.

Guessing he meant the signs, not the dogs themselves, she stepped forward and turned over the signs. Magnum's read I Love You while Jake's asked Marry Me?

Lucy felt her entire body trembling.

"How do you know it's real?" she asked, even though Logan still remained out of sight.

He walked from around the side of the house. She noted he looked thinner and as if he hadn't slept well. But even so, there was something different about him.

It was his eyes, she realized. They were smiling. The gold that dusted his brown eyes sparkled brightly.

Logan stopped when he reached her.

"I never thought of myself as a coward," he said. "But I was where you were concerned. I saw what we had as special and I guess I thought it would go on that way until we both decided it was over. Except everyone around us saw it differently. I felt…" He searched for the right word. "Manipulated." His face mimicked Lucy's wince. "Please, hear me out," he said quickly, as if afraid she would go back in the house and lock him out. Not that he could blame her. He'd put Lucy through hell when she didn't deserve it. Now she stood there looking beautiful and ready to listen to him. He suddenly wished he knew what to say to make things better. He decided his best bet was to speak from the heart.

"All right," she said.

He knew he wasn't home free. She hadn't invited him inside, and she stood in the open doorway. Magnum and Jake abandoned him and now sat on either side of Lucy.

"I let memories of Shannon color any woman who tried to come close to me," he said slowly. "You were the first woman I felt such a strong attraction to. Except you didn't want anything to do with me." His lips twisted. "Then…then I realized how much there was to you. That you're nothing like Shannon. You never tried to make me into something I'm not and you didn't believe in vengeance."

A tiny smile curved Lucy's lips. "On that point you would be wrong. I did imagine you taking a bath in a very large vat of boiling oil. I have a dark side," she admitted with the tiniest of smiles.

"I think I was in love with you all along. I just didn't want to admit it. Then I did something very wrong. I walled myself off from you without any explanation. I might as well have left the state."

"That was cruel." Her voice trembled with remembered hurt.

"It was, and I am more sorry than I can say." He held his hands out to the sides. "I know I can't make that hurt go away, but I'm hoping you'll forgive me for being an idiot and give me a chance to make it up to you."

"Even if making it up to me meant you'd have to go away?"

Logan's face fell at her words. He seemed to steel himself.

"Even if," he whispered. He started to turn around.

"But that would be too easy, wouldn't it?" Her words

stopped him. "My son would tell you I torture him every so often because I'm the mom and I can do it. Maybe I need to broaden my skills to concentrate on a larger target. Besides..." Her hands dropped down to stroke each dog's head. Jake tipped his head up, his tongue lolling happily, while Magnum remained his stoic self. "These dogs need a good role model."

Hopeful, Logan took a step forward, then a second step. Encouraged, even though Lucy hadn't said another word, he kept moving until he could pull her into his arms. His kiss betrayed the hunger that had been raging in him for a long time. More than that, it showed the love he'd been afraid to admit.

Lucy pulled back slightly. "If I accept your proposal, it's forever," she said fiercely with her eyes blazing. "I won't be talking about you moving the practice out of the area or changing the way you are, so don't think there's a chance it will happen. We'll have enough going on once Nick starts dating. Not to mention whatever trouble our own kids stir up. And I don't expect to wait too long. You're not getting any younger, you know!"

Logan rested his forehead against hers. His shoulders shook with his laughter. "You don't waste any time, do you?"

She framed his face with her hands. She could feel the slight roughness of his skin against her palms.

"I should make you suffer." Her voice shook with tears. "I should make you grovel."

"I am groveling." He brushed his mouth across hers.

But it wasn't enough.

He cupped her face with his hands and took her lips in a full-onslaught kiss. He let the kiss say all the things he couldn't find the words to express.

"I love you, Lucy," he finally said when they broke apart.

"I love you, Logan." Lucy gave him one of her patented wicked smiles. "But there's one more thing."

Was this going to turn into yet another test of wills? He

hoped not. He just wanted to get her somewhere alone. "What is it?" he asked.

"I'm not getting any younger, either." She grabbed his hand and pulled him through the doorway. "So come on in."

Logan grinned. "I always knew you were my kind of woman."

Epilogue

There was nothing like a wedding in the Walker family, even if the family member involved might only be related by marriage.

Abby, Gail and Nora were Lucy's bridesmaids, and Ginna acted as her matron of honor.

Logan said it was only proper that Nick be his best man. Magnum and Jake were attired in formal bow ties for the occasion, and Judge Kincaid officiated at the ceremony, where he announced to the guests he was only too happy to marry off his son.

At the reception, the youngest Walker sibling, Nikki, announced to everyone she was not following the family tradition of getting married.

"We did it," Logan said, as he danced with his wife of one hour.

Lucy's smile rivaled his own. "Yes, we did. And it even looks as if we'll survive to tell the tale."

He ducked his head. "You know what I think," he whispered in her ear. "I think we should go down to the Mañana every year to celebrate."

"Our wedding anniversary?" she teased.

He shook his head. "No, I think we should go there to celebrate the night you became my wicked woman."

"And you turned into my wild man. I think it's a wonderful idea, but only on one condition."

"What's that?"

"Your suit coat has to come, too."

THE BRIDE AND GROOM were so engrossed with each other they didn't notice that Lucy's son and Logan's father were over in a corner. Frank Kincaid held up a glass of champagne in a toast to the new couple and thoughtfully ignored Nick holding up the same. Of course, Nick would only be allowed a sip before the glass would be confiscated.

"We did it," Nick told his step-grandfather with a grin stretched from ear to ear.

Frank nodded. "Yes, my boy, we certainly did."

Nick looked at his mother and new stepfather. "Now if they'll just get to work on a baby brother or sister so they won't worry about me as a teenager."

Frank choked on his champagne.

* * * * *

Spring in the Valley (#1061) is the third book in Charlotte Douglas's popular series A PLACE TO CALL HOME. The previous titles are *Almost Heaven* and *One Good Man*.

When you read *Spring in the Valley,* you'll meet local police officer Brynn Sawyer and New York City attorney Rand Benedict, who's come to Pleasant Valley with his orphaned nephew. Brynn and Rand quickly develop a relationship—but Rand has a secret agenda that's going to affect not only Brynn but the whole town. Still, Rand will find himself enchanted by Pleasant Valley…. It's the kind of place where neighbors become friends and where people care—small-town life as it was meant to be!

Hiking her long silk skirt above her boots, Officer Brynn Sawyer slid from the car and used her Mag-Lite to guide her steps to the idling Jaguar she'd pulled over. At her approach, the driver's window slid down with an electronic whir.

The driver started to speak. "I have a—"

"I'll do the talking. This is a state highway, not a NASCAR track," Brynn said in the authoritative manner she reserved for lawbreakers, especially those displaying such an obvious lack of common sense. "And the road's icing up. You have a death wish?"

"No." The driver seemed distracted, oblivious to the seriousness of his offense. "I need to—"

"Turn off your engine," Brynn ordered, "and place your hands on the wheel where I can see them."

She shined her flashlight in the driver's face. The man, who was in his mid-thirties, squinted in the brightness, but not before the pupils of his eyes, the color of dark melting chocolate, contracted in the light. She instantly noted the rugged angle of his unshaven jaw, the aristocratic nose, baby-fine brown hair tousled as if he'd just climbed out of bed…

And a wad of one-hundred-dollar bills thrust under her nose.

Anger burned through her, but she kept her temper. "If that's a bribe, buster, you're in a heap of trouble."

"No bribe." His tone, although frantic, was rich and full. "Payment for my fine. I can't stop—"

"You can't keep going at your previous speed either," she said reasonably and struggled to control her fury at the man's arrogance. "You'll kill yourself and someone else—"

"It's Jared. I have to get him to the hospital."

Labored breathing sounded in the back seat. Brynn aimed her light at the source. In a child carrier, a tow-headed toddler, damp hair matted to his head and plump cheeks flushed with fever, wheezed violently as his tiny chest struggled for air.

Brynn's anger vanished at the sight of the poor little guy, and her sympathy kicked in. She made a quick decision.

"Follow me. I'll radio ahead for the E.R. to expect us."

With *Discovering Duncan* (#1062), Mary Anne Wilson launches a brand-new four-book series, RETURN TO SILVER CREEK. In these stories, various characters return to a Nevada town for a variety of reasons—to hide, to come home, to confront their pasts. In *Discovering Duncan*, a young private detective, Lauren Carter, is hired to track down a wealthy client's son. When she does so, she also discovers the person he really is—not to mention the delights of this small mountain town!

"I'm a man of patience," D. R. Bishop said as his secretary left, closing the door securely behind her. "But even I have my limits."

Lauren Carter never took her eyes off the large man across from her at the impressive stone and glass desk. D. R. Bishop was dressed all in black. He was a huge, imposing man, and definitely, despite what he said, a man with little patience. He looked tightly wound, and ready to spring.

Lauren sat very still in a terribly uncomfortable chair, her hands in her lap while she let D. R. Bishop do all the talking. She simply nodded from time to time.

"My son walked out on everything six months ago," he said. "Why?"

He tented his fingers thoughtfully, with his elbows resting on the polished desktop, as if he were considering her single-word question. But she knew he was considering just how much to tell her. His eyes were dark as night, a contrast to his snow-white hair and meticulously trimmed beard. "Ah, that's a good question," he said. For some reason, he was hedging.

"Mr. Bishop, you've dealt with the Sutton Agency enough to know that privacy and discretion are part of our service. Nothing you tell me will go any farther."

He shrugged his massive shoulders and sank back in his chair. "Of course. I expect no less," he said.

"So, why did your son leave?"

"I thought it was a middle-age crisis of some sort." He smiled slightly, a strained expression. "Not that thirty-eight is middle-aged. Then I thought he might be having a breakdown. Maybe gone over the edge." The man stood abruptly, rising to his full, imposing height, and she could've sworn she felt the air ripple around her from his movement. "But he's not crazy, Ms. Carter, he's just damn stubborn. Too damn stubborn."

She waited as he walked to the windows behind him and faced the city twenty floors below. When he didn't speak, she finally said, "You don't know why he left?"

The shoulders shrugged again. "A difference of opinion on how to do business. Nothing new for us." He spoke without turning. "We've always clashed, but in the end, we've always managed to make our business relationship work."

"What exactly do you want from the Sutton Agency, Mr. Bishop?"

"Find him."

"That's it?"

He turned back to her, studying her intently for several moments before he said, "No."

"Then what else do you want us to do?"

"As an employee of Sutton, I want you to find my son. I also want him to come back willingly."

"Okay," she said. She'd handle it. She had to. Her future depended on finding the mysterious Duncan Bishop.

We're thrilled to introduce a brand-new writer to American Romance! *Mad About Max* (#1063) is the first of three books by Penny McCusker. They're set in Erskine, Montana, where the residents gather at the Ersk Inn to trade gossip and place bets in the watering hole's infamous betting pools. Cute, klutzy schoolteacher Sara Lewis is the current subject of one of the inn's most popular pools ever. She's been secretly (or not so secretly!) pining for rancher and single dad Max Devlin for going on six years, and this story sees her about to take her destiny into her own hands.

Penny writes with the perfect mix of warmth and humor, and her characters will have you cheering for them right to the end.

"Please tell me that wasn't Super Glue."

Sara Lewis tore her gaze away from the gorgeous—and worried—blue eyes of Max Devlin, looking up to where her hands were flattened against the wall over his head. Even when she saw the damning evidence squished between her right palm and her third-grade class's mangled Open House banner, she refused to admit it, even to herself.

If she admitted she was holding a drained tube of Super Glue in her hand, she might begin to wonder if there'd been any stray drops. And where they might have landed. That sort of speculation would only lead her to conclusions she'd be better off not drawing, conclusions like there was no way a stray drop could have landed on the floor. Not with her body plastered to Max's. No, that kind of speculation would lead her right into trouble.

As if she could have gotten into any more trouble.

She'd been standing on a chair, putting up the banner her third-grade class had created to welcome their parents to Erskine Elementary's Open House. But her hands had jerked when she heard Max's voice out in the hallway, and she'd torn it clear in half. She'd grabbed the first thing off her desk that might save the irreplaceable strip of laboriously scrawled greetings and brilliant artwork and jumped back on her chair, only to find that Max had gotten there first. He'd grabbed one end of the banner, then dived for the other as it fluttered away, ending up spread-eagled against the wall, one end of the banner in either hand, trapped there by Sara and her chair.

She'd pulled the ragged ends of the banner together, but just as she'd started to glue them, Max had turned around and nearly knocked her over. "Hold still," she'd said sharply, not quite allowing herself to notice that he was facing her now, that perfect male body against hers, that heart-stopping face only inches away. Instead, she'd asked him to hold the banner in place while she applied the glue. The rest was history. Or in her case infamy.

"Uh, Sara…" Max was trying to slide out from between her and the wall, but she met his eyes again and shook her head.

"Uh, just hold on a little longer, Max. I want to make sure the glue is dry."

What she really needed was a moment to figure out how badly she'd humiliated herself this time. Experimentally, she stuck out her backside. Sure enough, the front of her red pleather skirt tented dead center, stuck fast to the lowermost pearl button on Max's shirt—the button that was right above his belt buckle, which was right above his—

Sara slammed her hips back against his belly, an automatic reaction intended to halt the dangerous direction of her thoughts and hide the proof of her latest misadventure. It was like throwing fuel on the fire her imagination had started.

Blood rushed into her face, then drained away to throb deep and low, just about where his belt buckle was digging into her—

"Sara!"

She snapped back to reality, noting the exasperation in his voice, reluctantly she arched away from him. The man had to breathe, after all.

"There's a perfectly reasonable explanation for this," she said in a perfectly reasonable voice. In fact, that voice amazed her, considering that she was glued to a man she'd been secretly in love with for the better part of six years.

"There always is, Sara," Max said, exasperation giving way to amusement. "There was a perfectly reasonable explanation for how Mrs. Tilford's cat wound up on top of the church bell tower."

Sara grimaced.

"There was a perfectly reasonable explanation for why Jenny Hastings went into the Crimp 'N Cut a blonde and came out a redhead. Barn-red."

Sara cringed.

"And there was a perfectly reasonable explanation for the new stained-glass window in the town hall looking more like an advertisement for a brothel than a reenactment of Erskine's founding father rescuing the Indian maidens."

She huffed out a breath, indignant. "I only broke the one pane."

"Yeah, the pane between the grateful, kneeling maidens and the very happy Jim 'Mountain Man' Erskine."

"The talk would die down if the mayor let me get the pane fixed instead of just shoving the rest of them together so it looked like the Indian maidens were, well, really grateful."

"People are coming from miles around to see it." Max reminded her. "He'd lose the vote of every businessman in town if he ruined the best moneymaker they've ever had."

Sara just huffed out another breath. It was a little hypocritical for the people of Erskine, Montana, to pick on her for something they were capitalizing on, especially when she had a perfectly good reason for why it had happened, why bad luck seemed to follow her around like a black cloud. Except she couldn't tell anyone what that reason was, especially not Max. Because he was the reason.

Veteran author Ginger Chambers returns to American Romance with *Love, Texas,* a warm, engrossing story about returning to your past—coming home—and seeing it in an entirely new way.... You'll enjoy Ginger's determined and delightful heroine, Cassie Edwards, and her rancher hero, Will Taylor. Cassie is more and more drawn into life at the Taylor ranch—and you will be, too. Guaranteed you'll feel right at home in Love, Texas!

When Cassie Edwards arrived at the Four Corners—where Main Street was intersected by Pecan—nothing in Love, Texas, seemed to have changed. At Swanson's Garage the same old-style gasoline pumps waited for customers under the same rickety canopy. The Salon of Beauty still sported the same eye-popping candy-pink front door. Handy Grocery & Hardware's windows were plastered with what could be the same garish sale banners. And from the number of pickup trucks and cars crowded into the parking lot on the remaining corner, Reva's Café still claimed the prize as the area's most popular eating place.

Old feelings of panic threatened to engulf Cassie, forcing her to pull the car onto the side of the road. She had to remember she wasn't the same Cassie Edwards the people of Love thought they knew so well. She'd changed.

Cassie gripped the steering wheel. She'd come here to do a job—to negotiate a land deal, get the needed signatures, then get out...fast!

A flutter of unease went through her as her thoughts moved to her mother, but she quickly beat it down. She'd known all along that she'd have to see her. But the visit would be brief and it would be the last thing she did before starting back for Houston. She glanced in the rearview mirror and pulled back out onto Main and continued toward the Taylor ranch.

Cassie drove down the highway, following a line of tightly strung barbed wire that enclosed grazing Black Angus cattle. The working fence ran for about a mile before being replaced by a rustic rock fence that decorated either side of a wide metal gate, on which the ranch's name, the Circle Bar-T, was proudly displayed in a circle of black wrought-iron. A sprawling two-story white frame house with a wraparound porch sat a distance down the driveway, the rugged landscape around it softened with flowers and more delicate greenery.

Cassie hopped out of the car, swung open the gate and drove through.

"Hey!" a man shouted.

Cassie looked around and saw a jeans-clad man in a long-sleeved shirt and bone-colored hat heading toward her, and he didn't look pleased. She'd had a thing for Will Taylor when she'd first started to notice boys. Trim and athletic with thick blond hair and eyes the same blue as the Texas sky, he was handsome in the way that made a girl's heart quicken if he so much as looked at her. But even if he had noticed her in the same way she'd noticed him, there'd been a gulf between them far wider than the difference in their ages. She was Bonnie Edwards's daughter. And that was enough.

"You forgot somethin', ma'am," he drawled. "You didn't close the gate. In these parts if you open a gate, you need to close it."

Will Taylor continued to look at her. Was he starting to remember her, too?

He broke into her thoughts. "Just go knock on the front

door. My mom's expectin' you." Then, with a little nod, he stuffed his hat back on his head and walked away.

Cassie stared after him. Not exactly an auspicious beginning.

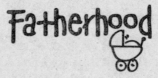

If you enjoyed what you just read,
then we've got an offer you can't resist!

Take 2 bestselling love stories FREE!
Plus get a FREE surprise gift!

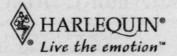